My Ticket Out

J.N. MARTON

ISBN: 978-0-578-77832-7 (paperback)

Interior design by FormattedBooks.com

Dedication

To Hollis, for showing me the beauty underneath the surface.

"If she favors you, love her. If she wounds you, love her. If she tears your heart to pieces —and as it gets older and stronger, it will tear deeper —love her."

—— Charles Dickens

Chapter One

"We did not come this far to roll over like a bunch of pigs! Take the ball and put it in the damn basket!" Falcons on three…one…two…three…FALCONS."

Twelve seconds left on the clock.

One more shot.

One more play.

One last chance.

Twelve seconds is all the time we need.

Defense pounces the second the ball is inbounded like a leach latching itself to the only available life source.

The fast break is swift—over before it even started. One hard dribble towards the middle and the ball is launched to the center of the court.

Seven seconds left.

What comes next is second nature. A hard cut to the basket and back out to the wing, my hands raise in the air as I catch the ball before defense has time to adjust.

Four seconds left… Three seconds… the ball rolls off my fingertips.

Two seconds… it swirls around the rim.

One second… and falls to the ground.

The sound of the buzzer erupts through the gymnasium, solidifying our defeat. Final score thirty-six to thirty-seven.

The rest of the Davenport bench rushes to the middle of the court, high-fiving one another while the spectators in the stands applaud their victory. My gaze scans the enthusiastic crowd, my eyes lingering on a tall woman dressed in a dark pantsuit seated in the corner of the bleachers. There's a notepad resting on her lap and a pen in her hand and she scribbles something across it. I drop my head as I realize she's the recruiter coach mentioned this week at practice. There's no way they'll consider me for a scholarship after I just missed the winning shot.

I inhale the musty stench of sweat, perfume, and hairspray as we sulk into the locker room. I'm starting to think no matter where we play—home or away—all locker rooms smell the same. We silently take a seat and wait for the aftermath that is Coach Stewart. I lean forward, resting my elbows on my knees and focus on the sweat dripping from my forehead, plummeting to the ground and leaving a minuscule puddle between my shoes.

One shot.

That's all we needed. And I blew it.

My main priority from the second this year started was getting a basketball scholarship out of this small town. From our very first game, it's felt like my life has been dependent on one specific goal. A single accomplishment—like making the game-winning shot—is going to make or break my future.

There's a soft knock at the door indicating Coach Stewart is about to enter. He comes charging through the door, letting it slam against the concrete wall as he steps in front of us. His eyes trace over us, one by one, pausing just long enough for us to feel the misery set in.

He dips his head, slowly shaking it back and forth before he holds up his index finger. "One shot. One damn shot. That's all we needed to be undefeated this season." He lifts his head, settling his hands on his hips. "We made mistakes tonight. And sometimes one mistake is the difference between winning and losing. The season's not over yet. We'll just have to practice a little harder to end it on a high. We've got a few games left, don't give up now. Practice tomorrow after school. Bring it in."

"Falcons on three…one…two…three…FALCONS."

I shuffle to my locker, ignoring the hushed conversations happening around me, and begin gathering my stuff.

"That was a nice shot, Charlie," Riley says as she pulls off her jersey, tossing it to the growing pile on the floor, and retrieves her t-shirt from the locker next to mine.

"Thanks," I mutter. "I'll see you tomorrow." I sling my bag across my shoulders and head for the door.

I round the corner and, glancing at the window of Coach's office, see the same tall woman from the stands sitting across from Coach, their heads bent in conversation. I slow my pace, wondering who and what they're discussing. Do I still have a shot at a scholarship after what she just witnessed in the game? I continue towards the exit, trying to push the thoughts from my mind as my stomach churns with distress.

I get about halfway when I'm cut off by Ben. He's wearing faded jeans, a red and black flannel over a plain white shirt, and boots with dried mud on the sides. The typical wardrobe of the boys that live around here.

"Hey, Charlie. Nice game."

"Thanks," I say, trying to brush past him.

He takes one long stride to the right, blocking my path. "I was thinking about checking out that new movie this weekend. Thought you might like to join me?"

"No thanks, I'm busy."

He leans in closer, the smell of popcorn lingering on his breath and I have to force the nausea back down. "C'mon, Charlie," he whispers. "It'll be fun. It wasn't too long ago you jumped at the chance to go out with me."

That's not actually true. I only went out with him because Riley insisted and I finally agreed in order to get her off my back, not because I found him even remotely attractive. Of course, he doesn't realize that—which isn't all that surprising when I really think about it. We did the typical dinner and movie date but he couldn't hold a conversation that didn't revolve around himself. Within the first twenty minutes of the movie, he was shoving his tongue down my throat. I managed to wrangle him off before awkwardly sitting there trying to pretend I was somewhat interested in the film playing on screen. I haven't gone out with him since.

"Ben, I need to get home. Can we talk about this some other time?"

"So," he straightens up, his tone chipper as a smile plays around his mouth. "You'll think about it?"

I stagger past him, picking up my pace as the EXIT-sign beacons above the door, hoping my silence will answer his question.

BluHaven, Oklahoma is like any other small, southern town. The same families, shops, restaurants and businesses have been here for generations. There's a church on nearly every street corner, everything shuts down on Sundays, high school sports are the main source of entertainment, and everybody knows everything about everyone.

They say you have the freedom to be whoever you want to be, to express yourself in your own way. But if that goes against the belief system that's been set in stone since before I was born, then don't even bother. It's not that I hate living here. It's just that I never felt like I truly fit in, like my place has always been somewhere else in this world.

The dreary evening air of late February envelopes the area in a blanket of darkness, except for the familiar yellow glow of the porch light. The minute I step through the door, I'm met with the satisfying aroma of coffee. There have been very few times I've come home and there hasn't been a pot of coffee brewing; Gramps and Nana are convinced it's the only way they're able to function properly.

The inside of our house reminds me of the old eighties movies Gramps loves to watch, with a modern twist to it. The floor is an old-fashioned parquet with a blend of deep homely browns. The walls are painted the green of a summer garden, with pictures of Matty, my brother, and me scattered about the entire house. It's an open floor plan, the living room blending into a small dining room, then remaining open as the kitchen appears behind it with just enough space for a family of four to move around without climbing on top of each other.

We may live in a neighborhood where each house is nearly identical to the others, but once I step inside it feels different. It's a place where the lungs choose to fill a little deeper and the heart beats a little steadier.

"Oh, Charlie, you're home just in time to help me finish cleaning up and load the dishwasher," Nana says as soon as I enter the kitchen.

I do a quick sweep of the area. "Matty can't help you?" I reply, trying to keep the annoyance out of my voice.

"He's upstairs working on a project or something and besides, you're already here."

I exhale slowly, debating if it's even worth arguing. I've been home less than ten minutes and I'm already roped into doing something Matty could've easily accomplished without me. It may be the twenty-first century but I swear my Nana is still stuck in the sixties with her borderline sexist ideologies.

"How was the game, sweetheart?" Nana asks.

"We lost."

"That's too bad, dear. I'm sure you'll do better next time."

I respond with a barely audible grunt as I place the last of the silverware into the dishwasher. I snag a clean bowl, spoon, and the unopened box of Lucky Charms and set them on the laminate white countertop.

"Hey, Monkey. Sorry to hear you lost," says Gramps as he hobbles into the kitchen.

I shrug, shoveling another bite of cereal into my mouth.

"Any word about the recruiter that was coming to the game tonight?" asks Gramps.

I drop my gaze to my bowl of cereal, the uneasiness fluttering in my stomach as I think back to the game. For some reason, I don't feel hungry anymore. I shake my head at Gramps and slide past him to put my bowl away before heading upstairs.

I lightly tap on the door before walking through. "Hey, Matty."

"Hey, Charlie," he says with a grin. "How was the game?"

"We lost," I mumble.

"Ahh man, that sucks. I'm sorry, sis. Any word on the recruit?" He picks up the slim screwdriver balancing on his thigh and inserts it at the corner of the small plastic box in his hands.

I shake my head. "Nope."

Matty's my younger brother but he has towered over me ever since his growth spurt in the ninth grade. He's got broad shoulders, curly brown hair (just like our father's), and the same emerald green eyes as me. His limbs are lean, and muscular which I always found odd because he hates working out or anything close to exercising. Ever since we were little, there was always something that drew people to him. He's charismatic and charming, but it was more than that. There's a sort of reservedness about Matty, not obvious to the naked eye, but he has a way of picking up on cues most people can't.

We've had our ups and downs, but he's the one person I can be myself with, the one person I can count on no matter what. I could tell him anything and he would love me just the same.

"What was the score?" he asks, as he pries the sides apart.

"Thirty-six to thirty-seven. I missed the winning shot."

"Dang, Charlie. I'm sorry I wasn't there. Don't be too hard on yourself; it was one shot."

I sprawl out on his bed, letting my chin rest in the palms of my hands. "One shot that cost us the game."

"C'mon, Charlie, cut yourself some slack." He lifts his head, his gaze softening. "You're going to get a scholarship to some fancy school halfway across the country and leave this all behind." He gestures to the room around him.

"We'll see. A scholarship is my only ticket out of this place."

"You and me both, sis. But would staying in BluHaven really be the end of the world?"

"Yes," I respond, without a second thought. Matty swivels in his chair, raising an eyebrow at me while he fidgets with the items in his lap.

"Don't you want to see what's out there, Matty? There's got to be more to life than high school football games and visiting the same shops and restaurants that've been here since before Gramps and Nana were born."

"What would you even want to do once you get out?"

I take a minute to consider his words before answering. "I'm not entirely sure to be honest. But I think I would like to do something that involved helping people. Maybe I'll become a social worker and help kids in the foster system. Or maybe I'll get a degree in something like business and keep my options open. All I know is that whatever I do, I want it to be somewhere that's not here."

"Do you even like kids?" he says with a smirk.

I grab the pillow from behind my feet and smack him with it. "I'm just kidding, relax."

"What're you working on, anyways? Please tell me it's not another one of your machines to help Nana with the chores?"

Matty looks at me with mild exasperation and rolls his eyes. The last time he tried to help Nana with the chores—he built a contraption that was supposed to help her dry the dishes—he nearly caught the house on fire.

"It's a project for my Engineering and Design class. We had to build a mousetrap structure that could trap more than one thing at the same time."

"Sounds riveting," I tease.

"It's actually more challenging than I originally anticipated but I think I'm almost finished." A childish grin spreads across his face when he finishes disassembling the now broken box in his lap.

"Have fun. I'm going to my room."

"Night, Charlie."

I toss aside the various pants and shirts lying askew on top of my full-size bed before crawling underneath the covers and picturing what life might be like when I'm far away from this place.

The sound of my alarm the next morning wrenches me from my subconscious. I roll out of bed and head for the shower, mentally preparing for the day ahead.

Scouring through my closet, I push aside the blouses and dresses Riley keeps convincing me to buy whenever she ropes me into shopping and Nana loves to put in the front until I find my grey BluHaven Falcons basketball shirt and favorite pair of jeans.

I throw my hair in a bun before slipping into my white Converse. I grab my basketball gear and head downstairs.

"You ready, Matty?"

He nods, shoving the last of his breakfast burrito into his mouth, and slings his backpack over his shoulder.

The early morning sun paints a soothing amber across the sky as we maneuver our way through the familiar streets to the high school. I pull into the parking lot, toss the keys to Matty, and head inside.

"Hey girl," Riley says cheerfully as I slump down next to her on one of the benches.

"What's up?"

"I heard Ben invited you to the movies this weekend?"

"Damn, Riley. It hasn't even been twenty-four hours."

"I'm your best friend; it's my job to know these things. So are you gonna say yes?"

I glance up towards the ceiling as if I'm considering her question. "I don't know."

"C'mon, Charlie. He's cute. We could totally double date."

I tilt my head, raising a brow. "Are you insinuating you dislike it when I tag along with you and Tyler?"

Riley gives me a playful shove. "Of course not. But I think it could be fun. Ben's cute."

I hold up my forefinger. "That's a matter of opinion."

She rolls her eyes, shaking her head slightly. "I think you should at least give him a chance."

"I did, and it didn't turn out so good, remember?"

"It could be different this time."

"I don't—"

The blaring ring of the bell cuts me off.

"I gotta go, Riley. Ms. Arden is a drill sergeant when it comes to tardies. I'll see you at lunch," I say, gathering my bag.

"Okay, but we're not finished with this conversation," she hollers.

I head towards the main corridor, shuffling through the crowd of students as monotonous conversations and laughter buzz around me. I catch a glimpse at the few couples failing to obey the no PDA rule and survey the area around them, before tightening the grip on my backpack and averting my gaze.

After a brief stop at my locker, I'm caught off guard by Ben standing in my path.

He's determined, I'll give him that.

We've gone to school together since middle school but always ran in different circles. His entire family has lived in BluHaven for generations. His older brothers were the star athletes during their time here, with Ben ending that tradition when he failed a drug test during our junior year and got himself kicked off the football team. Now, he spends his time trying to overcompensate for what his family deems a failure. If he wasn't such a jerk, I might even feel a little bad for him.

His eyes drift to the couples still cuddled up in the crooks of the lockers. He raises his eyebrow ever so slightly as a smirk tugs at the corner of his mouth.

"Hey, Charlie. We on for this weekend?"

"I think I'll pass. There's a test I need to study." I try to side-step past him.

"Let me know if you change your mind," he says as he saunters past me down the hall.

The morning begins with an introduction to Hamlet in English, followed by a science experiment that goes horribly wrong and ends with a pop quiz in Calculus; a typical day at BluHaven High School.

At lunch, I hop in line with Riley, watching as people slowly stagger into the cafeteria.

"You make a decision about Ben yet?" Riley says without missing a beat.

"I told him I can't. I need to study for Calculus this weekend."

Riley crosses her arms over her chest and stares at me, her eyes questioning.

"What?"

"Why'd you turn him down? He seems like a sweet guy."

I shrug my shoulders as we each grab a turkey sandwich. "I just don't like him like that."

"How do you know? You didn't even give him a chance."

"Not true. What makes you think this time would be different?"

"That was weeks ago, I'm sure it would go a lot smoother this time around. Besides, I heard he's a good kisser."

"Gross. And also not true."

She cocks her head, pursing her lips at me. "C'mon, Charlie. You can't just say no to every guy who asks you out. You at least need to give them a chance."

"I do. It's not my fault there's nothing between us."

"But how do you know that if you only go on one date?"

"How'd you know you liked Tyler that way after just one date?"

She shrugs her shoulders. "I just knew. It's hard to explain but I could just feel it, ya know?"

"No I don't and that's the point, Riley. It's not like that for me. The way you talk about being with Tyler—how elated he makes you feel. I can see it on your face whenever he's around—how much you love him. That's never happened to me."

"And you're never going to have the opportunity to have that happen to you if you constantly say no."

"Say no to what?" Emily says as we arrive at our usual table.

I shake my head at the same time Riley says, "To every guy that asks her out."

Emily leans forward, quirking an eyebrow and grinning. "Who asked you out?"

I let out an exasperated breath. "Ben. I said no."

"Like she always does," Riley chimes in.

"I think I'm with Charlie on this one. Ben is kind of a jerk."

"Thank you, Emily." I tilt my head at Riley. "At least somebody's on my side."

We're interrupted by the sudden applause from Tyler and John. Tyler gives him a high five for successfully breaking his record of chugging two cartons of milk in less than twenty seconds. And Riley questions why I don't want to date any of the boys from around here?

"You guys meet the new girl?" says Sara.

"What new girl?" Riley asks.

"Her name is Aspen Sullivan," Skylar cuts in. "She just moved here from Texas. Apparently her dad grew up here, was the star of the football team and was a major hottie."

"Eww, Skylar. He's probably super old now," Emily says, her nose crinkled in disgust.

"What? I'm just telling you what I heard. He joined the military right after high school to put himself through college, and now he's a hotshot businessman that's running the factories for the poultry plant. I also heard his wife died not too long ago after some scandal involving Aspen and another girl. So they packed up and came back here."

It's absolutely no surprise that Skylar knows intimate details about a family that literally just moved here. Her family owns all the car dealerships in town, is outlandishly rich, has ridiculously high standards for just about everyone, and are notorious gossipers. It doesn't help that they go to one of the biggest churches in town. The kind of church that uses God to camouflage messages of hate. Last year, their church took a trip to Westray to protest a new independent film that got a lot of press because of the subject matter. Apparently it involved the love story of two males, instead of the expected male and female love duo.

"What kind of scandal?" Sara asks, intrigued.

Skylar shrugs. "I'm not sure. My mom had to get off the phone before I could hear anything else."

"Well, I heard she got into some trouble at her old school and her dad brought her here to set her 'straight'. Whatever that means," John chimes in.

The sight of heads turning and voices quieting causes our table to look in the same direction as Aspen Sullivan strolls through the cafeteria. She's flanked by two boys, Brandon and Alex. They're both seniors, play football, and are known for their legendary keg stands. Not exactly the brightest guys around. But it's not surprising that they're glued to her like lost puppies. Aspen Sullivan is breathtaking.

I size her up and down, deciding that she's shorter than me by about two inches. She has a lean, slender figure and long slim legs. My gaze travels up her body, lingering on her face for a second too long, before tracing her outline back down. Her caramel brown hair cascades around her face in beachy waves. Her facial features are enthralling and utterly captivating. Her ocean-blue eyes are set above a small, curved nose and her lips fame a beautifully shaped mouth. She's wearing black jeans, a cream-colored blouse that highlights her curvy figure, and black ankle boots.

It's no wonder people are staring; she walks with a presence of confidence and purpose. She's guided to the table across from ours and I catch a glimpse of her tan, smooth skin peeking out as she sits down.

"You gonna stare at her all day, Charlie?" Skylar says.

"What? No, I—" I drop my gaze to my tray, not sure how to finish my sentence.

"Dang, I'm surprised Brandon hasn't proposed to her yet," Emily says, her head tilted in Aspen's direction. "He's practically drooling over her."

Skylar turns her head, giving Aspen a once-over before she swivels back to the table. "I don't see what is so interesting about her."

"She's the first new kid we've had in over a year. Of course everyone is going to be fixated on her for a few days."

"Whatever," Skylar huffs.

The bell shrieks through the cafeteria indicating the end of lunch. I jump up from the table, hurriedly gathering my things as the lunch group begins to disperse. I head towards B wing, turning to get one last glimpse of Aspen before she disappears into the crowd.

I have study hall sixth period but Mrs. Ryzinski lets me come to the gym instead to get some extra shots in during basketball season. I open the locker room door, surprised to see Riley here as well.

"What're you doing here? Don't you have Spanish sixth period?"

"Yeah, but I finished the project we've been working on last week so Mr. Ramirez let me come to the gym."

"Sweet. I could use the extra practice."

"Charlie, you missed one shot. Relax."

"Yeah and that one missed shot is the last thing on the recruiter's mind."

"I think you're forgetting how well you played last night. They'd be stupid not to take you."

"Easy for you to say. You already have how many offers?"

"Three," Riley whispers.

"Exactly. You know if I don't get a scholarship I'm stuck going to community college until I can save up enough money to transfer. I know my grandparents would help me out if they could but Gramps spent the last of his pension on my mess of a mother."

"Hey, let's just have some fun today. Take your mind off things for a bit."

"What'd you have in mind?"

She cracks a smile. "A little game of one-on-one, loser buys ice cream on the way home?"

I move my hand in a circular motion on my stomach. "You're on. I'm feelin' a strawberry milkshake today."

"Ha-ha, you have to win first."

"We'll see." We head out of the locker room and I jog over to the rack, tossing a ball to Riley so we can warm up.

I take a deep breath, letting the familiar sensation of stepping onto the court rain down on me. Our gymnasium is one of the best features of our high school. The polished, hardwood floor sparkles when the lights from above hit it just right, reminding me of a stage. The navy-blue bleachers encircle the court, rising all the way up to the second level. There's a ledge on either side of the court behind the goals, allowing plenty of space for spectators. In my opinion, it's the best place to watch the game—never missing a minute of the action.

"You ready?" Riley says with a sly grin as she jogs to the top of the three-point line.

"Let's go."

I pass Riley the ball and take my defensive stance. She casually dribbles the ball in front; her gaze locked with mine. I lightly shift my weight on the balls of my feet, my fingers twitching with exhilaration. We've played ball together since we were nine; I can anticipate her first move just as easily as she can anticipate mine.

Without missing a beat, she lunges forward with one hard dribble and powers towards the basket. I shuffle my feet, keeping pace with her as she goes in for the layup. I spring upwards, tipping the ball before it's able to make contact with the rim. I hustle to get the rebound, returning to the top.

I dribble the ball in between my legs, debating my next move. My gaze shifts to Riley, a whisper of a smile flicks across my face before I charge past her, stopping just below the elbow to pull up for a shot. It glides into the basket with ease.

"Nice shot," Riley says, as she jogs to retrieve the ball.

She returns to the top of the key, but this time there is no negligence to her dribble, her expression is fierce. *Game on.*

She hurls past me, but my feet are swift, staying in sync with her like it's second nature. She goes in for the layup but my arms are outstretched above my head, blocking her shot before it connects with the backboard.

She's quick. The second the ball hits the floor, she lunges for it, dribbling back out to the wing before I'm able to grab it. I hustle to get in front of her, shuffling my feet as she drives around me. She stops at the elbow, pulling up to shoot a jump shot. It goes in without missing a beat.

"Lucky shot," I say as I fetch the ball rolling towards the other side of the court. I slowly walk towards the top of the key, catching my breath as I glance around the gym, my eyes resting on a figure observing from above. I do a double-take, recognizing that wavy brown hair immediately. I slow my pace, once again sensing her entrancing presence. Our eyes lock for a moment, a tiny smile playing about her mouth. Riley tips the ball out of my hands, diverting my attention back to the game at hand.

Riley gently tosses the ball back to me. "What're you looking at?" she asks, her head tilted upwards in the same direction.

"Nothing."

"Well c'mon then." She takes her defensive stance. "We gotta finish before practice starts."

I hustle to the three-point line, glancing at the top of the bleachers before I dribble. But Aspen is nowhere in sight.

We finish just in time to take a breather before practice starts. I won by two points, although it was tied up until the very end.

The rest of the team slowly trickles onto the court, everyone stretching as we wait for Coach to make his appearance. We run through our normal practice routine, focusing on the fundamentals—shooting, ball handling, defense, offense—running through the motions as Coach barks orders at us from the sidelines.

But all through practice, I couldn't ignore the inkling feeling I got; like someone was watching me. My eyes continuously traveled to the top of the bleachers, wondering if my admirer was going to return.

We finish with a brief five-on-five scrimmage.

"Baker, Perkins, come here a sec," he hollers as the rest of the team disperses.

Riley and I exchange a curious look before turning on our heels and jogging over to Coach.

"Yes sir?" Riley says.

"I'm sure you both noticed the representative from LittleWood University in the stands last night?"

We both nod; the knot in my stomach increasing with his words.

"Well I talked with her for a bit after the game, and apparently she liked what she saw in the two of you. Unfortunately, she only has room for one."

I glance at Riley, her face expressionless. "So what happens now?" I ask tentatively.

Coach cocks his head to the side. "She's going to come back next week. She wants to watch another game or two before they make a decision."

I nod. My emotions are a mixture of exhilaration at the thought of a school actually being interested in me, and trepidation knowing they're just as interested in Riley.

"Thanks Coach," Riley mumbles as we slowly walk to the locker room.

"What was that about?" Emily asks as we start to gather our things.

"Uhh the recruiter that was at the game last night."

"No way? They're offering you two a scholarship?"

I look towards Riley, unsure of how to respond. She turns to gather the last of her gear. "Something like that," she says.

"That's awesome."

Riley nods, turning towards me. "You ready?"

Since Matty and I share a car and I always have to stay late for practice, Riley drives me home. I finish gathering the last of my gear and notice my math book missing. "I think I left my math book in my locker," I say to Riley. "Can I meet you at your car?"

She nods and heads towards the exit as I take the back way to my locker. I slip my phone out of my pocket as I round the corner.

SMACK

The collision sends my phone sliding across the tiles and an assortment of papers descends to the ground.

"Sorry about that," a voice says.

I bend down to retrieve my phone and the papers littering the tiles. "No worries." I stand up, the now disorganized papers clutched in my hands. My gaze falls on the familiar face of Aspen Sullivan.

"Hey." I fumble with the papers all of a sudden. "You're new here, aren't you?"

She nods, her expression attentive as her eyes travel over my face. "Yeah, we just moved here. I'm Aspen."

"Charlie." I extend my hand with the papers. "I believe these are yours."

"Thanks." She reaches for them, our fingers brushing as she gathers them into her grasp. Her gaze shifts down my body, lingering on the bag slung over my shoulder. "You just finish practice?"

"Yeah, but I needed to grab a book before I left."

"I saw you playing earlier." A tiny smile tugs at the corner of her mouth. "You're pretty good."

A small shudder trickles down my spine at her words. "Thanks. What're you doing here so late?"

She gestures to the pages in her hands. "Art project."

I nod, all of a sudden feeling a nervous sensation snake into my stomach. I drop my gaze to the floor, not sure what to do next. My phone buzzes and I pull it out to check it. Aspen raises an eyebrow, as if curious to see who I'm talking to.

"My ride's waiting on me," I mumble.

Her gaze travels once more up and down my body before she says, "I'll see you around, Charlie," and walks off.

I stand there for several seconds, admiring the way her hips sway as she walks down the hall, before turning on my heels and heading to Riley's car.

"Hey, sorry," I say, still somewhat flustered.

"You okay?"

"Yeah."

We pull out of the parking lot and head towards downtown. I stare out the window, debating if I should bring up the scholarship or just brush it off. Riley and I have been best friends for a long time.

When I first moved to BluHaven, I begged my grandparents to let me play basketball. I was finally old enough to be on a legit team and craved the feeling of being part of something bigger than myself. During the first practice I tripped and faceplanted in front of everyone, parents included. Everybody started pointing and laughing.

Except for Riley; she walked over to me, reached out her hand, helped me back up to my feet. We've been best friends ever since.

It's not like Riley and I have never gotten into an argument before or competed for the same thing. But this is different.

Riley's mom is a pediatrician and her dad owns the local coffee shop across town. They're by no means what people consider 'rich' but they are comfortable.

I can't say the same for my family. Gramps was a police officer for over thirty years, and Nana was a teacher, but having to unexpectedly raise two children gets pretty pricey. They'd give us an arm and a leg if we asked them, but tuition for a university? That's a whole different ball game—one where there's no right answer.

"Do you wanna talk about it?" I ask.

Riley shrugs, her eyes staying glued to the road in front of us. "I don't know, Charlie. I don't know what we're supposed to do now."

"That makes two of us."

"I guess we shouldn't be all that surprised that LittleWood is interested in both of us. And we both want to play ball next year. Maybe we should just drop it until they decide who they want to offer the scholarship to?"

"Okay," I reply, trying to hide the apprehension in my tone. But Riley's always been able to read me like an open book.

She glances towards me, her eyebrows furrowed. "I know that's probably not what you want to hear but I want out of this town just as much as you do."

"I know. But don't you have three other schools that want you? LittleWood is the only school that's interested in me."

"But none of them have officially offered me anything."

"Yet. There's still plenty of time. You could at least tell LittleWood you have other schools interested in you."

"Why would I do that?"

"So they would know you're keeping your options open."

"Seriously, Charlie? You really think that's a good idea? I'd thought you'd be happy for me."

"I am happy for you," I snap. "But let's face it Riley, even if you don't get a scholarship you have a lot more options than I do."

"That's not necessarily true."

"Yes it is. You can go pretty much wherever you want. We both know you have the resources. But me? The furthest I'd be going is to the other side of town."

"So you want me to just give up a potential scholarship? That's not fair, Charlie."

"None of this is fair, Riley. If it was, we wouldn't be having this conversation."

"Can we just drop it?"

"Fine with me," I huff. I turn back towards the window, very much aware that the tension has yet to dissipate. I sink back into the seat as my mind runs through the only options left if I *don't* get the scholarship.

We make a pit stop at the local ice cream parlor before Riley drops me off but neither one of us has much of an appetite.

I give my grandparents a kiss hello, heading straight for the stairs before they're able to bombard me with questions. I toss my things to the side and collapse on my bed. My mind wanders back to my unexpected interaction with Aspen after practice.

I sit up and retrieve my laptop from my desk. I log into Facebook and type Aspen Sullivan in the search bar. It doesn't take long to find her profile. I click on it and scroll through her newsfeed, photos, generic info, and friends list.

She has the typical posts about weekend activities, complaints about school, wardrobe updates, and the most recent one being about her move. I scroll through her photos. There are several pictures of her and a group of kids I don't recognize—most likely friends from back home—a few of her family, and a couple of her and another girl, posing against the backdrop of green fields and a deep blue sky. I slow down, zooming in on the features of her and the mystery girl, not entirely sure why I'm so curious about these specific pictures.

I open a new tab, log onto Instagram, and repeat the same search. I scroll through many of the same photos I saw on Facebook, but there are several more of her and that same girl. My curiosity continues to grow as I study these photos, trying to decipher any clues to tell me who she is. After a few more minutes of playing detective, I close my laptop and crawl into bed.

I'm not sure why I felt the sudden need to do a deep dive into Aspen's social media accounts. There's just something about her that I can't seem to wrap my head around. I close my eyes, replaying today's events in my head and somehow always coming back to Aspen.

Chapter Two

Head to my locker first thing the next morning. I catch a glimpse of Aspen leaning up against the wall across from the lockers, book in hand. I slow my pace, my gaze trailing the outline of her slim frame. She's wearing low-cut jeans that show off her hips, a yellow blouse that hugs her frame, and brown boots.

I glance around her, scanning the area for any sign of Brandon or Alex. She lifts her head, our eyes meeting. A gentle smile spread across her face, sending a chill down my spine. I drop my head, turning to bury my face in my locker as a familiar shape appears next to me.

I turn, not surprised to see Ben standing next to it. "Hey, Charlie." He props his arm against the wall.

"Hi," I say, unamused.

"I was gonna check out the new candy shop that just went in at the mall this weekend, what'd you say you join me?"

I exhale an exasperated breath, peering past him for my best escape route. "I told you I have to study."

"Ah c'mon, Charlie. You can't possibly study all weekend." He takes a gradual step forward. "Take a break and hang out with me."

I shuffle backward slightly, not wanting to be closer to him than I have to be. "Ben," I say impatiently. "I already told you I can't."

"C'mon, Charlie," he pleads. "Give me another chance. I'll make it worth your while."

Oh hell no.

"Jeezus, Ben can't you take a hint? I'm not interested." I slam the locker closed and push past him as the warning bell echoes through the hall, not bothering to look back.

Thankfully, the rest of the morning carries on without another sign of him. I hang back in Calculus after the bell so I'm late getting to lunch. I survey the cafeteria line, looking for any sign of Riley or the other girls but I don't see them.

"Hey, Charlie," a familiar voice says.

I turn and see Aspen Sullivan standing next to me in line. I peer around her but see no sign of Brandon or Alex.

"You expecting someone else?" she says.

I turn my attention back to her, as her wavy brown hair falls in front of her face. "What? Uh no."

"Saw you talking to that boy this morning, thought you might be waiting for him."

"Ben? What—Oh no. Gross. It's not like that."

She nods, smiling as she tucks her hair back behind her ear.

"So how're you liking it?" I ask.

She shrugs. "It's alright. Different from my old school but also the same."

"Yeah," I mumble as we shuffle forward in line. My gaze drops to the floor as I rake my brain for something else to say.

"How long have you lived in BluHaven?"

"Since I was seven." I nod my head towards the direction of my usual table. "You wanna join us?"

"Sure."

I set my tray down next to Riley and motion for Aspen to take the empty seat next to me.

"Where've you been?" Riley asks.

"I had to ask Mr. Murphy a question about the quiz." I take note of the lack of tension between me and Riley today and feel my body slightly relax.

"Who's your friend, Charlie?" says Emily.

"Oh my bad. This is—"

"I know who you are," Skylar cuts in. "You're Aspen. Aspen Sullivan. You and your dad just moved here from Texas."

"You've done your homework," Aspen replies without missing a beat.

Skylar gives Aspen a once-over, leaning forward and placing her hands in front of her, almost as if to create a barrier. "Heard you got into some trouble back in Texas." She raises an eyebrow, daring Aspen to react. "That's why your dad brought you back here to where he grew up. Thought it might do you some good."

Riley waves Skylar off, reaching her hand out towards Aspen, "I'm Riley. It's nice to meet you."

"You too." Aspen extends her hand before turning to me. "You have Mr. Murphy for Calculus?"

I nod, my mouth full of sandwich. "I wanted to ask him about the quiz, it was brutal."

"Tell me about it. Calculus is not my best subject."

"Charlie is a whizz when it comes to math," Riley chimes in.

The heat slowly begins to rise to my cheeks as I shake my head. "I'm alright."

Riley rolls her eyes. "She's just being modest. If it wasn't for Charlie I would've failed trig last year."

The bell rings for fifth period before I have a chance to respond. I reach to collect my backpack, fumbling to grasp the straps as the heat continues to trickle up my neck.

"You wanna study this weekend?" Aspen asks when I've got everything situated. "I could really use the help."

"Sure."

"Saturday?"

"Yeah but is it cool if we do it at your house? It's my grandparents' turn to host the monthly luncheon for church and my brother already called dibs on the car."

"Sure, I'll pick you up around noon?"

"Sounds good to me." I slide my phone out of my bag. "Put your number in my phone so I can text you my address."

She nods, typing her name and number into my phone. She hands it back to me, her fingers grazing mine before she moves past me, the smell of coconut lingering in her wake. I glance down at my phone, smiling at the sight of the winky-face emoji she typed next to her name.

"What's gotten you up out of bed this early on a Saturday?" Nana says as I come into the kitchen, grabbing a Gatorade.

"I'm studying with a friend later and wanted to get a workout in."

"Who are you studying with, dear?"

"Aspen. She's new and we have the same teacher for Calculus."

"You're hanging out with the new girl? The drop dead gorgeous one from Texas?" Matty says with his eyebrow quirked up.

"Yeah."

"I heard her family is super rich. I mean have you seen the clothes that girl wears and the car she drives?"

My ears begin to turn pink as the words tumble out of his mouth. I quickly drop my gaze and head towards the front door. "I hadn't noticed."

"Oh Charlie, would you mind vacuuming this morning? I need to run to the store to pick up some last-minute goodies for lunch today."

"Can't Matty do it? He's not meeting up with Alec until later and I need to practice."

"You know you do a much better job than he does and I want the house to look nice for our company."

"The only reason I do a better job is because the majority of the time you make me do it instead of him. He is more than capable of pushing the vacuum around the living room. It's not difficult."

Nana turns, resting her hand on her hip and giving me her famous 'teacher look' as she narrows her eyes at me. Nana taught English at the local community college, giving her plenty of time to perfect the look that made college kids squirm.

"Charlie Marie, the longer you stand here arguing with me, the less time you will have to practice." She settles her purse onto her shoulder. "Now I expect the house to be vacuumed before you leave, is that understood?"

"Yes," I mumble, resisting the urge to roll my eyes in protest.

Matty smirks and he rises from the table. "Have fun, sis. I'll see you later."

I ignore his jab and head outside, soaking in the warm sunlight before grabbing my basketball from the garage.

It took me weeks of begging and countless hours of chores before my grandparents agreed to get me a basketball goal for the driveway. They were convinced the ball was going to bounce off the rim and somehow manage to smash through one of the windows, even though it's set up at the end of our driveway. After some serious persuading—my main argument being I'll no longer have to walk to the old tattered park down the road *alone* anymore—my grandparents finally gave in.

I spend the next two hours practicing layups, jump shots, dribbling, ball handling, and anything else I can think of to prepare for next week's game. I'm drenched in sweat by the time I head back into the house.

After my shower, I rifle through my closet, trying on four different shirt and pant combinations, before deciding on my royal blue t-shirt with a front pocket and black jeans. I take a minute to examine my selection in the mirror, smiling when I notice how appealing my legs look in the jeans.

I'm not sure why I'm suddenly meticulous about my outfit. I don't usually put this much effort in. But there's a part of me that *wants* Aspen to be impressed with my choice.

I take one last look in the mirror as my phone buzzes with a text from Aspen.

On my way. See u soon :)

I sling my backpack over my shoulder and head downstairs. "I'll be back later tonight," I holler on my way out. I step outside as Aspen's black Lexus pulls into the driveway.

"Hey, Charlie," she says as I slide into the passenger seat. She's wearing dark skinny jeans, a green blouse, and her caramel brown hair is hanging loose around her shoulders. My eyes wander up the length of her body, following her curvy figure till they rest on her face, lingering on her lips. After a moment, I realize I'm *staring*.

"Hey, Aspen. How're you?" I say, trying to play it cool.

"Better now." She flashes me a gentle smile.

She pulls out of the driveway and heads towards the west side of town. We turn onto Washington Street, which doesn't surprise me at all. It leads to the only high-end developments in town. After another minute or two, we turn into the neighborhood, Summit Valley. Two left turns later, she pulls into a long, curved driveway.

I lean forward in my seat, peering at the structure towering in front of me. The first thing I notice is the three-door garage attached to the end of the house. My gaze tracks the outside of the house, wondering if one day I'll see it on the cover of a Southern-Living magazine.

We climb out of the car and I follow her inside, which is just as stunning as the outside. My eyes are immediately drawn to the paintings dominating the wall., Every color is bold and painted with such precise lines that they almost look like a mosaic.

"And who might you be?" says a deep voice, jarring me from my admiration of the interior.

"Dad, this is Charlie," Aspen whispers. She twirls a strand of hair between her fingers as she turns to me. "Charlie, this is my father."

Aspen's father has a large, broad physique, one that suggests years of constant exercise. I guess that's to be expected considering he played QB in high school and served in the military. He's wearing black pressed slacks, a salmon-colored polo, brown loafers, and a gold Rolex watch. His slicked-back hair is dark brown, similar to Aspen's but thinner. They weren't kidding when they said her father was some hotshot businessman. Even on a Saturday his outfit is pristine, like he's on his way to a board meeting.

"Hi," I say more enthusiastically than I mean too. "You have a beautiful home, Mr. Sullivan."

"Thank you." His eyes study me, his gaze traveling up and down for a moment. He tilts his head to the side, our eyes meeting, before he turns back to Aspen. "I didn't realize you were having company."

"Charlie is here to study. We both have Calculus with Mr. Murphy."

"I see." He shifts his gaze back to me. His eyes are the same color blue as Aspen's but there's a darkness to them. I produce a feeble smile, hoping it looks more genuine than it feels.

"I thought you were getting together with that nice young man down the street?" he says to Aspen.

"We had to uh… reschedule. We have a test in Calculus next week and Charlie is helping me study."

"Uh huh. Well, I suppose that's a good enough reason to reschedule." He takes one last look at me. "I've got some work to get done, but don't forget your grandparents and Aunt Beth are coming over for dinner tonight at seven."

She nods as he walks between us towards the living room, the faint smell of whiskey trailing behind him.

"Sorry about that," Aspen says when her dad is out of earshot. "He's not really the friendliest around company, my mom usually handled that."

"It's okay."

"Shall I give you a tour?"

"Sure."

I follow her through the rest of the house, stopping to do a double-take of the luxury pool and basketball goal in the backyard through the large glass door, before she leads me upstairs to her bedroom.

Her room is at least twice the size of my room and just as furnished as the rest of the house. A four-poster bed with a coffee-colored comforter is positioned against the back wall. A TV is mounted directly across from the bed; a dresser and desk sit opposite each other on either wall. A small jacuzzi tub sits in the attached bathroom, and her walk-in closet has enough space for an entire department store worth of shoes. There's similar artwork pinned to the wall above her desk, but these pieces seem much more personal. There are sketches of animals, scenery, flowers, even a few people. Every stroke is carefully thought out and precise, down to the pupils of the animals.

"Did you draw these?" I walk over, taking a closer look.

"Yeah, it's just a hobby of mine," she says shyly.

"They're incredible."

"Thanks." She moves closer, our bodies only inches apart. "Maybe I can draw you sometime?"

I shift my head, our eyes locking as I catch a whiff of the peppermint on her breath. "Sure, I'd like that."

We stay like this for another moment, both of us waiting for the other to move. She tilts her head slightly, a strand of hair falling in front of her face and I have the sudden urge to tuck it back into place.

"So," I say, breaking the silence as I slip my backpack off my shoulders. "You ready to study?"

She walks to the window and peers out, as if she's looking for something. She spins around, a childish grin spread across her face. "I have another idea."

I raise an eyebrow, waiting for her to elaborate.

"What if you show me around BluHaven instead?"

"But what about the test?"

"We can study later," she says waving off my question.

I cock my head to the side, considering her request.

"C'mon, Charlie, please," she pleads, interlacing her fingers and placing them underneath her chin. She lightly bounces up and down on the balls of her feet, as if she's a child begging to a parent. "I need somebody to show me places other than the mall and school."

"What about your dad?"

"What about him?"

"You told him I came over here to study, and he didn't exactly seem pleased either. Isn't he going to be a little curious as to why we are all of a sudden leaving?"

"We'll just say you forgot something at your house, no biggie."

"Alright." I zip my backpack closed.

"Yay," she says, excitedly. She walks over, grabs my hand and pulls me towards the door, "C'mon."

There's a slight drop in my stomach when her fingers touch mine. She lets go as we descend the staircase.

"I thought you two were studying?" We freeze at the sound of her father's voice.

Aspens spins around, continuing to shuffle backward to the door as she speaks. "We are. We just have to get a couple books and things from Charlie's house. We'll be back later."

She nudges me towards the door before her father has a chance to respond. She tosses me the keys before heading to the passenger side door.

I stop walking. "You want me to drive?"

"Well duh. You're the one showing me around, remember?"

"But what about your dad?" I use my thumb to motion back to the house. "What if I wreck it?"

"Relax, Charlie," she says with a grin. "I trust you." She slides into the passenger seat before I can argue.

I sigh, climb into the driver's seat and turn on the car. I ease out of the driveway, careful not to hit the curb, and head towards town.

"Where to?" I ask.

"Anywhere is fine with me."

I lean back, resting my arm on the center console next to hers as I mull over where we should go.

She leans forward, the hem of her shirt rising up just enough for me to catch a peek of her smooth, tan skin underneath. She fidgets with the buttons on the radio, turning the knob until a familiar pop song plays through the speakers.

She leans back, grazing my skin ever so slightly as she positions her arm next to mine.

A few minutes later, I pull into the parking lot of *The Book Worm*.

"Where are we?" Aspen asks, peering forward.

"Just one of my favorite places."

I watch as her eyebrows furrow before she flashes me a wide grin as we step foot into the outdated structure. It was built sometime in the fifties, originally used for some sort of office space before it was turned into a used bookstore. It's scattered with an assortment of bookshelves of all shapes and sizes. They're so close together it's almost as if you're weaving in and out of a maze.

"What'd you think?" I ask after she's had a minute to take it all in.

She whirls around, her lips pulled back into a gorgeous smile. "It's fantastic. I didn't even know this was here."

"It's a little outdated." I glance around. "Most people prefer *Barnes & Noble* or ordering online but this place has so many different kinds of books you just wouldn't believe."

"Let's go explore." She grabs my hand and pulls me forward.

We meander through the numerous bookshelves around us, pausing here and there to pull out a book and skim through it.

"Why'd you bring me here?" Aspen says, looking up from the book opened in her palms.

I tuck the book in my hand back in its place on the shelf, glancing at her. There's a few strands of hair dangling in front of her face and I have the inexplicable urge to run my fingers through her hair, tucking away the loose strands in the process.

"I don't know," I finally say. "I just thought you might like this better than the mall or movie theater. Would you rather go somewhere else?"

"No," she says quickly. She reaches her hand out, gingerly grabbing my forearm. "This is perfect." She turns, heading for the next row of shelves, the touch of her fingertips leaving a warm trail on my skin. "C'mon, let's keep going."

I follow, not needing to be told twice.

We spend another ten minutes wandering through the store before we both grab a couple books and make our way to the chairs in the back corner. We sit, our legs barely inches apart.

"What kind of books do you like to read?" I ask.

"I'm open to just about anything and everything. Lately, I've been into the older, classic type books. I just got done reading *Pride and Prejudice*."

"What'd you think of it?"

She shrugs lightly. "Not bad. Most girls swoon over Mr. Darcy, but he's not really my type."

"Oh yeah? I haven't read that one yet. We had to read a couple 'classic' books for English last year." I put air quotes around classic. "All of the kids complained about it the entire time but I have to admit, I enjoyed them more than I thought I would."

"Really?" she says with a playful smirk. "I didn't peg you for the classic literary type."

I give her a grin in return. "Now what in the world would make you think that?"

She pauses, her eyes glancing up and down. "You just seem like somebody who'd rather be doing something active."

A soft laugh bubbles out. "Don't get me wrong, I love playing ball. I'd do it all the time if I was given the opportunity. But when I was a kid reading was my favorite thing to do."

"Until you started playing basketball," she teases.

"I still enjoyed reading, I just enjoyed playing basketball a little more."

"But I know what you mean," she says with a mild nod. "My mom used to read me all sorts of books when I was a kid, everything from fairy tales and Dr. Seuss to poetry and fantasy. She was the one who made me fall in love with reading."

I smile, encouraging her to continue.

"Every night, she'd crawl into my bed and read me a book. No matter what was going on, even if we had gotten in an argument that day, she would still read to me at night. When I was old enough to read on my own, I still wanted her to read to me; it just wasn't the same without her. I'd lay down beside her, our heads nuzzled on the pillows next to each other, and just get lost in the story. It was like we were on our own little adventure. She had this ability when she was reading to make the rest of the world just fade away, it would just be me, her, and the characters in the story. When she finished a book, she would always ask me about my favorite part. I always thought it was when the hero comes out on top, but it turns out my favorite part was listening to her tell it." She drops her gaze to the floor. "And then one day she just stopped. I guess she thought I was too old to be read to anymore."

Without realizing it, I reach out and gently lay my hand on her knee. "Sounds like you and your mom were close. I'm really sorry. I can't even imagine how much you miss her."

She looks up, our eyes meeting as she timidly places her hand on mine. The tingle from her touch sends a shiver down my spine. "Thanks, Charlie."

After a moment she stands up, ending the moment. "You hungry?"

"I could eat."

We exit the bookstore and climb back in the car.

"What're you in the mood for?" I ask.

"Doesn't matter to me. You're in charge, remember?"

I nod, rolling the windows down as we drive towards downtown. We spend the drive listening to the radio while I peek glances at Aspen's hair blowing around in the wind. I pull into the parking lot of *Barry's Old Fashioned Burgers* and shut off the car.

"What's this?" Aspen leans forward to look out the windshield.

"Only the best burger and milkshake joint in town."

"Never heard of it."

"Aspen Sullivan, you have not lived till you've eaten at this place." We climb out of the car and walk inside.

The second we step inside, we're met with the pungent aroma of fried food. The diner is a small hole-in-the-wall restaurant that you wouldn't notice unless you knew what to look for. The booths and tables are worn, with tears and wrinkles in the upholstery. The interior design looks like it hasn't been updated since it first opened in the sixties but the dim lighting creates a sort of retro atmosphere so it works. We maneuver around the tables and chairs and slide into an empty booth in the back.

A young waiter with an unkempt mullet walks over to our table, pulling out a small notepad from his apron. "Good afternoon," he mumbles. "Can I getcha' somethin' to drink?"

"Coke," says Aspen.

"Same," I say.

He nods, drops the pad back in his front pocket and walks away.

"So what's good here?" says Aspen as she pulls out a menu.

"Pretty much everything. My go-to is usually a burger and fries but the sandwiches are really good too."

The waiter returns, setting our drinks down. "What'll be?"

"I'll have a cheeseburger, fries, and a strawberry milkshake with extra whipped cream."

He nods, turning to Aspen and raising a brow.

"I'll have the same thing but we'll just share the shake." She looks at me. "If that's okay with you?"

"Sure."

He nods, scribbles on his pad and then walks back towards the kitchen.

My eyes find Aspen. Her hair is a bit tousled from the car ride over here, causing several pieces to fall in front of her face. My hand twitches at the urge to tuck it back into place. I pick up my straw wrapper, folding it into a tiny square as a distraction.

"So you've been here since you were seven?" she asks.

I nod.

"And you live with your grandparents?"

"Yeah."

"What about your parents?"

I exhale slowly, rolling what's left of the straw wrapper into a tiny ball.

"I'm sorry, I didn't mean to overstep."

I shake my head. "No, it's okay." I begin by telling her the story of how my parents got together and how they eventually lost custody. "There's a reason people say marrying your high school sweetheart is a bad idea—that it usually never works out in the end. I guess they thought they were the exception, at least until everything went to hell."

"I'm so sorry, Charlie," she says, her tone sincere. "I can't imagine how difficult that must've been."

"It's okay," I say. "I'm grateful my grandparents took us in. We never went to bed hungry; never had to wear the same clothes every day of the week without washing them. The first Christmas we spent together was the kind of Christmas we had always dreamt about—the ones we would see in the movies and wonder if we would ever get to experience it for ourselves. That morning, we woke to a thin layer of snow on the ground, just enough to cover everything in a white blanket. There were two brand new bikes waiting for us nestled beside the tree."

I smile to myself as I replay the memory in my head. "Mine was green with flowers on the frame and Matty's was red and decorated with superheroes. We rode those bikes up and down the neighborhood all the time. We'd stay out till dark, usually until Gramps dragged us back inside."

"That sounds like it was really special."

I nod. "Yeah. It was the first time we opened something that wasn't from a flea market or garage sale. They've given us everything we could possibly want. We're lucky."

"Sounds like your grandparents really care."

"They do." I drop my gaze to the table.

She tilts her head to the side, her eyebrows raised. "What is it, Charlie?"

I glance up, my eyes fixed on Aspen's. "It's just, there's a part of me that can't help but wonder what life might've been like if my parents were able to get it together. I know that sounds messed up. But we were a family once, and we were happy. I just don't know what went wrong. I tried talking to my grandparents about it but they would never answer me. They always just brushed it off and changed the subject."

"I'm sorry," she says softly.

I run my fingers through my hair, pushing the memories to the back of my mind. "It's weird." I lean forward, resting my hands around my cup of water. "I don't normally open up to people like this." I glance up, her deep blue eyes sparkling with emotion. "But you're easy to talk to."

She leans forward and lightly caresses the top of my hand before pulling away. "I could say the same about you. I don't normally tell people that story about my mom right off the bat."

"Well, I'm glad you did."

"Me too."

We're in the middle of a laughing fit over the time Matty dove headfirst into his birthday cake at his eighth birthday party when our food arrives.

"So did you still eat the cake?" Aspen asks in between bites of her burger.

"Well, Matty had the cake that was smeared all over his face and Gramps did his best to salvage what was left of the rest of it. On the bright side we still had ice cream."

She giggles. "You and your brother seem really close."

"We are." I dip a fry into the milkshake and pop it in my mouth. "I mean he gets on my nerves all the time and we always fight over the car but at the end of the day, he's the one person I can count on no matter what. When everything went down with my parents, all we had was each other. He was the only other person that knew what I was feeling."

"That must've been nice not having to go through that alone."

"Yeah," I say with a sigh. "I just wish I could've done more to protect him."

Aspen reaches over, placing her hand on mine and my heart rate increases. "You were there for him," she says gently. "That's all that matters."

I smile at her, making no move to pull my hand away. Her touch is oddly comforting. We sit like this for a few more seconds, soaking up the moment as it passes between us, before she leans against the booth, sliding her hand back with her.

We finish eating, pay the check and head back to her place.

"You ready to study?" I ask as we pull into her driveway.

"I guess." She throws her head back in a dramatic fashion and I chuckle.

We make our way inside and head straight for her bedroom. I grab my backpack from the floor, set it on her desk and begin removing my textbook, notes and a couple pens. I glance at Aspen, who is sprawled out on her bed, making no effort to retrieve her notes.

"It'll probably be easier to study if you get out your book and notes," I say.

"Or," she says with a grin. "You can come over here and show me yours instead." She delicately pats the empty space next to her—an open invitation.

Her hair is still disheveled from the wind, stray tendrils falling freely around her face. She's laying on her side, her head propped up with the palm of her hand. The hem of her pants slide down as she readjusts to make room for me, the curve of her hips peeking out. I avert my gaze and quickly gather the rest of my notes as heat rumbles low in my belly.

I sit on the bed, leaning against the wall as I lay out the notes in between us. We spend the next hour and a half reviewing everything we've covered in class from the beginning of the semester to now.

"I think it's time for a study break." Aspen pushes the book to the front of the bed.

"Didn't we do that earlier?"

She gives me a playful grin. "You can take more than one study break."

"Okay." I lean back against the pillows.

"So have you dated a lot of boys from school?"

"Not exactly."

She raises an eyebrow, rolling over so she's facing me.

"I've dated a few guys here and there, but nothing ever really serious. What about you?" I say, deflecting. "You date a lot of boys back at your old school?"

She nods. "A couple but it didn't last very long."

"Oh yeah? Why's that?"

"Turns out they weren't really my type," she says, inching closer.

"I see. And what is your type?"

Her cheeks blush as a tiny smile tugs at the corner of her mouth. She glances up. "I don't know, someone who's fun to be around, knows how to make me laugh, and is a decent person."

"Well no wonder none of your relationships lasted long. You have ridiculously high standards."

She laughs and gives me a gentle shove. "Shut up."

"I'm just teasing."

"I've had a lot of fun today, Charlie."

"Me too." I smile.

She looks up, running her fingers through her hair and letting it fall back into place. "I'm really glad I met someone like you."

"Me too." I lift my gaze, our eyes locking as I gradually inch my fingers closer towards hers, the warmth from her skin radiating as our hands connect.

The presence of her father in the door severs the connection and we both immediately sit up, careful to leave plenty of space in between us. He takes a step forward, glances in my direction and a hint of indignation flickers behind his eyes. A moment later, it's gone.

He turns to Aspen, "Aspen, dear. Your grandparents and Aunt Beth will be here soon. Why don't you put on that pretty yellow dress your grandmother got you for your birthday last year?"

Aspen flashes him a bright smile. "Sure, Dad."

I hop off the bed, taking his glare as a sign that it's time for me to leave. "I should go." I shuffle around the room, gathering my things.

"I'll drive you home," Aspen says, standing up.

Her father sighs loudly enough to make a point. "Please be quick about it. You know your grandparents don't like to be kept waiting."

She nods, heading for the door. I follow, mumbling a 'nice to meet you' as I pass by him in the doorway.

"I don't think your father likes me that much," I say once we're safely in her car.

"He wasn't always like that. We were really happy once. We used to do things as a family all the time. You know that thing where you can just look at two people and tell they're in love?"

"Yeah."

"That was my parents. I know it seems hard to believe given how stand-offish my dad is but my parents loved each other. He used to work less, sulk less, drink less, and seemed genuinely happy. They'd do stuff that'd be super cute in some cheesy romantic comedy but cringe-worthy in real life. I mean, they'd just look at each other and get these goofy grins—like they were back in college and seeing each other for the first time. I know it might sound weird, but after seeing how they interacted with each other, I always thought how nice it'd be to have someone look at me that way."

I resist the urge to reach over and take her hand. "So what happened?" I ask, tentatively.

She exhales slowly, like she's mustering up the energy to continue. "Then my mom and I were in a pretty bad car wreck. We were coming back from an art show in Dallas. My dad was supposed to come with us but he had been working more and more lately and couldn't make it. It was dark and she'd just got off the phone with my dad and didn't seem too happy about how the conversation went. Then a truck crossed over the median on the interstate and we didn't see it until it was too late. It slammed into the side of the car causing us to veer off the road and crash into a tree."

I glance over, watching as the tears slowly spill down her cheeks. She quickly wipes her face with the back of her hand before continuing. "My mom didn't make it and I did."

Instinctively, I reach over and squeeze her hand, hoping my gesture will communicate what words cannot. "I'm so sorry, Aspen."

"I think my dad blames himself for what happened. And maybe a part of me blames him too. God, that sounds so awful of me to say. But my parents had been fighting constantly; it was like no matter what we were doing, an argument was bound to ensue. I think that's why he'd been staying at work late all the time. I think he may have purposefully missed the show. I could tell my mom was upset that he bailed. But part of me felt a little bit of relief because for those couple hours, it was just me and her and I could pretend that everything was fine. Until it wasn't. He's never been the same since. Neither of us have."

"I can't even imagine what that must've been like."

We pull into the driveway. The moonlight casts a shadow across her face, the tears shimmering on her cheeks. I make no move to get out, my hand still firmly grasping hers.

"I'm sorry, Charlie. I didn't mean to unload that on you. It just felt good actually saying it out loud for a change."

"It's okay. I'm glad you told me."

"Thank you," she says.

"For what?"

"For today."

I smile at the tender squeeze of her fingers around mine. "Anytime."

"I'll see you at school?" she says.

"Of course." I climb out of the car, watching as she pulls back onto the road and drives away.

I make my way towards the house, wondering when was the last time I spent the day with someone who made me feel this good, made me feel this *alive*. It's like I'm on an emotional high, one like I've never experienced before. Aspen....she's different—different from anyone I've ever met. There's a strange sense of longing for her; like the day is over but I'm just not ready to leave her yet.

Chapter Three

On Monday morning, the aroma of pancakes summons me from my fog of slumber. I scurry out of bed and head for the shower, thoughts of Aspen winding their way into my mind. The idea of running into her before school makes me shudder with anticipation.

Still having an inclination to impress her, I deliberately choose a pair of jeans with tears in the thighs, and a white V-neck. I tame the last few strands of my hair before slipping on my grey converse and heading downstairs.

My phone buzzes and my heart skips a beat thinking it's from Aspen. My stomach sinks when I realize it's from Ben.

Would love 2 see you this week if u r free :)

I ignore it, once again wondering why he can't take a freaking hint.

I head straight for my locker when we arrive at school. Aspen's leaning against the locker next to mine, a book balanced in her palm. I slow my pace, taking my time to admire her from a distance.

"Hey."

A timid smile spreads across her face. "Hey yourself."

"I brought you something." I slide my backpack off my shoulders.

"Oh yeah?" she says, the smile growing wider.

I retrieve a book from my bag, *Bellow From Beneath*, and hand it to her. "It was one of the books we had to read in English last semester. Thought you might enjoy it since you're into the classics right now. It's about a guy on a fishing expedition in the nineteen-hundreds.

His boat capsizes in the middle of a horrible storm, and he washes up on a supposedly deserted island."

She turns it over in her hands, studying the cover before tucking it away in her bag. "Thanks, Charlie."

The warning bell echoes through the hall, abruptly ending our conversation. She reaches over, resting her hand on my forearm, the feel of her fingers on my skin sends a tingle rippling up my arm.

"I'll see you at lunch?" she asks.

I nod. "Yeah."

She slips past me, the smell of coconut lingering behind her as she strolls down the hall.

"Hey, Charlie," Ben says. I let another moment pass as I watch Aspen saunter down the hall before begrudgingly turning my attention to Ben.

This time, he's accompanied by Will and Trey and I resist the urge to roll my eyes at the thought of him bringing backup.

I've had several classes with Trey but our conversations never went anything beyond the assignment or sports. Will and I had used to be good friends in middle school. He was a short, stocky kid who had just moved here at the beginning of seventh grade. He got branded the 'Teacher's Pet' on his first day and it stuck with him up until the summer before high school. He went out of town and came back, tan, muscular, and had all the girls fawning over him. It became very clear where his priorities were after that.

"What do you want?" I say, irritation seeping through.

"Just wondering if you got my text?"

"I told you I'm not interested." I try to shuffle past him. He takes one long stride to the left, blocking my path. "Saw you talkin' to the new girl."

"And?"

"C'mon, Charlie. Our families go way back. You really think they'd be happy with you hanging out with someone like her?" He nods his head in the direction Aspen went.

"Just because our grandparents grew up together, doesn't mean anything."

Our grandparents have been friends for years. Our grandfathers had worked together in the sheriff's department before retiring. Now,

Ben's father runs the department, along with his two oldest brothers. Ben might be quite the charmer when he's around adults, always knowing just what to say, but that usually doesn't carry over when it comes to people our age.

Ben shakes his head, making a *tisk-tisk* noise. "C'mon, Charlie don't you think you're better off hangin' with a guy like me?"

I do my best to stifle a laugh. "Ben, my grandparents have no idea what I want, but I know it's not you." I use my shoulder to push past him and head towards class.

By the time lunch rolls around, I've nearly forgotten about my interaction with Ben this morning.

I hop in line next to Riley. " Hey, girl. Tyler and I are going to the mall this weekend with a couple of his friends. You should come with us. I think they wanna check out the new movie that's playing."

I roll my eyes, thinking back to the last time Riley roped me into hanging out with her, Tyler and some of his 'friends'. Turned out that when she was referring to 'friends', she just meant one of his friends, Noah. It didn't take long to figure out that she'd set me up on a blind date.

We went to the carnival that was in town for the weekend. It started off pretty decent; we played a couple different carnival games like Ring Toss, Shooting Gallery, and the one where you use darts to pop the balloons. Tyler won an orange and yellow polka dot teddy bear for Riley. Noah and I, on the other hand, didn't have much luck.

I was having a great time until Riley and Tyler decided to run off to ride the Ferris Wheel. Noah wasn't big on rides and neither was I, so we just wandered around the area instead. We ended up behind the concession stand and before I knew it, Noah had me pinned up against the fence trying to force his tongue into my mouth. I managed to squirm out of his grasp, mumbling a 'goodnight' as I fled.

When I told Riley what happened, she said I needed to give him another chance, that I need to relax and let my instincts take over. Reluctantly, I agreed to another date, if you can even call it that. This time we went bowling. The bowling part was actually pretty enjoyable, even though my ball ended up in the gutter more than it connected with the pins. When we were walking back to our cars, he kissed me again. I tried to stay calm and let my instinct kick in, but it was like he was trying to swallow me. Riley stopped trying to set me up after that.

"I don't know, Riley. The last time you tricked me into a blind date."

She laughs. "I promise it's not a trap. C'mon, it could be fun."

"I'll think about," I tell her, knowing damn well I'm not actually going to go.

"I called you Saturday, but you were MIA."

"Oh my bad. I was studying with Aspen all day, I guess I didn't hear my phone."

We head towards our usual spot, my eyes scanning the tables scattered about, searching for Aspen and hoping it's not too obvious. I watch her stroll into the cafeteria, conscious of how some people are still as captivated as I am. The knot in my stomach tightens as she turns back to Brandon, giggling at something he said. I take a seat, diverting my eyes to the now unappetizing food sitting in front of me.

"Can I join you?"

I glance over, surprised to see Aspen standing behind an empty chair. I peer around her, looking for Brandon but he seems to have vanished. I realize I never answered her when I hear Riley say, "Of course."

Aspen sits, her knee bumping against mine.

"You coming to the game this week?" Riley asks.

"Uhh I hadn't really thought about it," Aspen says.

"You should come, it'd be fun," I say.

"Yeah." Riley nudges me with her elbow. "Charlie and I have a college that's interested and they'll be at the game this week. I'm sure we could use your support."

"Yeah, let's just hope she doesn't blow it at the end like in the last game," Skylar cuts in.

I roll my eyes, ignoring her comment.

"So is it the same school that's interested in both of you?" Aspen asks.

I glance at Riley, waiting for her to answer.

Riley nods her head. "They're interested in both of us, but they only have room for one of us."

"Oh," Aspen says softly.

"So how is that going to work exactly?" Skylar says. "Are they going to pit you against each other? Make you play a game of one-on-one and see who wins?"

I shrug. "No idea."

"Riley, don't you already have some other schools that want you?"

"Yes," Riley says.

"I see. And Charlie, any other schools interested in you?"

"Nope."

"Huh. Well that's quite the predicament then."

"Thank you for that astute observation, Skylar," I deadpan.

"We're going to let them decide who they want, right Charlie? It's up to them in the end anyways."

"Right," I drop my gaze to the tray, trying to ignore the discontent building inside of me when I feel the gentle embrace of Aspen's hand on my knee.

My heart skips a beat at her touch—something I realize happens often when she's around.

The tender touch of her hand is exhilarating and comforting at the same time, like the calm of the sea just before a summer storm. I'm not usually one to seek physical contact but for some reason when it comes to Aspen, I can't seem to get enough.

I chance a sideways glance, and a whisper of a smile flickers across her mouth as she catches my eye. The bell echoes through the cafeteria before I can reciprocate the touch.

"I'll see you around, Charlie," Aspen says as I feel the light grasp of her hand on mine as she shuffles past me down the hall.

It's game day. My favorite day of the week. Coach Stewart is a little (more like a lot) superstitious and requires us to wear our matching BluHaven Falcons Basketball shirt and jeans every game of the season. He's convinced that's one of the reasons we've done so well this season, but I'm not so sure I agree with him.

I'm perpetually nervous on game days, no matter how pre-pared I am. And today my nerves are at an all-time high given the circumstances surrounding tonight's game. This is my chance to show this recruit that I deserve a scholarship, that I have something to offer.

The sight of seeing Aspen leaning up against the lockers waiting for me is just what I need to simmer my churning stomach.

"Hey," she says with a smile.

"Hey."

"You okay?"

I nod. "Yeah, just a little nervous for tonight's game."

"I'm sure you're going to do great," she says, her expression sincere.

"I hope."

"You'll be fine." She takes a small step forward, a coy grin etched at the corner of her mouth. "And besides I'll be there, cheering you on the whole time. I can be your good luck charm."

A soft laugh escapes. "Yeah, that'd be great."

The bell rings and we head our separate ways, but not before the fleeting touch of her hand grazes my arm.

The rest of the day continues in a blur. I make my way from class to class, going through the motions of note-taking, but failing at concentrating on anything other than tonight. When the final bell rings, I meet up with Riley and we head to our usual sandwich shop across the street.

"You okay? You seem a little off today?" Riley asks, taking a bite of her turkey club.

"Yeah, I'm just nervous about tonight."

"You and me both."

I give her a sheepish smile before taking a small bite of sandwich.

"You sure there's not more to it than that?"

I shrug. Riley's always been able to tell when something's up, no matter how well I try to mask it. But this is not the time nor place to unload on Riley about these sudden feelings I have when I'm with Aspen. And besides, there's too much at stake right now. I need my focus to be on this game.

"You think it'll be the same woman at tonight's game or someone different?"

"No idea. Have you talked to her at all?"

"No. Have you?"

"I did a little bit at last week's game but it was only for a few minutes."

"Oh." I drop my gaze, doing my best to feign excitement. "That's good."

We spend the next few minutes eating in silence; the only sound coming from the *ding* of the door opening and closing.

"Why didn't you tell me?" I ask, shyly.

"I'm sorry, Charlie. But I didn't want to upset you. I know how badly you want out and I don't want to be the reason you miss your chance but I need a scholarship too."

"Look, I don't want to fight right before the most important game of our high school career. So can we just drop it?"

"You brought it up."

"You're right. And you answered my question. Now can we move on please?"

"Alright." She throws her hands up like she's surrendering. "So you and Aspen seem to be spending quite a lot of time together."

"Yeah?" I say, more as a question than a statement.

"You blew off a date with Ben to hang out with her?"

"So? Ben's an asshole and we were studying. She's also brand new to town, I was just being friendly."

Riley shrugs, shoveling the last bite of sandwich into her mouth. "I was just curious, that's all."

I ball my wrapper and stuff it into my empty chips bag, "You ready? I'd like to get some extra shots in before the game."

"Yeah, we can go."

There's a tradition during sporting events at BluHaven. It began when my grandparents went to school here and just stuck. See, we didn't always dominate in sports like we do now. We used to be pretty awful actually. One year, the principal was determined to boost morale and school spirit. He bet the student body that if they came out to support our players and show their school spirit, he would dress like a chicken for an entire school day. Surprisingly, it worked.

They sold more tickets that year than any of the previous years. The students covered themselves from head to toe in our school colors, blue and white. They would wear blue sweaters in the summer heat, long white pants, blue socks and shoes, and some of them even painted their face. I must admit, I always thought it was a little extra but there's nothing quite like the feeling of being on the court and experiencing the thrill of the crowd cheering you on.

I'm doing my best to drown out the usual humdrum conversations around me and focus on the game at hand, while we wait for Coach to deliver his 'before the game speech.' The only problem is, thoughts of Aspen keep slithering into my mind. The thought of her up in the bleachers, cheering me on tonight, makes my heart beat like a wild animal trying to escape my chest.

"You ready, Charlie?" Skylar's question jars me from my thoughts.

"What? Oh, yeah."

"Maybe you should stop daydreaming and focus."

There's a knock on the door and Coach enters before I'm able to respond, probably a good thing. He steps in front of us, clapping his hands and flashing us a bright smile, before he settles his hands on his hips. "We play Crossroads tonight. We played them once before and destroyed 'em and there's no doubt in my mind that tonight will be any different." He turns towards the board, grabs a marker and begins drawing a make-shift court on the whiteboard in front of us. "Now, they have two decent guards that know how to handle a ball. Charlie, Riley, you stick to them like glue; wherever they go, you go. They've got one really tall girl who usually stays by the basket, shuffling back and forth between the blocks. Emily, you stay on her." He sets the marker down, turning back towards us, "Now the rest of you, cover your man, stay low, and let's get this win.

"Falcons on three…one…two…three…FALCONS!"

I have yet to discover anything that compares to the adrenaline rush that ignites as we charge out of the locker room and onto the court. Feet stomping, hands clapping, and the whooping and hollering of the crowd erupts like an auditory volcano, rising to a crescendo as we begin our warmup routine.

I lay the ball in the basket, jogging to the back of the line as my eyes survey the crowd for Aspen. I spot Matty standing next to his best friend, Alec. They both wave enthusiastically, a goofy grin etched across their faces. I give them a nod of acknowledgment before catching the ball and pulling up beside the free-throw line for a jump shot.

At the end of our last warmup, Coach calls us over to the bench before I'm able to continue my search. I take my seat next to the other starters, wait for my name and number to be announced through the speakers, and then run through the tunnel of cheerleaders and players.

Still no sign of her.

We take our positions for tip-off. One last glance before we start... there she is! Aspen's in the upper right corner, her hair falling effortlessly around her shoulders. She flashes me a tantalizing smile when our eyes meet.

Now, I'm ready.

The first half flies by, ending with a score of twenty-four to eleven, BluHaven in the lead. I peek at Aspen as we jog into the locker room, her lips curled back in a devilish grin. Did she just wink at me?

Coach plows through the door right behind us, beginning his halftime speech with the basic fundamentals.

A smile flutters across my face as I picture Aspen cheering from the bleachers. The *thrum thrum* of my heartbeat steadily increases with each passing second as thoughts of Aspen continue to inhabit my mind.

"Baker are you with us?" Coach barks, jolting me out of my trance.

I bring my gaze up from where I was staring at the floor. "Uh...yes sir."

"I hope so, because we still have another half to play. Just because we're up doesn't mean they're going to roll over and give it to us."

I rub the back of my neck, attempting to divert my attention back to the game as we exit the locker room.

"What'd you keep looking at?" Skylar says, coming up behind me.

"Nothing." I trot over to the baseline, taking my spot for the second half, but not before I notice Skylar's head turning in Aspen's direction.

Crossroads has possession at the start of the second half. My man dribbles the ball down the court, lobbing it to the wing as she makes a hard cut towards the basket. I shove my way through the sweaty defenders, anticipating their next move. Out of the corner of my eye, I catch sight of the ball hurtling towards her. I extend my arm just far enough to interrupt the pass and tip the ball out in front of me.

I sprint down the court, pushing the ball out in front of me as my feet pound against the hardwood floor. The crowd explodes with applause as I go in for the layup. I hustle back on defense, catching a glimpse of Aspen bouncing on the balls of her feet as she cheers, her lips pulled back into a bright smile.

Crossroads is able to get a few shots off by the end of the third quarter, but we're still leading, with a score of thirty-nine to eighteen. We huddle around Coach, a contagious energy dispersing among us, eager to finish what we started.

"One quarter. Eight minutes. That's all that's left. Look at the scoreboard," he says, motioning with his thumb. "They're not coming back from that. Keep playin' hard but we don't have to pick 'em up as soon as they inbound the ball. Pick 'em up at half court. Let's finish this.

"Falcons on three...one...two...three...FALCONS!"

The fourth quarter begins with Riley shooting a three after a glorious pass by yours truly. We hustle back on defense, the adrenaline infectious as the yellow digits of the clock tick away. I peer into the stands, immediately finding Aspen. Our eyes meet briefly and a grin flickers across her face. I return the smile before shifting my concentration back to the game, all of a sudden having a surge of energy.

I watch as Riley's man dribbles the ball down the court, hand raised in the air, signaling the play. I keep my attention centered on my man as the scene unfolds around me. She cuts to the top of the key, palms facing outward. I lunge forward, my hand connecting with the ball as it soars through the air. I drive the ball towards the other end of the court, laying it in the basket with ease. I'm able to get a few more shots off before the final buzzer sounds, ending the game with a score of forty-seven to twenty-three.

I felt good tonight. Really good.

We jog back into the locker room, clapping and slapping each other on the back as Coach strides in behind us. His speech is short—a few congratulatory remarks—before dismissing us with one last 'good job'. I saunter back to my locker, still relishing the victory as the locker room buzzes with laughter and conversation. I can't help but wonder if me playing so well tonight had anything to do with who was up in the stands?

"What the hell was that, Charlie?" Skylar barks after Coach exits the locker room.

"What the hell was what, Skylar?"

"That little stunt you pulled in the fourth quarter. Coach said to play D at half court but you just did what you wanted instead."

I roll my eyes, yanking off my jersey and tossing it into the growing pile in the middle of the room. "I stole the ball and I scored. Last time I checked, that was a good thing."

She takes a step forward, placing her hands on her hips. "But Coach said to ease back. It wasn't necessary. We were up by like twenty points. You were just trying to show off for your little 'friend'," Skylar snaps, putting air quotes around the word 'friend'.

"What's your problem Skylar? First you're on my case about not screwing up in the game and now that we've won, you're on my case about doing too much? I saw an opening and I took it."

"Oh c'mon, Charlie," she says, throwing her hands in the air. "The only reason you were playing so hard was because of who was sitting in the bleachers."

"That's bullshit and you know it. I give it my all every damn game."

She rolls her eyes and slowly shakes her head before turning back to her locker. "Whatever."

I finish changing and throw the rest of my gear into my bag, purposefully avoiding Riley's eye.

"Just ignore her, Charlie. You gotta stop letting her get to you like that."

I throw my bag over my shoulder, mumble a 'see you tomorrow' to Riley and head out the door.

"Baker," Coach calls as I turn the corner. "There's someone I'd like you to meet."

Shit. I completely forgot about the recruiter from LittleWood. I take a breath, regaining my composure before I plaster a smile to my face and walk over to him.

I'm led to a woman wearing a black pants with a cream-colored blouse, and red high heels. Her makeup is thick and flashy, making her look older than she probably is. Her hair's pulled back into a tight bun, and she's carrying a slim leather briefcase in her right hand.

She steps forward and extends her free hand. "Charlie, my name is Juliet McCalister. I'm a recruiter from LittleWood University in Arizona. I understand you're interested in playing for us next year."

I reach out my hand, returning the gesture. My head swirls as I comprehend the words that have just come out of her mouth. "Yes ma'am."

She nods toward the court. "You seem to know what you're doing out there. You and Ms. Perkins have quite the chemistry when it comes to playing ball."

I nod, the heat rushing to my cheeks as I try to think of something to say.

"I'm sure Coach Stewart has already told you that we are interested in you and Ms. Perkins. Unfortunately, we only have enough room for one of you."

"Yes ma'am," I squeak as I try to contain my composure. I catch a glimpse of Coach waving to someone; a few seconds later, Riley is standing next to me. I keep my attention focused on the woman in front of me.

"Riley," Ms. McCalister says with a smile as she reaches out her hand. "It's good to see you again. Great game."

"Thank you."

She glances back and forth between the two of us. "I've watched game footage of both of you and like what I see. I like it even more now that I've seen you two in person a few times. You guys gave it your all out there and that's what we're looking for in players. But we also want to see you transfer that same determination and hard work off the court. I'm going to talk to your Coach some more and discuss everything with my colleagues back in LittleWood."

We both nod.

"For now, I'm going to give you both my card and a brochure about our school." She reaches in her bag, pulls out several different papers and hands them to us. I glance down at the one on top, noticing the few pictures of students strolling around campus, the mascot (a bright orange tiger) and a list of activities offered.

"I'll be in touch soon," she says before turning back and following Coach into his office.

I watch them walk away, turning to look at Riley after they've disappeared into his office. The knot in my stomach tightens as I realize I'm no closer to getting out of this place than I was before this game.

Riley turns back around, meeting my gaze. "You okay?"

I shrug. "I guess."

A few more moments pass as we stand there staring at each other, both of us unsure of what to say.

"Well, I'll see you tomorrow then?" she says it almost as if it's a question.

"See you."

Riley turns, heads up the bleachers and joins the rest of the team. I readjust the bag on my shoulder and head towards the exit. I pick up my pace slightly when I see Aspen waiting for me at the other end. I'm forced to a halt when Matty slings his arm around me.

"Great job, sis. You killed it out there. How many points did you get? Like twenty?"

I laugh, feeling some of the tightness alleviate as I wrap my arm around his lower back. "I did alright."

"Just alright? C'mon, Charlie, you gotta give yourself a little more credit. I mean when you just took the ball from 'em at the end; they didn't know what hit 'em."

"He makes a pretty valid point," Aspen says as we make it to the other end.

"Matty, this is Aspen." I gesture towards her. "Aspen, this is my brother, Matty."

"Hi Matty, it's nice to meet you."

"You too." He turns his head towards me, releasing me from his grip. "Saw you talking to a lady after the game, was that the recruiter?"

I nod. "She's from LittleWood University in Arizona."

"And?" Matty waves his arm in front like it's an invitation to elaborate.

I shrug trying to brush it off. "She's interested in me and Riley. But they only have a spot for one of us."

"When are they going to make a decision?"

"She said soon. Whatever that means."

"Well I'm sure you'll get it. I've seen you on that court. They'd be stupid not to pick you."

"We'll see."

"I need to drop something off at Alec's before tomorrow. Is it cool if I take the car?"

"I can give you a ride home," Aspen cuts it.

"Sweet. See you at home. Bye, Aspen," Matty hollers as he scampers out the door.

Aspen turns towards me. "You ready?"

I nod. "Yeah, but can we make a detour first?"

"Of course. You have something in mind?"

"I've got an idea."

She tosses me the keys and we climb into the car.

"Matty, was right you know. You were pretty great tonight," she says.

"Thanks, but not everyone thought so."

She tilts her head, raising an eyebrow so I elaborate about what happened in the locker room after the game.

"I don't understand; you scored. What's the big deal?"

"Right? She said I was trying to impress my 'friend'."

After a beat Aspen says, "Oh you mean me?"

"Yeah," I whisper, tucking my bottom lip between my teeth. I peek a glance at Aspen, unsure of what I'll see.

Her gaze is fixed on me, her mouth pulled into a flirtatious smile. "Well it worked. I'm impressed, Charlie Baker."

"Really?"

"Yeah, you were great out there. I'm glad I came."

"Me too."

She turns her head, peering out the window. "Where are we?"

"This is just somewhere I like to go when I wanna be alone."

We pull into an empty lot of an abandoned park that used to serve as some sort of day camp for kids. There's a lake in front of us that extends out into the horizon. The trees surrounding it ascend upwards, creating an archway of shadows. The moon is suspended above us illuminating the lake below, generating a sense of tranquility throughout the area. I lean back in the seat, taking in the scenery around us.

"I'm really glad I met you," Aspen says. She shifts slightly, her fingers brushing the back of my hand. When I don't pull away, she settles her hand on my arm, tracing nonsensical patterns with her fingertips.

"I'm glad I met you too, Aspen."

We sit there in silence for a few minutes, conscious of the sudden ambiance surrounding us. Her hand gradually comes to a stop just below my wrist. I inch my fingers apart, my heart rate increasing as she threads her fingers through mine. The feel of her skin on mine ignites tiny sparks through my entire body.

I glance over at her luminescent silhouette, acutely aware that the erratic thrum of my heartbeat hasn't stilled. She turns towards me, my lips forming a gentle, almost involuntarily smile as our eyes meet.

"You wanna hang out Saturday?" she says, reciprocating the action.

"I'd like that."

We stay there for what seems like hours, before turning the car back on, and reluctantly heading back towards town.

"Evening, sweetheart. How was the game?" Nana says when I step into the house.

"It was great. We won."

"Hey, Monkey. Matty was just tellin' us how great you played tonight," Gramps hollers from the living room. He's laid out in his recliner with his feet propped up watching one of his favorite shows, Wheel of Fortune.

Matty's sprawled out on the couch next to him, trying to guess the answer before the contestants. "Yeah, and Charlie talked to the recruiter that was at the game. She's from a school all the way in Arizona. How cool is that?"

That gets Nana's attention. She stops loading the dishwasher and straightens up, turning towards me. "Oh wow, that's great, honey. Now tell me. Is this a good Christian school? Arizona is a ways away, I wouldn't want you goin' somewhere so far without knowing a little more about it."

I shrug my shoulders. "She gave me some information about everything, but I haven't gotten a chance to look at it yet."

"Well I want a little more information about this school. What kind of classes do they offer? How big is it? What kind of people attend this school?" She finishes loading the dishwasher and wipes her hands on her apron.

"I don't know, Nana." I say harsher than I intended.

"Well we're going to need some more information before we can consider if you'll be able to go."

"What do you mean? If I get the scholarship, I'm going. There's no way I'd turn it down."

"Well I just want to make sure it's a school we approve of."

"Why wouldn't you approve of it? My tuition and expenses will be paid for. What more could you want?"

"I understand that, dear. But I want to make sure it's a place where you could potentially find someone to settle down with."

"There's more to college than finding a husband, Nana."

"Yes, well I just want you to find someone that'll take care of you."

"I'm more than capable of taking care of myself."

"I'm just saying, there's a lot more to taking care of yourself when you're out there." Nana points towards the door with the spatula in her hand as if indicating the world beyond this town. "There's nothing wrong with wanting to find a decent young man to share that with."

"Because that worked out so well for mom." I wince, waiting for Nana to scold me for bringing up the forbidden topic that is our mother.

Instead she purses her lips into a taut smile, pointing a finger at me. "Your mother should've spent more time paying attention to her family instead of trying to find her next fix." She spins around, snatches the dish towel from her shoulder, and vigorously scrubs the counter. "Maybe then your father wouldn't have left her," she whispers loud enough for me to hear.

"I think you're forgetting who started using to begin with. She took care of us just fine before he got her hooked on that stuff."

She exhales, her shoulders sulking slightly. After a beat, she turns back to me with a forced smile. "We're not going to discuss this tonight, Charlie."

"Why? Why can't we ever talk about what happened? I'm not a little kid anymore. I can handle it."

"Because," Nana says through clenched teeth, "It's in the past. We don't need to be digging up stuff that happened years ago."

"But—"

"Charlie," Matty hisses from the doorway, "Just drop it. It doesn't matter now."

I cock my head to the side, giving him a baffled look. "Doesn't matter? Matty, she's our mother. Of course it matters."

"She sure didn't seem to act very motherly to me."

"That's not true."

"Yes it is," he snaps. "Think about it Charlie. She got so high she lit the apartment on fire. Don't you remember how terrifying that was? Waking up to me screaming at you and then getting dumped at some stranger's house. It was messed up. Don't tell me you've never thought about what might've happened if dad had stayed? If *she* hadn't driven him away."

"Oh that's bullshit and you know it," I fire at him. "He was never around to begin with, and when he was, he was so stoned off his ass he couldn't see straight."

"Not all the time."

"Whatever. The minute dad got that bogus record deal, he bailed. You're forgetting that *he* walked out on *us!*"

"Enough," Nana cries. She looks back and forth between the two of us, her eyes lingering on me. "We will not discuss this matter further, is that understood?"

"Yes," we mumble at the same time.

"Good," she soothes. "Now, on to more pressing matters; we have the bake sale with the church on Saturday, I expect both of you to help out."

My face falls. "But I kinda already had plans on Saturday"

She places her hand on her hip and raises a brow.

I choose my next words carefully. "Aspen and I are supposed to work on a school project this weekend."

"Is this the same Aspen you spent last Saturday with?"

"Yeah."

"Uh huh. You seem to be spending a lot of time with her lately. Tell ya what, invite her over for dinner on Friday so we can get to know her and you can explain your project and I'll think about letting you off the hook for Saturday?"

"Okay, I'll see if she's free." I say, turning to head for the stairs.

Exhaustion sinks in as I finally crawl into bed. My mind replays the scenes from today—lingering on the memory of our tangled fingers resting on the center console in the car.

Being with Aspen just feels different and I can't figure out why. It's not just that I enjoy spending time with her, I yearn for it. It's like there's this sensation of being fully awake, like every fiber in me comes alive when I'm with her. I can't seem to get enough, always aching to have just a few more minutes.

Chapter Four

The next day begins with fist-bumps and high-fives from several kids at school.

"Look at you, Ms. Popular," Aspen teases as I exchange my books from my locker.

"They're just being friendly," I say as we stroll aimlessly down the hall.

"You say that, but they're not wrong. You were pretty on fire last night."

I drop my gaze to the tiles underneath our feet, a shudder snaking down my spine. Why do her compliments always have this effect on me?

"You free Friday night?" I ask once my nerves are under control.

"I think so, why? You have something in mind?"

"Well my grandparents have a bake sale at the church on Saturday and want Matty and I to help. But I told Nana I already had plans with you, so now they want to have you over for dinner to get to know you."

"Alright. What time?"

"Sixish?"

"I'll be there."

I feel the faint cradle of her hand on my arm as she walks past me down the hall. The rest of the morning continues on as normal. I make my way from class to class, doing my best to pay attention while thoughts of Aspen having dinner at my house swirl in my mind.

"Hey, girl!" Riley says as she hops in line next to me at lunch. "What's up?"

"You wanna hang this weekend? We can play some ball at that old park down the road from my house?"

"You sure playing ball together is a good idea?"

"Why wouldn't it be?" Her expression shows genuine confusion.

"Because of everything going on with the scholarship and stuff."

"C'mon, it'll be like old times from when we were kids and we'd spend more time playing ball than anything else."

"From what I remember, I was such a clutz when we were kids, I spent more time on the ground."

She laughs. "But look how far you've come. I don't think I've seen you fall once this year."

"Alright. I made plans with Aspen on Saturday but I'm free Sunday afternoon."

"Sunday works. But you and Aspen seem to be getting along quite well," she says with a smirk and cocked eyebrow.

"She's fun to hang out with." I shrug. "What's the big deal?"

"Nothing, you just seem happier when she's around."

I tilt my head to the side, my eyebrows furrowed. "Really?"

"Yeah, I haven't seen you smile this much in a while."

"I don't know. There's just something about her. She doesn't really care what people think and I admire that, especially living in a narrow-minded town where people can be super judgmental."

"C'mon, these people aren't that bad. We've gone to school with nearly the entire student body since grade school, and most of our families go way back. I'd like to think most of them can be somewhat open-minded."

"Not when it comes to anything that goes against 'tradition'. My Nana is convinced a woman cannot survive without a man and thinks finding a husband should be a top priority when I go off to college."

"There could be worse things, Charlie. I think she just wants to make sure you're taken care of. And besides, the plethora of boys *is* one of the perks of going to college."

I shrug. "I guess."

"Oh, c'mon on, Charlie. You're like the only person I know who hasn't seriously dated anyone. I figured you were waiting till we go off to college to find your man."

I crinkle my eyebrows at her. "I'm not the only one who hasn't seriously dated anyone."

"I didn't mean it as a bad thing, but you've never really shown any interest in the guys around here. Hell, you don't even give them a chance."

"That's not true."

"What's not true?" Emily asks, ending her rant about some reality tv show as we take our seats at the table. I swear that girl watches more reality television than anyone else I know.

"Charlie thinks going on one date with a guy constitutes her giving him a chance." Riley says.

"What? Why would I want to lead them on when I know there's nothing there?" I say, defensively.

"But can you really know that if you've only been on one movie date?" Emily says.

"Yes. Can we just drop it? I don't know why my dating life has become the topic of every conversation lately."

"Your non-existent dating life," Riley chimes in.

I give her a playful shove before popping a chip into my mouth.

"Where's your friend, Charlie?" Skylar says.

"Not sure."

And just like that, Aspen plops her tray down next to mine and takes a seat.

"Where've ya been?" I ask her.

"I stayed back to ask Mrs. Rabens a couple questions about the homework. What'd I miss?"

"We were discussing Charlie's non-existent dating life," Skylar tells her.

"Oh, really?" Aspen says, smirking at me.

"No. But Emily was telling us about last night's episode of Romance Island," I say.

"Never heard of it."

"Girl! You have to check it out. It sucks you in right from the start. It's so good," says Sara, who's also a big fan of reality television.

Between her and Emily, they could probably come up with their own show.

"I'll add it to my list," says Aspen.

"So did you come to the game last night? I thought I saw you up in the stands," Skylar cuts in.

"Yes I did."

"Really?" Skylar leans forward and folds her hands in front of her. "Did you stay for the boys game? I can't remember if I saw you."

"Nope."

"Mhmm," she says after a moment. Her eyes jump over to me, "Charlie, I seem to recall you leaving rather quickly after the game as well."

"Your point?" I answer, dryly.

She lifts her shoulders, picks up her fork, and pokes at the make-shift salad on her plate. "Nothing, just curious is all."

The bell rings, I gather my things, mumbling a goodbye to the rest of the table before I head down the hall with Aspen.

We're about a third of the way down when Will, Ben and Trey fall into step beside us.

"Hey, Charlie. Hey, Aspen," Ben says. Will and Trey give us a soft head nod in acknowledgment.

"What'd you want, Ben?" I say, not bothering to hide the irritation in my tone.

He takes one long stride to the left, forcing us to stop. He pivots on his heels, his eyes darting back and forth between us. After a pause he says, "Wanted to see if you two wanted to hang out this weekend? Maybe hit up the mall or bowling alley?"

"Actually, we already have plans."

Will takes a step forward, cocking his head to the side, a smirk curled at the corner of his mouth. "C'mon now, don't be like that. Let us show you a good time. We're just tryin' to give a warm welcome to our new friend here." He reaches over, attempting to tuck a strand of hair behind Aspen's ear before she smacks his hand away. When did he become such a tool?

Ben inches forward. "We heard all about your little 'adventures' from your old school," Ben whispers, putting air quotes around 'adventures.'

"Yeah. Heard your daddy thought bringing you to a place like BluHaven would straighten you out, isn't that right?"

"We just thought we might try to help ease the transition," Will cuts in.

Aspen elbows Ben, creating an opening and charges through. I rush to catch up with her, the warning bell echoing in the background, but I ignore it. I hear the distant laughter as the boys stroll down the hallway, curious as to what they're referring to but more concerned about Aspen at the moment.

"Aspen, wait up," I say, reaching out to grasp her forearm.

She spins around, shrugging off my grip as her eyes glisten with tears. I'm tempted to reach out and take her hand but I don't. "Are you okay?"

"I'm sorry, Charlie."

"What? Why? What're they talking about?" I gesture back towards the direction we'd just come from, but the area is deserted.

She turns towards the wall, leaning against it as a tear trickles down her cheek and springs to the floor. I inch closer, resisting the urge to eliminate all the space between us. "Aspen, please," I whisper. "You can talk to me. Tell me what's going on." She uses her thumb to wipe the bottom of her eye. "People hear a couple stories about you, half of which are just bullshit, and suddenly they think they know everything there is to know. They don't even bother trying to get to know the real you."

I stare at her, giving her a gentle smile and nod while I wait for her to elaborate, the curiosity growing inside me.

"I got into some trouble at my old school," she says. "That's part of the reason why my dad moved us back here. He thought coming back to where he grew up would somehow fix everything." She pulls out a tissue and uses the corner to wipe the mascara from underneath her eye. She turns towards me, her gaze fixed on the floor. "You were the first person to hang out with me and not ask questions or make assumptions and it was really nice. I just didn't want to ruin everything by bringing up my past."

Without thinking, I bring my hand up and brush the hair back from her face, tucking it back into place.

Did I really just do that?

I look up at her, watching as she wipes the last of the tears away, and takes a gradual step closer. Slowly, I reach out my hand and tip her chin up, conscious of the shivers pulsing through me as our skin connects.

"It's okay," I say when she meets my eye. "We can talk about it whenever you're ready or we don't have to talk about it all if you don't want to. But all I know is that I enjoy spending time with you and I would very much like to keep spending time with you if that's alright."

"Really?"

"Yes. Don't think it's that easy to get out of dinner with my grandparents," I tease.

A soft laugh escapes, as a smile tugs at the corner of her mouth. "Thank you, Charlie."

"Anytime."

"I guess we should probably get to class now."

"I'll see you later, Aspen."

I'm a bundle of nervous Friday night just thinking about Aspen coming over. I'm not sure why I'm so jittery—it's not like this is the first time we're hanging out. But this is the first time she'll be inside my house and meeting my family. Will she find my grandparents sweet and charming or overbearing and intrusive? Will she think of my house as cozy and inviting or outdated and mediocre?

Relax, Charlie. She's just coming over for dinner, not for an inspection of the house.

I run a brush through my hair one more time, spray just a hint of perfume, and head downstairs.

Nana's bent over scrubbing the countertop for the umpteenth time. She glances up, her lips curled back into a smile as she wipes her hands on her favorite apron tied neatly around her waist. "Charlie dear, come help me set the table." She hands me the stack of plates and silverware before double-checking the press of her yellow-colored polyester pants and matching floral blouse.

"Would it really be the end of the world to ask Matty to do something as domestic as set the table?" I mumble under my breath. I'm setting the last fork down when the doorbell rings.

I open the door, my mouth dropping into a small *O* when I see Aspen standing in the entryway. Her hair is hanging in loose curls around her shoulders, her makeup is exceptional, just enough to compliment her already perfect features, and she's wearing a black dress that hugs her body like the closed petals of a flower.

My lips part into a soft smile as the heat floods through me. "Wow," I say after a moment.

"Too much?" she asks, shyly.

"No," I say a little too quickly. "You look great, c'mon in."

She steps inside, her eyes wandering about, taking in the surroundings. "You have such a cute home, very cozy."

"Thanks. Dinner's almost ready."

We make our way into the kitchen and I gesture to my grandparents. "Gramps, Nana, this is Aspen. Aspen, these are my grandparents."

Gramps steps forward sticking out his hand, his lips pulled back into a smile. "It's so nice to finally meet you."

"It's nice to meet you too," Aspen says, returning the gesture.

Nana refolds the dish towel and lays it next to the sink before she shuffles over to us, beaming. "Aspen, honey. It's such a pleasure having you over. Please come in and have a seat." Nana ushers her towards the table and I motion for her to take the seat next to mine.

"It smells delicious," says Aspen.

"It's Nana's famous lasagna. Just wait till you take a bite of this," Matty says, coming in from the living room.

Once everyone is seated and the table is set, Nana motions for us to hold hands so we can pray before we eat.

Without missing a beat, Aspen settles her hand into mine and reaches across the table, taking Matty's.

We bow our heads, my body focused on whose hand I'm holding instead of what Nana is saying. There's a soft chorus of 'Amen' and then we start loading our plates with food.

"So Aspen, what made you all move to BluHaven?" Nana asks.

Aspen finishes chewing before she answers. "My dad grew up here and wanted us to have a fresh start somewhere familiar to him."

"I see. Are you liking it so far?"

"Yeah. It's similar to where we used to live but it's kinda cool getting to see where he grew up."

"And what does your father do?" Gramps asks.

"He oversees the plant operations at the poultry factories or something like that. I've never been completely sure of what his job actually entails." I scoop some salad onto my bowl and offer some to Aspen.

"Ahh yes, I heard about Bill Davidson hiring an outsider to run the plant. I guess I didn't realize you two were related," Gramps says between bites of bread.

"What church do you and your father attend, dear?" Nana asks. I duck my head and stab my lasagna with my fork, rolling my eyes at Nana's question. Just because we live in a small southern town doesn't mean every single person is required to go to church.

"It's the same one my dad went to when he was a kid. Everlasting Glory I think is what it's called," she says, glancing down at her plate.

"Ahh yes, that is a pretty popular church around here. We go to the one down the street with Reverend Charles."

"I'm pretty sure Skylar's family goes to that church," I whisper to Aspen.

"I thought I saw her there but wasn't sure. Although now that I'm thinking about it, that makes sense."

"Coach Stewart goes there too. That's part of the reason why he's so tight with Skylar's family."

"I knew he looked familiar when I saw him at the game. I just couldn't place him." She raises an eyebrow. "Is that weird? Them going to the same church?"

I shrug. "Not really. Skylar likes to mention it occasionally to suck up to him but he usually doesn't fall for it."

"Do you have any plans after high school, Aspen?" Gramps asks, diverting our attention back to the conversation. "Any colleges you're interested in?"

"I'm applying to a couple different colleges but I'm hoping to get accepted into the art program at the Waltson Institute. It's a highly competitive program; they only take about twelve to fifteen students a year."

"I see and where is that located?"

"In Sumon, Arizona."

"Hey, Charlie," Matty says, nudging my arm. "Isn't that the same place the recruiter's from?"

"Same state, different city. But they're not that far away from each other actually, maybe a couple hours."

"Well if you two both go there, you'll at least know someone."

"Yeah, that would be nice," says Aspen.

"Wait, if you go all the way to Arizona and take the car, how will I get around? That's not fair."

"But how will I get to college without a car? Face it. I need it more than you do. Plus, I'm older."

"So? The deal was we share the car. We can't really do that when you're in a completely different state."

Gramps holds his hand in the air, signaling us to stop. "Now, now, please do not start bickering when we have company over. Matty we'll take you car shopping before Charlie leaves. I'm sure Grant will be able to give us a good deal."

"So what is this school project you are working on? Charlie tells me it'll take you all weekend to finish?" Nana asks, quickly changing the subject.

I freeze, my gaze instantly dropping to my plate. I completely forgot to warn Aspen about the school project excuse I came up with to get out of the bake sale. Think, Charlie.

"Uh, it's just a project for Calculus," I say as casually as I can.

"What sort of project?" Nana inclines.

I shovel the last of my pasta into my mouth, trying to buy some time.

"Mr. Murphy wants us to create a presentation that explains how calculus can be used to solve real world problems," says Aspen.

Damn. That's super believable.

"I see," Nana says thoughtfully, "Well seeing that this'll take you all weekend, I guess we'll have to make do without you, Charlie."

"Speaking of school projects," Matty cuts in, "I'd still like to put some finishing touches on my Engineering and Design assignment."

"Nice try, son," says Gramps. "We already know you finished that last week. Looks like you'll be joining us tomorrow."

Nana stands up. "Now, let me clear the dishes so I can bring out dessert. I made peach cobbler, Charlie's favorite."

"I can help," Aspen says, getting up.

"Nonsense, you're our guest. Please have a seat. Charlie, you can help me."

I roll my eyes. God-forbid she asks Matty to do something like clearing the table instead of me.

After dessert, I offer to show Aspen the rest of the house. The tour is short considering the size of the house and the fact that she saw the majority of it as soon as she walked through the door.

"Your grandparents are really sweet," she says when we've entered my bedroom.

"Yeah, they like you too." I watch her eyes dance around the room, taking in the mundane features of my bedroom.

"So I didn't realize we had a project to work on this weekend?"

I flash her a sheepish smile as the heat on the back of my neck rises. "Yeah, well I sort of told my Nana we had to work on a project this weekend so I didn't have to help with the bake sale on Saturday. I probably should've given you a heads up. You saved my butt down there."

She pivots towards me, her lips twisted into a playful grin. "Charlie Baker, did you lie to get out of helping your sweet, sweet grandparents?"

"Maybe," I say with a shrug. "But they don't actually need my help, Matty is more than capable of carrying the boxes by himself. And besides, the last time we helped with something like this, I got stuck next to Mrs. Wilma's grandson and he smells like egg salad. I deserve a break."

"Hey, I'm not complaining," she says with a soft laugh. "I'd much rather have you hanging out with me than stuck next to somebody who smells like an old sandwich. I had a fun time tonight." She walks over to the dresser, peering at the photograph on top.

"Me too."

She picks up, studying it. "Is this when you were little?"

"Yeah," I walk up behind her to stare at the picture.

"Are these your parents?" She points to the man and woman crouched beside us.

"Yeah." I whisper as the memory runs through my mind like an old film on a projector screen.

"You guys look happy."

"We were. Our parents were still together back then; Matty was about three or four and I was five. My dad had just landed a gig that was supposed to help boost his music career, so they wanted to celebrate. It was one of the few times I remember us actually acting like a family, before everything went to hell. They were so happy, so full of hope. "

Aspen sets the frame back on the dresser, her hand resting on top of my forearm. "I'm so sorry, Charlie," she whispers.

"It's okay," I look up at her. "It was a long time ago." I walk over to the bed and take a seat, feeling the mattress sink as Aspen sits next to me.

"Do you and your family ever talk about your parents?" she asks.

"Not really." I twist a loose thread in between my fingers. "I tried asking questions when we first moved here but every time I did, it just made Nana upset so I stopped. I actually brought it up the other night and we kind of got into it. You'd think after all this time we'd be able to talk about it." I shake my head. "But no, it's still off limits."

"Do you have any idea why it makes her so uncomfortable to talk about?"

"I don't know. I get that she's upset about the entire situation but it's still my mom. Don't you think I have a right to talk about her, to know her—not just the details that led to her losing custody?" I run my fingers through my hair, willing myself to relax. "Maybe Nana's afraid I'll turn out just like my mother."

Aspen scoots closer, gently resting her hand on top of mine. "I'm sure she doesn't think that."

I glance up, my eyes finding the soft blue hues of hers. "Maybe *I'm* afraid I'll turn out like my mother," I whisper.

"You don't really believe that, do you?"

"I don't know. My Nana is convinced that a woman's worth is derived from the man she marries and I'm not sure I'm going to live up to her expectations. I know she wants me to be happy but I think we have very different ideas on what that means. I just…I just don't want to disappoint her the same way my mom did."

"Well you're not doing drugs so you've got that going for you."

A soft laugh escapes as I feel the tension in my chest ease ever so slightly. "True, but Nana acts like all the mistakes my mom made are some sort of a betrayal against her and now it's like she despises her own daughter. I don't want that to be how things turn out with me and Nana."

"Maybe your Nana blames herself for what happened to your mother?"

"But that wasn't her fault. If anybody's to blame it's my father. He got her hooked on that stuff and then just bailed. I've done some research on addiction and stuff like that. I became curious after we moved here and was old enough to understand what happened. Anyways, when you have an addiction like that—a disease really—and you're so wrapped up in it, I'm not sure if there was anything anyone could've done to help her. Not until she was ready."

"Did you try telling your Nana that? Maybe that would help her understand."

"I tried a few times but she didn't want to hear what I had to say."

"I'm sorry, Charlie."

"It's like she has this notion in her head about how the world works and I just don't see it the same way she does. I just don't want her to end up resenting me like she does my mother because we don't see things the same way."

"Your Nana loves you, Charlie. And I'm sure her intentions are good and that she just wants what is best for you."

"I'm sure you're right but I don't think what Nana wants for me is the same thing that I want for me."

"I get it, trust me. It's like the minute we're born our parents have our entire lives planned out for us, only to realize they never stopped to think about what *we* actually wanted to do with them."

"Exactly."

We sit in silence for several seconds before I say, "Can I ask what your mom was like? If you don't mind."

"She was my favorite person. We would watch these horribly cheesy movies and always try to guess the ending. She was right, nearly every time. On the nights I didn't have a lot of homework, we would always cook a new recipe, something she found online or in a magazine. One time, we had this orange citrus chicken that she raved about after reading the recipe. It tasted like an old can of sour prunes. It was so bad."

She laughs as her ocean blue eyes mist over with emotion, like she's watching the memories play out in her head. "We did everything together. She was my favorite person to hang out with. I know most kids would rather spend their free time at the mall or with their friends, but I won't forget the times I spent with her, especially now that she's gone. I just wish we had a little more time."

I reach my hand out, gently laying it on top of hers. "At least you had the time you did with her. I'm sure it meant everything to her."

"I'm sorry, Charlie. Here I am crying about all the time I got to spend with my mom when you didn't even get half of that with your parents."

"Hey, that still isn't nearly enough time. Just because I lost my parents earlier than you, doesn't mean what you're feeling isn't valid."

"My mom would've loved you."

"You think?"

"Definitely. She was a good judge of character."

I let out a soft laugh as I lie back and stare up at the ceiling. Aspen joins me, our heads barely an inch apart. We spend the next two hours listening to music and discussing any and every gossip topic we can summon. When we've exhausted that list we move on to favorite songs, then movies, then books. Our ability to feed off each other's brains is incredible and in a way not all that surprising.

It's nearly ten o'clock by the time we come out of the bedroom and I walk her to the door.

"We still on for tomorrow?" she asks.

"As long as you're not sick of me yet."

"Never." She walks to her car and flashes me a smile. "I'll pick you up around noon?"

"Sounds good."

"Goodbye, Charlie."

"Bye." I stand in the driveway, watching as her taillights recede into the darkness of the night.

I saunter back upstairs and collapse on my bed. I pull out my phone and thumb through Facebook. An image of Ben, Brandon, Will, and a couple of other boys from school pops up on my newsfeed. The caption "Bros 4 lyfe" is underneath it and my mind jumps back to when they stopped us in the hallway from school. I replay the scene in my head, looking for any clue as to what they were referring to. They weren't the first people to mention Aspen's past and it's hard to ignore the growing curiosity building inside me.

Chapter Five

The daylight trickling in from the slits in the window beckons me from my somber trance. It dawns on me that today is Saturday and I have plans with Aspen this afternoon. I spring out of bed, checking the time before slipping into some workout clothes and heading downstairs.

"Charlie, my dear, we're heading out for the bake sale. We'll be back later," Nana says to me as I hurdle down the stairs.

"Alright. I'm not sure how long this project is going to take so I don't know when I'll be home."

"Okay, honey. Just don't stay out too late."

"Have fun," I holler as they wave goodbye. Matty rolls his eyes, sticking his tongue out as he trails behind them. I return the gesture before I grab a Gatorade and head out front for my run.

A shower and change of clothes later, Aspen pulls up in her shiny, black Lexus.

"Hey," she says as I slide into the passenger seat. My gaze sweeps over her, drinking in all that is her. She's wearing skintight jeans and a striped white and grey V-neck that hugs her torso. Her long caramel hair is hanging loosely around her shoulders, giving me the same tantalizing urge to run my fingers through it.

"What'd you want to do today?" I ask.

"I thought we could get a bite to eat, then head back to my place to watch a movie. My dad has to go into the office later today so we should have the house to ourselves."

"Sounds good to me."

"Maybe you can even show me some of your basketball moves?" I flash her a sly grin. "I'd be happy to."

I lean back, watching the ever-changing landscape as we head into town. I feel the tenuous graze of Aspen's hand on top of mine, the warmth from her fingers pulsing through my veins. She pulls into the parking lot of *Sally's ShortStop Grill* and shuts the car off.

"Is this alright?" she asks. "I heard a couple kids talking about it at school and thought we could check it out."

"Yeah, this is actually a pretty popular place. Good choice."

Inside, the diner is tiny and crowded with people. I recognize a few kids from school and acknowledge them with a simple head nod. The interior is decorated with bizarre paintings all over the wall, each one more peculiar than the next. The tabletops are coated with multi-colored patterns, almost resembling some sort of maze. The piercing scent of fried foods is overwhelming as we stroll to a booth in the back corner.

"How'd you do on the Calculus test?" Aspen asks after we order our drinks.

"I think I did alright. What about you?"

"I don't know. It's definitely not my strongest subject."

"But we studied all day Saturday?" I tease.

"Maybe we need a few more study dates?"

"I think that can be arranged."

The waiter returns with our food and we waste no time digging in. We're in the middle of laughing after Aspen squirted ketchup all over the place, when I hear the high-pitched *ding* of the door being opened. Instinctively, I glance towards the entrance, immediately recognizing Skylar. She's followed by Harper, Emily, John and two other boys from school. I pop a fry into my mouth, silently debating if I should act like I don't notice them or be the first to say hello.

"Now, don't you two look cozy," Skylar says, her face scrunched as she wags her finger between the two of us.

So much for trying to ignore them.

"Hey," I say to them.

"Hey, Charlie. Hey, Aspen," Emily says with a smile. Harper waves from behind Skylar, before heading towards the open seating to the right and settling next to one of the boys.

"Hey, Emily," Aspen says, ignoring Skylar's stare. "I've been meaning to tell you that I was able to check out that show you mentioned at lunch the other day."

Emily takes a step forward, her eyebrows raised in curiosity. "Oh yeah? Sucks you in right from the start, doesn't it?"

"You know, I hate to say it but it does. Before I knew it I was six episodes in."

"I told you. Sara and I are planning to binge watch the new season they're about to release on Netflix in a couple weeks. You should totally join us."

"Sure, that sounds like fun."

"Great. I'll see you around." She turns, heading to the other side of the diner and settling in next to John.

"I have to admit, I'm a little surprised to see you here, Aspen," Skylar says, gesturing to the restaurant. "I figured you would prefer something a little more high class with your daddy being rich and all."

"I could say the same about you considering where your family comes from," Aspen snaps back.

"Hmph," Skylar says with a smug smile.

"Can we help you with something, Skylar?" I ask curtly

"Oh no, I just wanted to say hello, be friendly." She glances back and forth between the two of us. "But it seems you two are already pretty friendly with each other." She spins on her heels, strolling to the table to join the rest of the group.

"She sure knows how to make a girl feel welcomed, doesn't she?" Aspen says once Skylar is out of earshot.

"I'm sorry," I say, rolling my eyes. "She can be a real witch sometimes. Do you wanna leave?"

"No, we have just as much right to be here as she does, let's finish eating and then we can go."

"Alright. I didn't realize you were a big reality tv fan now?" I glance up at her, a smirk tugging at the corner of my mouth.

Aspen shrugs as her cheeks begin to turn crimson. "I was bored. I didn't realize how quickly I would get hooked." She shoves another fry into her mouth. "Oh. I almost forgot. I finished the book you gave me."

"*Bellow From Beneath?* What'd you think?"

"It was different. Definitely didn't see that twist coming at the end."

"Me either. That's why I really enjoyed it. I mean this whole time he thinks he's all alone just to discover there's an entire tribe of people already there."

"I know right? And the writing was incredible, really sucked me into the story."

"Well I'm glad you enjoyed it."

"Me too."

We finish the last of our meal, pay the check and climb back into the car.

"So tell me about this art school in Arizona?" I say as we pull onto the main road.

"Oh it's nothing. They just have a really good art program and I've always wanted to get out of the south. See what else is out there."

"I know exactly what you mean. A basketball scholarship is the only chance I have at getting out of this place. BluHaven is nice and all but I always knew this was never where I wanted to stay. There's just so much more out there to explore."

"I couldn't agree more. I've been working on this application all year. I'm almost done but I have to choose the right pieces. That's why I've been staying late after school. I want to show them that I can handle it, that I'm worth taking a chance for."

"Well if it's anything like what's in your room, there's no way they can say no. Your art is pretty incredible, they'd be stupid not to pick you."

Her cheeks flush as a smile skirts across her face. "It would be pretty neat if we ended up going to colleges near each other. At least we would've already made one friend."

"Yeah, that'd be pretty awesome."

"What would you want to do? Once you get out of BluHaven, I mean?"

"I'd like to help people. One of the reasons I wanted to play basketball so bad was because I wanted to be a part of something greater than myself. I'd like to continue that when I go to college.

I want to work at a place where I feel like I'm actually making a difference, no matter how small." I shrug, wondering if I sound as idiotic as I feel. "I don't know. Maybe I'm being naive."

"No, Charlie. That's incredible. And I think you could do it."

"Really?"

"Yeah. You're a hard worker, determined, and it's obvious you care. I think you can do anything you want."

"Thanks, Aspen. That means a lot."

We pull into the driveway, her house looking just as unsullied as I remember it. I follow her into the kitchen, nearly bumping into her when she suddenly stops in the doorway to the kitchen. I peer past, wondering what made her freeze all of a sudden. My eyes land on the rigid figure, sitting at the island, newspaper in hand.

Ever since Aspen told me the story about the accident, it's much easier to understand why her father is acting the way he is. If you look past his rigid and distant facade, you can see the pain so evident in his eyes.

"Oh, hey, Dad," she says softly. "I thought you had to go into the office today?"

"I'm just about to head out." He stands up, folding the paper on the counter. He smiles, turning to Aspen without any acknowledgment in my direction. "How was your date last night with that nice young man from down the street? You two have a nice time?"

"Yeah," she whispers, avoiding my eye.

His eyebrows perk up, his mouth almost representing a smile. "That's great. You two make plans to see each other again soon?"

"I don't know, maybe," she mumbles as she twirls a strand of hair in her fingers, her eyes looking anywhere other than her father. "We're gonna go upstairs." She quickens her pace, heading for the stairs as I trail behind her.

"I'll be back later tonight," Mr. Sullivan calls after her.

The minute we enter her bedroom, Aspen pivots around, running her fingers through her hair several times before saying, "I'm sorry, Charlie. I lied to my dad and told him I was on a date with a boy last night instead of telling him I went to your place for dinner."

I shrug. "No worries. I definitely lied to my Nana about what we were doing today."

"He's just been harder to be around lately. He was convinced coming back to where he grew up would be good for everyone. When we first got here, he genuinely seemed like he was trying to move past everything. But that lasted all of eight days. Now, I feel like I'm suffocating."

"Maybe it's harder than he thought it would be. What he and your mom had was special, you said so yourself. Maybe he's still working through everything."

"But he never wants to talk about her. It's like he doesn't understand that he wasn't the only one that lost someone." She sits on the bed and braces her elbow on her knees, her head resting in her hands.

"I miss her every day. And I know he does too. But every time I mention anything that relates to mom, he gets all weird and changes the subject. So I try to act like nothing's wrong and everything is fine, hoping that'll help. But he still looks at me like he doesn't even know who I am anymore." I watch the tears plummet to the ground, darkening the carpet between her feet. I walk over and sit next to her, wanting nothing more than to take the pain away.

"I understand that he misses her. But half the time it feels like he's grieving the loss of two people instead of one. I'm still here, Charlie. And I lost someone too. It hurts just as much for me as it does for him. Why can't he see that?"

I grab the box of tissues resting on her bedside table and hand one to her. I give her a moment to wipe her eyes as I resist the urge to wrap my arms around her.

"Maybe you just need to give him some time. You lost your mother but he lost his best friend. Maybe he wants to be there for you but he doesn't know how?"

"Then why won't he just talk to me and tell me that?"

"I don't know, Aspen. I wish I had all the answers. But when my dad left, my mom was a wreck. I'd never seen her in this kind of state. She wouldn't eat, she slept all day, she lost weight, it was like she was a ghost. The few times she was awake enough to utter a few words, I looked into her eyes and it was like the light had gone out. It's like she was there, but she wasn't. I don't know your dad, but he moved you all the way here to give you a fresh start. That's gotta count for something right?"

She sniffles, wiping her eyes with a balled-up tissue. "Yeah, I guess it does. It just sucks feeling so alone sometimes."

"Well you don't have to be alone anymore because now you have me."

"Thanks, Charlie. I appreciate that." She gathers the used tissues laying on her lap and tosses them in the trash can.

I smile at her. "You still wanna watch a movie? Maybe it'll help take your mind off things?"

"Sure."

We decide on a romantic comedy based on a book that was written in the nineties. We settle on top of her bed, leaning against the back wall. We're about halfway into the movie when the bed shifts as she repositions to her side, her head propped up with her elbow. I glance over at her, immediately noticing the way her V-neck accentuates the subtle swell of her breasts. I force my gaze up, our eyes locking.

"Thank you, Charlie. I know you didn't come over here expecting to see me blubber like that. It just feels really good to actually have someone to talk to. I'm really glad I met you."

I adjust my body, angling towards her. "I'm glad I met you too."

Aspen tilts her head ever so slightly, her blue eyes swimming with emotion. She slides her hand closer, her fingers threading through mine, sending a tremor down my spine.

"I really like you, Charlie."

"I like you too."

"No, I mean I *really* like you."

Very deliberately, she glides her hand up my arm, the touch of her fingertips leaving a warm trail on my skin. She inches closer, our legs brushing against each other.

She leans in and I inhale the sweet scent of peppermint on her breath. "Tell me no and I'll stop," she whispers.

I close my eyes, feeling a quick peck at first. When I don't recoil, she does it again, moving her hand to the back of my neck, pulling me in. I part my lips, surrendering my mouth to hers. The kiss is intense and open-mouth, and nothing like I've experienced before.

I breathe in the smell of her breath and find it intoxicating. Heat floods through my veins at her touch, like every atom in my body is on the verge of bursting through my skin.

Finally, she pulls back slightly, breaking contact. I let a few seconds pass before I push myself up to a sitting position.

And then reality comes crashing down. Did we really just do that?

"Are you okay?" she asks, her tone timid.

I lightly run my index finger over my still-moist lips, trying to digest what just occurred. We *really* did just do that. I glance over to Aspen as she gradually sits up. I immediately stand up, running my fingers through my hair, trying to get a grip on myself. My head feels like it's spinning, everything that's happened the past two weeks comes surging back to me all at once.

"Charlie?" Aspen whispers, her voice sounding a million miles away.

"I gotta get home," I mumble, my voice shaky and hoarse.

"I'll drive you home," she says, rising from the bed.

"No, it's okay. I can walk." I pace to the other side of the room, stuffing my feet into my shoes.

"Charlie, wait a minute," she pleads.

I rake my fingers through my hair, avoiding her eye as I head for the door. She grabs my arm, forcing me to stop.

"Charlie, can we please talk about this?"

I turn to face her, her hand still firmly gripped on my arm. I glance down, the butterflies in my stomach slowly morphing into a lump. I know I should talk to her but how can I articulate something that I don't even understand myself?

The best I can do is offer her a weak smile. "I gotta get home. I'll see you later, Aspen." And I walk out the door.

Chapter Six

I'm lying in bed, fully awake for what feels like hours, my mind racing a hundred miles an hour to a hundred different destinations, all twisted in thoughts of Aspen. I shut my eyes, my pulse hammering in my chest as the images of her replay in my mind like a record caught on a loop.

Aspen kissed me last night.

And I kissed her back.

I bring my fingers up to my mouth. I can still feel the tingle of her lips on mine. Kissing her was not like kissing Noah, or any other boy for that matter.

When I kissed Noah, I closed my eyes, praying it would be over quickly. The idea of having to do it multiple times repulsed me. But when I kissed Aspen, I closed my eyes, begging for it to continue.

But this isn't how it's supposed to be.

At least, that's what I've been told my entire life, by everyone—Gramps, Nana, people from church, kids at school, even Riley. Girls are *not* supposed to kiss other girls. Girls are *supposed* to date boys. And marry them. And have a family with them. And cook and clean, live in a tiny house with a white picket-fence and tend to their every fucking need. That's the notion that's been crammed into my head for as long as I can remember. A woman's place is to serve her husband, no question about it.

But when I stop and think about it, is that really what I want? Nobody ever stopped to ask what I wanted for my life. When I pictured myself growing up and settling down, did I really think it would be with a man? If the idea of kissing a boy is repulsing to me, what makes me think I can commit to marrying one?

I step into the shower and let the steaming hot water drown out the world around me. I rest my head against the tiles as the water beats against me. I take several deep breaths and tell myself to focus on the task ahead—church.

Great. Just what I need, to be surrounded by a bunch of pretentious people who wouldn't think twice about shaming me for what I'd done.

Relax, Charlie. You haven't done anything wrong.

You hung out with a friend from school. It's not like you broke the law and committed a crime. You two just happened to share an intimate moment, one that involved your lips connecting with hers and you just happened to like it.

It doesn't mean your gay, or you're going to hell.

There's nothing wrong with kissing a girl and liking it. I'm sure lots of people have encountered this experience before. Surely they didn't beat themselves up about it, so why does it feel like I swallowed a boulder?

I don't have to have everything figured out right this second. Just take it one step at a time. Get through today, and then we can worry about what's next.

I've never been thrilled to attend church every single Sunday morning, but unless I have a basketball tournament or a legitimate reason to miss (school work and practice are not legitimate reasons to miss, trust me I've tried) my butt better be in that pew by eleven a.m.

I throw on my staple of jeans and t-shirt and finger comb my hair, before heading downstairs.

"You feelin' okay, Monkey?" Gramps says from the table. "We didn't hardly see ya last night when you came home."

"Yeah, I'm fine."

"You two get that project knocked out?" Nana asks.

"Yeah," I croak.

"Can I see it?"

I freeze, trying to think of some excuse to give her. "Uh, I left it at Aspen's. I'm gonna go shoot hoops till it's time to leave." I practically sprint out the door, eager to escape Nana's inquiries.

I grab my ball and start shooting. I miss every shot. I shoot another three, watching it bounce off the rim as Matty closes the front door behind him. He catches the ball before it can roll into the grass.

"You okay?" he asks.

"Yeah, I'm fine," I huff, not meeting his eye.

"You don't seem fine." He takes a seat on the curb and pats the spot next to him. "Talk to me Charlie. Maybe I can help."

Stubbornly, I take a seat next to him. He gently bumps my shoulder, giving me the *I know something's bothering you* look. If anybody's willing to listen to what's going through my head right now, it's Matty. He's the one person who's seen me at my worst and still loves me; the one person I've always been able to count on.

"Matty," I say slowly. "Do you think we're able to choose who we're attracted to? Or do you think it's already been decided for us?"

"What do you mean?"

"I don't know, do you think we get to choose who we love as in like…" I pause, scanning his face to see his reaction. He nods his head, quirking his eyebrow so I continue. "Like if we're attracted to boys or girls?"

"Huh. I don't know. I never really put a lot of thought into it to be honest."

"We've been told since we were little that boys are supposed to date girls and live happily ever after. It's what they say at church, what Nana and Gramps have always told us." I glance over, making sure I haven't lost him. "But what if it feels like your heart is pulling you in another direction? Is that so bad?"

Matty glances up towards the sky, as if he's searching for an answer. "Charlie, I'm not sure what's going on with you right now or who it involves." He turns to look me in the eye. "But you have the freedom to love whoever you want. It shouldn't matter what people think or say. You have to do what makes you happy. If you want to be with someone that other people might not approve of, then screw them. If they can't support you, then they don't deserve to be a part of your life to begin with. I love you, Charlie and I always will, no matter who you love."

I stare at my brother, digesting everything he just said. He makes a pretty strong point. Should it really matter if I love a boy or a girl, as long as whoever it is makes me happy? So what if that makes me gay? As long as I'm happy, should it really matter? Do I care that much about what other people think? Riley? The team? Nana and Gramps?

Yes, I do.

But should I care more about the opinions of others at the expense of my own happiness?

The slam of the front door snaps me back into reality. My phone buzzes inside my pocket as I slide into the backseat of the car. I pull it out of my pocket, not surprised to see it's a text from Aspen.

Hey Charlie. Can we plz talk?

I stare at the words on my screen, until they blur together, merging into a jumble of letters. Deep down, I know that what I'm feeling for Aspen goes beyond 'just friends'—that the longing and desire I feel for her is unlike anything I've ever experienced. How just the sight of her is calming and electrifying at the same time, causing butterflies to explode in my stomach and the nerves to settle all at once.

But I also can't ignore the knot that binds my stomach at the thought of how people might react. Am I ready for that? Is it worth denying myself what I want to make other people comfortable?

Gramps pulls into the church parking lot and the dread sinks in like a heap of rocks plummeting to the bottom of the ocean. I do my best to avoid mingling with anybody before service starts. I follow behind Matty and slump into the pew. My phone buzzes again but I don't bother checking it, knowing I have a pretty good idea of who it's from.

I couldn't tell you a single thing about Reverend Charles' service today. My body was present, but my mind was somewhere else entirely. He finally finishes the last prayer and I head straight for the door, mumbling something to Gramps about not feeling well. The longer I'm inside these four walls, the harder it is to breathe.

I collapse into the backseat of the car, pulling my phone out as it buzzes yet again. I glance down surprised to see it's a text from Riley.

Hey girl. We still on 4 later 2day?

Ahh shit. I forgot I'm supposed to get together with Riley today. I toy with the idea of coming up with a lame excuse to bail but I don't. Maybe shooting hoops with Riley is just what I need to clear my head? I reply.

Yep. Leaving church now.

I glance up at the sound of the car door expecting it to be Gramps and Nana, but Matty slides into the backseat instead.

"You sure you're okay?" he asks.

I stare at the back of the headrest, asking myself the same question. Gramps and Nana climb into the car before I can respond, and for that I'm grateful. I sense Matty's eyes on me, waiting for a response as we pull out of the parking lot. I lean my head against the window, watching the obscure land drift by, searching for an answer I know isn't there.

I step outside in sweats, an old t-shirt, and a basketball tucked under my arm as Riley pulls into the driveway.

"Hey girl," she says when I've climbed in the car. For someone wearing baggy sweatpants and a long-sleeve shirt, she looks a helluva lot better than I do.

"Hey."

"You okay?"

"Yeah, just a lot on my mind."

"You wanna talk about it?"

I shake my head. "I'm okay, just need to play some ball."

She opens her mouth to protest then abruptly shuts it. We ride in silence until she turns into the old park that's not too far from her house. Anytime Riley and I want to practice outside of school, this is where we come. It's hardly ever occupied so it's perfect for when we want to play some ball and forget all our troubles.

We spend the next two hours shooting around, running through a couple different ball handling drills, ending with a game of one-on-one. Riley won by four points. Today was not my best day. But it sure felt good having a ball in my hand and pretending my problems don't exist, even if it was only for a short time. We spread out in the grass, sipping on Gatorade as we catch our breath.

"What's goin' on with you?" Riley asks.

"What do you mean? Nothing's going on with me?" I say defensively.

She tilts her head, giving me the look that says she knows there's more than what I'm letting on. I try to deflect by bringing up next week's game but she shoots me down, not letting it go.

"Charlie, we've been best friends for years. I know when something's bothering you. And I know there's more to it than this whole scholarship feud. Just talk to me."

I pick at the grass below me, debating what I should tell her. The entire time I've known Riley, we've always been straight with each other. She's the one person, besides Matty, that's always had my back.

When we were in middle school and I was finally old enough to understand the severity of what my mother had done, I was furious, hurt, and pretty miserable to be around. I was angry at my grandparents for not doing enough to help; I was angry at my father for leaving us the way he did; and I was angry at myself for feeling like somehow I was responsible—that if I could've been a better daughter, we might've been able to stay together.

I spent more time at Riley's house during that time than I did at my own. When I was with Riley and her family, it was so easy to forget everything and pretend all was right in the world. Riley never got sick of me. She was always just as excited as I was to hang out—even if that meant just lying around watching tv all day.

She was there for me when I needed it the most. I owe it to her to be honest. But how can I be honest with her if I still haven't been honest with myself?

"Charlie," Riley says, warily. "Does this have anything to do with Aspen?"

"What'd you mean?" I say, avoiding her eyes.

"Well, I've just seen how you two are. I see the way she looks at you…" She pauses, her tone gentle. "And I've seen the way you look at her."

She stares at me as if she's waiting for me to fill in the missing pieces. I drop my gaze to the ground, willing myself to disappear.

Riley knows.

Is it that obvious?

I brace myself for what might come next. Is she going to freak out? Hate me? Forget about me because I'm not like everybody else?

But she's my best friend, and has been for nearly ten years. That's gotta count for something, right?

"Charlie," Riley begins. "Do you—do you like her? As in a 'more than friends' kind of way?"

I freeze, my attention riveted to the numerous strands of grass clutched in my hands. "Yes," I finally say. "I do."

"Okay."

I jerk my head in her direction, wondering if I misheard her. "What?"

"I said okay."

"That's it? Just okay? You're not mad?"

"Mad? Charlie, why the hell would I be mad? You're my best friend and if Aspen makes you happy then so be it."

"Really? You're not gonna freak out? Or forget about me because I'm not like everybody else?" I lean in closer to whisper. "Because I like a girl?"

"What? Charlie c'mon," she gives me a light shove. "We live in the twenty-first century, who cares who you like? I mean is it really that big of a deal if it's a boy or a girl, just as long as it's what you want?"

I shrug my shoulders, "I don't know. Everybody's always said that girls are supposed to date boys. Nobody's really said anything about girls being able to date other girls."

"That's because some people can't understand the idea that people can date people of the same sex. It's not like it's the end of the world. There's far worse things you could be doing." She turns to face me, her expression sincere. "People are gonna have their opinions, and they're gonna say what they wanna say. Doesn't mean you have to listen to them."

"But what about the kids at school? The team?"

"What about 'em?"

"What if they're not as accepting as you are?" I say.

"You mean Skylar?"

I nod. "It's not like she welcomed Aspen with open arms."

Riley rolls her eyes. "Who cares what Skylar thinks. She's gonna say what she wants no matter what or who it involves. Just ignore her. And if she gets too ugly, you know I've got your back."

I smile at her. "Thanks, Riley. I'm sorry I didn't tell you sooner."

"I guess now I know why you kept turning down all those guys."

I shrug. "Honestly, I thought there was something wrong with me. Dating guys seemed so easy for everyone else, and I tried, but every time was worse than before. I thought the issue was with me."

"Why didn't you tell me any of this?"

"I don't know. I just thought it might be different when I went off to college—that I'd find someone I could actually relate to. And then I thought maybe I don't need anyone, that I'd be fine just taking care of myself. I didn't even think I liked girls that way until Aspen came along." I drop my head, shaking it slowly before twisting to look at Riley again. "And then I started having these feelings for her and it was terrifying and invigorating all at the same time." I shrug. "I don't know, I'm not really sure how to explain it."

"Well, I'm just glad she makes you happy."

"Thanks, Riley."

"So tell me more. How long?"

"How long what?"

"How long have you and Aspen been, I don't know, dating I guess?"

I hang my head and sigh. "See…about that…"

"What?"

I lift my head up, a sour look on my face. "I don't know if we are what you consider 'dating'," I say, putting air quotes around the word dating.

"What do you mean? What happened?"

"Well we sort of kissed last night…" I pause, raking a hand through my hair. "Okay, not sort of. We definitely kissed last night."

"And?"

"And then I don't know. I kind of freaked out and took off."

"What? She kissed you and you left. Charlie, what the hell's the matter with you? You like her, why'd you run?"

I throw my hands up in mock surrender. "I don't know. I didn't know what was happening, I'd never kissed a girl and still wasn't sure I liked her in that way and then we kissed, and it was all happening so fast. I just freaked out and ran out of there."

"Well?"

"Well what?"

"Did you like it?"

"Yeah, I did." A smile draws across my face as I recall the memory of last night. "I liked it a lot actually."

"So what are you waiting for?"

"What'd you mean, what am I waiting for?"

"March your butt over there and tell her how you feel."

"But she kissed me and then I just bolted, without an explanation or anything. You think she'll still want me?"

"Charlie, girl. You've gotta give yourself a little more credit. I've seen the way she looks at you. You need to tell her how you feel."

"Yeah, I guess you're right."

"Alright, get up. Let's go."

"Why? Where're we going?" I gather my things, trying to keep up.

"We're going to get your girl."

I follow her towards the car. "But I don't even know if she's home and her dad doesn't seem to be my biggest fan. And besides, it's getting late, maybe I should——"

"Charlie, do you like her?" Riley cuts in.

"Yes."

"So stop your whining, use your phone and see if she's home. I'll be waiting in the car." She turns before I can say another word. I pull my phone out and scroll to her name.

Hey r u home? Can I come over 2 talk?

I head to the car, not expecting her to respond so quickly.

Yes u can.

"Well?" Riley says when I slide into the car.

"She's home."

"Yay." She claps her hands. "Let's go."

"But I——"

She turns, pointing her finger at me. "Stop making excuses, Charlie Baker. You're going."

Ten minutes later, we pull into her driveway. My stomach is a mixture of fireworks and nausea and I have absolutely no idea what I'm going to say when I see her.

"Good luck," Riley calls as I stumble up the driveway.

I knock on the door, completely caught off guard when Mr. Sullivan opens the door. He gives me a once-over, his expression a mixture of annoyance and disapproval.

"Can I help you with something?" he says in a tone that reminds me of a parent reprimanding a child.

I rack my brain, trying to come up with an excuse as to why I'm over here on a Sunday night, when Aspen peeks out from behind him.

"Charlie was just coming over because she left something here," she says.

I sidestep past him, not bothering to wait for a formal invitation to come inside. I quickly follow Aspen up to her room. I awkwardly stand in the middle of her bedroom, fidgeting with my fingers as she closes the bedroom door. I open my mouth to speak but she starts before I'm able to get a word out.

"I'm so sorry," she fires. "I didn't mean to make you upset. We started hanging out and getting to know each other and it was really nice. You're the first real friend I've had here and I just don't want to ruin everything or do any—"

I take a step towards her and grab her hands, stopping her before she can continue. I interlace our fingers, welcoming the familiar tingle of her skin on mine. "Aspen," I say gently as I use my finger to lift her chin. I gaze into her deep blue eyes, the *thump thump* of my heart ringing through my ears. "I should be the one apologizing. I just freaked out and left without any explanation. Everything was happening so fast and this is all new to me and I panicked so I ran."

"So you're not mad?"

"No, of course not."

She runs her fingers through her disheveled hair. "I was just so afraid I ruined everything and—"

Before she can say anything else, I pull her into me and kiss her. Our mouths open, finding each other. Her lips are firm and wet, and just as hungry as mine. I slide my hands down her torso, hovering dangerously low on her hips. Her hand comes up to my face and she gently caresses my cheek as the kiss deepens.

I smile when we come up for air. "Believe me now?"

"Yes."

Aspen leads me to her bed and we sit, our fingers still intertwined. I lean in, eager to get another taste of her lips when I feel the pressure of her hand against my chest.

"Wait, Charlie. There's something I need to tell you."

I glance up, the hesitation in her eyes evident. I lightly stroke the back of her hand. "What's wrong?"

She hesitates, taking a breath before answering. "There's a reason my dad just packed us up and moved us here in the middle of my senior year." She stops, her voice shaky. I give her a light nod, encouraging her to continue. "I told you how my parents were perpetually fighting, but I didn't tell you *why*.

"Last summer, I got involved with another girl. We started dating or whatever and before I knew it, things were out of control. I've known I was gay for a long time, but I never acted on those feelings. And then—and then I met this girl and everything changed. We tried to keep it quiet, and we did for several months, but then word got out. And that's when everything went to hell." She rises from the bed and begins pacing back and forth.

After a moment I ask, "So what happened?"

"My dad lost it. I've never seen him so angry before. I mean, I've seen my dad upset but this was a whole new level of anger. He started yelling and throwing things, saying stuff like 'he did not raise his daughter to turn out gay' and 'he will not have me embarrass the family like this'. At first I tried to explain that it's not my fault, I can't help who I'm attracted to. I'm still the same person I've always been. But he wouldn't listen, he was too worried about how this would look on *him*, how it would affect *his* reputation. He didn't care about me being happy, or what I wanted—he was only concerned about himself." Her voice cracks at the end, her lashes glistening with tears.

I step in front of her, blocking her path. "Hey," I say, softly. "You can talk to me. I'm not going anywhere. Tell me what happened next."

She exhales a staggering breath and wipes at the corner of her eye before continuing. "My mom sided with me. I think she was just as shocked by his reaction as I was. I mean, I knew my dad had a strong religious upbringing but I don't think either of us realized the effect it had on him. She tried to get him to understand that me being gay wasn't the end of the world, that I was still the same girl they raised. But he didn't want to hear it."

"So what happened next?"

"He couldn't accept the fact that I was gay. No matter how my mom tried to explain it, or how much I tried to prove to him that I'm still the same person I've always been. It was just an endless debate where everybody loses. He was convinced that it was a phase; that it was all just in my head. He would constantly hound me about guys and try to set me up with his colleague's kids. He was seriously convinced if I just dated a guy, it would somehow fix everything. We were walking on eggshells around each other. The constant tension always surrounding us like a blanket, reminding me that this is my fault."

"Aspen," I say softly. "That wasn't your fault. There was no way to know he would react the way he did."

"Maybe you're right, but if I had just waited till I was off at college, maybe he wouldn't have freaked out the way he did. He started working more; he was angry and temperamental whenever he was home. If I had just waited then maybe they wouldn't have been fighting all the time—fighting about me and my sexuality. I did my best to stay out of his way but I couldn't help feeling like everything was all my fault."

I brush the hair out of her face, tucking it behind her ear. "But it wasn't your fault, Aspen."

She dips her head, wiping her face with the palm of her hand. "And then my mom and I were in that terrible accident. When she died, he was so angry. I remember waking up in the middle of the night not too long before we moved here and I could hear my dad crying, but this wasn't your normal grieving crying. He was sobbing, crouched on the floor, pounding his fist into the ground. He was mumbling something into the carpet, but I could only make out a few bits and pieces about asking God why? Why was He punishing him? I'd never seen my dad so vulnerable like that—so broken."

"Did you say anything to him about it?"

She shakes her head. "No. I wasn't sure how he'd react and I didn't want to upset him even more. Not too long after that I came home one day and he told me we were moving here. He said going back to his roots was just what we needed. The look in his eyes told me there was no point in arguing."

"I'm so sorry, Aspen. I can't imagine how difficult that must've been for you. I'm so sorry you had to go through it alone."

"Thank you, Charlie." She smiles and grabs my hand. "I really don't know what my dad'll do if he finds out about us. We don't really talk about what happened, not since my mom died. He pretty much just acts like it never happened. But that doesn't mean he's suddenly okay with me being gay. But I really like you, Charlie. And I would very much like to be with you but I just don't think it's a good idea if my dad knows—at least not right now. We only have a few months of school left and then we graduate. After that I'll be free to live my life however I want."

"Okay, I don't want to do anything that would put you at risk." Now that I'm thinking about it, it might not be a terrible idea to keep it on the down-low, at least for right now.

"Really?"

"Of course." I lean in, pulling her lips to mine. It's scary and freeing all at once, allowing myself the pleasure of her.

I freeze, drawing back.

"What's wrong?" she asks.

"There's something you should know."

"What?"

"Riley knows. She's the one that drove me over here." I give her a rundown of the conversation Riley and I had in the park. When I finish, sheer terror is written all over her face.

"But I'll talk to Riley, explain the situation. She's my best friend, she won't say anything."

"You're sure she won't say anything?"

"Yes, I know Riley. We can trust her."

A knock on the door sends me flying to the other side of her room. Her dad opens the door before Aspen can say anything. "Aspen, honey. It's almost time for dinner. I ordered a pineapple and spinach pizza, your favorite." He turns towards me, "I'm sure you need to be getting home as well."

"Right, Dad," Aspen says, springing from the bed. "Let me just drive Charlie home real quick."

"I hope she's reimbursing you for all these drives around town." Ouch.

Aspen waves him off. "It's fine. Charlie's house isn't that far away, no big deal."

I follow behind her, muttering a 'goodbye' to her father.

"Your dad really doesn't like me," I say once we're safely out of earshot and in the car.

Aspen shrugs, "He's never been the most welcoming parent. Even before my mom passed, he was always awkward around my friends. My mom usually took the lead."

I nod, not wanting to escalate the situation.

We back out of the driveway and turn onto the main road. She reaches over, gathering my hand in hers, and I lean in closer to her. "Can I ask you a question?"

"Sure."

"The girl from back home, the one you got involved with last summer." I hesitate, not wanting to overstep.

"What about her?"

"What happened with her? Do you two keep in touch?"

"Oh. No, not really. When everything got out, my dad made it very clear I wasn't allowed to see her again. Her family, on the other hand, was much more supportive. From what I heard they seemed to be okay with her being gay. I can't say I wasn't a little bit jealous, but I was happy for her. They ended up moving to California or somewhere on the east coast. It didn't seem worth it to keep in touch." She shrugs as if she's saying something as casual as what to pick up for dinner.

I debate if I should press the issue but the curiosity is too much. "Do you miss her? I mean, it sounds like it was pretty monumental, especially how everything played out."

"I missed her a lot at first. But as time passed on, I found myself thinking about her less and less. Looking back, it was probably really stupid that we got together in the first place. But I was so wrapped up in the excitement of it all that I never really stopped to think about the consequences of our actions."

"Aspen, you got into a relationship with a girl. It's not like you robbed a bank."

"True. But we didn't exactly make the smartest choices either. We got into quite a bit of trouble while we were together, more than I care to admit."

"What? Did you two vandalize the school or something?"

"Or something," she whispers.

I lean forward, my curiosity only increasing. "What'd you do?"

"Nothing, it's not even a big deal."

"So tell me."

"Why do you want to know?"

"Look around, babe. This town isn't exactly crawling with excitement. The most interesting thing that's happened here recently is when Deion's house party got busted by his parents. And that happened nearly four months ago."

"It's nothing, we may have gotten wasted one night and trashed her dad's basement."

"Seriously?"

"I told you we didn't make the smartest choices."

"Did her parents walk in on you two wasted and shit?"

"No, I snuck out the morning after before her parents got home. When her folks came home they freaked but she was too hungover to remember what happened, or that I was ever there. I feel bad letting her take the fall for it but there was no way I would've been able to talk my way out of that."

"Damn. You are just showing me a whole new side of you tonight," I say with a quirked grin.

She brings my hand up to her lips and smiles as she kisses the back of my hand. "Whatever."

We pull into the driveway. I lean over, giving her a slow kiss before I get out of the car.

"I liked the little nickname you called me earlier," she says.

"I'll keep that in mind."

"Goodnight, babe."

"Night."

I head straight for my bedroom as soon as I walk through the door.

Riley answers on the first ring. "So how'd it go?" she asks.

"It was good. Really good actually."

"Yay! Charlie, I'm so happy for you!" I can practically hear her jumping up and down through the phone.

"Thanks, Riley. But there's something we need to talk about."

"What's up?"

I spend the next fifteen minutes explaining everything that happened at Aspen's.

"So we have to keep it on the downlow. Please don't say anything, Riley."

"Of course I won't say anything. You know I wouldn't do that to you."

"Thanks. That means a lot."

"Sucks how everything played out though."

"Yeah, it really does."

"Don't worry your secret's safe with me."

"Thanks, Riley. I'll see you tomorrow."

"Bye, girl."

It takes me several hours to get everything finished. It doesn't help that I'm distracted from texting Aspen the entire time. I don't crawl into bed until after midnight. I'm exhausted from this weekend, but it was worth every second.

Chapter Seven

The most difficult part about being in a secret relationship is acting like you aren't. When you're totally head over heels for someone, it's pretty hard to hide the pure bliss written all over your face. I know people have noticed a change in me; Gramps, Nana, Matty, Riley, even some of the girls from the team.

I carry myself differently since Aspen and I have started dating. I smile more. I laugh more. I walk with a confidence that I didn't have before. Just the sight of Aspen is enough to send shivers coursing through my body. I count the minutes until I get to see her again, feel her hand tangled with mine, the tender press of her lips. When you're attracted to someone, it's because of the details. Their kindness. Their eyes. Their smile. Their laugh. It's the little aspects that most people breeze over in day-to-day life, not taking the time to notice. I feel all of those things for Aspen.

Every morning, I meet up with Aspen by my locker. Some days we'll walk around the courtyard if it's nice outside. Some days we'll sit together at the far end of the cafeteria. Other days we'll stand by the lockers, laughing until we can't breathe. I've never met someone who can make me laugh the way she does.

At lunch, we go back and forth between eating with the team and eating lunch outside by ourselves. On the days Aspen stays late working on her art application, which is most days, I catch a ride home with her after practice. We usually make a couple detours to make out before arriving at my house.

"The party this year is going to be off the chain," Tyler says to the table when we arrive for lunch that day.

John gives him a high five. "And we're seniors, which means this is our last end of season party so we have to make it count."

"And my parents just happen to be out of town that same weekend and my brother is bringing in some kegs for us," says Skylar.

"What party?" asks Aspen.

"Just the biggest party of the year," Riley tells her, her voice bursting with enthusiasm. "Every year we, and by we I mean Skylar's family, throw a party celebrating the end of the season. It's at Skylar's mansion and her family goes all out for it."

"That sounds like a lot of fun," says Aspen.

"Oh it is. You should totally come," says Emily

"Yeah, you should," says Riley, glancing back and forth between Aspen and myself. Heat trickles up my neck as she raises her brows slightly.

Skylar makes a noise that sounds like a forced cough.

"I'm not sure how I feel about an outsider crashing the party," says Skylar.

"That's bullshit, Skylar. You literally invite the entire school," I snap back at her.

"Yeah, I invite the entire school but that's after the team has our own get together beforehand."

"It sure doesn't feel like it's just for the team considering John, Tyler, Liam, and all those other boys join us before the rest of the school shows up," I say.

"That's because they're all dating someone from the team. They cheer us on at the games. It's like a 'thank you' for being supportive."

"So just because they're dating they——"

Aspen cuts me off before I'm able to finish.

"It's fine, I'll just show up when everyone else does. How 'bout that?" she says.

Skylar rolls her eyes. "Fine. Whatever."

I glance over at Aspen but her eyes remain fixed on anything other than me. The bell rings, ending lunch and everybody disperses. I take my time gathering my things. When Aspen and I are left alone I stare at her until she meets my gaze.

"Why'd you cut me off like that?" I ask.

"It's fine, Charlie. It's not a big deal."

"But it is to me. Skylar doesn't get to boss me, or you, around like that."

She takes a breath. "Charlie, people can't know. I know it's not fair but we have to be careful. I was afraid you were gonna say something you shouldn't so I cut you off. I'm sorry."

I run my tongue over the back of my teeth, considering her words. "No, you're right. I need to do better. I'm sorry."

"I'll see you after practice?"

I nod, feeling the swift caress of her hand on mine as she walks past me down the hall. I try to squeeze back but she lets go by the time I realize what happened.

I'm still pretty pissed at Skylar about the whole lunch situation by the time practice rolls around. I know I need to let it go but the more I think about it, the angrier I get. I do my best to avoid being next to Skylar during practice. We go through our normal routine and end with a scrimmage.

Skylar and I get put on the same team. Great.

I deliberately avoid passing her the ball almost the entire scrimmage.

"Baker, pass the damn ball. Make the defense work for it," Coach yells from the sidelines.

I dribble down the court, making note of the time displayed on the clock; we've got just enough time left for one more play. Sara cuts down, setting a screen for Harper, who moves to the left wing. I pass the ball to Harper, spreading to the other side. At the same time, Emily moves from the block to the right wing, setting a screen for Skylar. Harper passes the ball back to me. I see Skylar wide open as she cuts to the basket. I fake a pass to her, throwing off Riley and the rest of the defense. I make a hard dribble to the right, shoot, and watch the ball glide into the hoop.

"What the hell was that, Charlie?" Skylar says when we're back in the locker room.

"What?"

"I was wide open. We made eye contact. You saw me but refused to pass me the ball, didn't you?"

I say nothing and turn back to my locker to finish gathering my things.

"This is about what happened at lunch isn't it? With your little 'friend'," she says, putting air quotes around friend.

"What the hell's that supposed to mean?"

Several of the girls have filed out of the locker room by now, trying to act like they can't hear the conversation. All that's left is me, Riley, Harper, Emily and Skylar.

"Oh I think you know exactly what I mean, Charlie," Skylar says, tilting her head.

"What's your problem Skylar? You've hated Aspen since the minute she got here. You made up your mind about her before you even got the chance to know her."

She narrows her eyes. "Oh I know enough. She's some spoiled rich kid who just waltzed in here thinking nobody would find out what she really is."

"Oh c'mon, Skylar. Like you have room to talk. Your family's one of the richest in town and go around acting like they're better than everyone else. What makes you think you have the right to judge Aspen?"

"It's not like I go around flaunting my expensive clothes, accessories, and fancy car. She could at least show a little humility."

"Says the person who throws a party in her family's mansion every year to show off their worth."

"It's not my fault you're jealous, Charlie."

"Fuck you." I hurl my bag to the ground and take a step towards her.

Riley steps in between us, placing her hands on my shoulder, pushing me back. "Let it go, Charlie."

I pick up my bag and stalk out of the locker room without another word.

"Hey, are you okay?" Aspen pushes off from where she was leaning on the car and takes a couple steps forward.

"Can we just go?"

She gives me a wary look. "Alright."

We climb in the car and cruise out of the parking lot. The drive home is silent and tense as I stare out the window avoiding her eye.

"You wanna tell me what's got you so riled up?"

"Practice was rough."

We sit in silence for a few moments before Aspen speaks again. "You sure there's not something else on your mind, babe?"

I exhale slowly as I turn to look at her. "It's fine. Can we just drop it?"

"Okay. There's no need to bite my head off."

I reach over and gather her hand in mine. "I'm sorry. Today was just a lot. I didn't mean to take it out on you."

She squeezes my hand. "It's okay. You have any plans this weekend?"

"Nope. You have something in mind?"

She bites her bottom lip. "I have an idea."

She pulls the car over a couple driveways down from my house. We always stop here so we can kiss goodbye without the risk of my grandparents seeing. I'm still not sure how they would react if they found out.

I lean over, pulling her in for a long sensual kiss.

"I'll see you tomorrow?" she says when we pull apart.

"Always," I reply, getting out of the car.

Our next game is against Mansfield. They're one of the better teams in our league. They have three guards that know how to handle the ball, and two girls the size of trees that rotate in and out around the blocks.

I'm a bundle of nerves on game day. I can't make myself focus on anything for more than a few minutes. Thoughts of the scholarship and what I have riding on tonight's game lingers in the back of my mind, like an itch I can't scratch. The day goes by in a haze as I make my way from class to class, going through the motions.

When the bell rings for sixth period, I head straight for the gym, hoping to get some extra shots in before the game.

I spot Aspen waiting at the end of the hall past the locker room door. I walk over to her, conscious of the fact that the hallway we're in allows us to be out of sight.

"What are you doing here? Shouldn't you be in class?" I ask her, my tone teasing.

"I wanted to see you before the game, wish you luck."

I lean against the wall next to her, tucking her hair behind her ear and smile. "And that's just what I needed." I reach out and take her hand.

She glances around us, making sure there's no one in sight before her hand relaxes in my grip. "I should probably get to class now."

"But you just got here and I feel like I haven't seen you."

She gives me a playful grin. "We literally saw each other at lunch not too long ago and I've already been late several times to this class. I don't need my dad breathing harder down my neck than he already is."

"Alright," I sigh, reluctantly releasing her hand. "I'll see you at the game?"

"Wouldn't miss it."

I wait several seconds until Aspen's around the corner before I follow behind her. I pause when I see Riley entering the locker room right before me. She turns to me, grinning and raising her eyebrows. I roll my eyes and follow her in.

"Thought you wanted to get some extra shots in before the game?" she says.

"I am."

"You sure you didn't just want to sneak over here to see Aspen before the game?" she teases.

"Actually, she's the one who snuck over here to see me. She's supposed to be in history right now."

"Awh, look at you two lovebirds, being all cute and shit."

"Shut up," I say, giving her a playful shove.

"I'm just messing with you. I think that's really sweet of her."

The locker room is buzzing with conversation while we wait for Coach. Everybody's feeling good about tonight's game, we beat Mansfield the last time we played so why should tonight be any different, someone says.

"I say we all head over to *Sally's* after the game to have celebratory milkshakes when we crush them. We only have two games left. We need to make the most of it," says Emily, who's lightly bouncing up and down in the corner of the room; her usual pregame routine.

Several 'I'm in's' echo around the locker room.

"What about you, Charlie?" says Skylar.

"What about me?" I ask.

Her lips tug into a smirk. "Are you down to go to *Sally's* after the game or do you have other plans with your new 'friend'?"

"Yeah, Charlie. You two seem to be all that anyone's talking about," says Harper, ducking her head to giggle with Skylar.

I roll my eyes and stay silent, trying to ignore them.

When they finish their laughing fit Skylar lifts her head. "What? No snarky come back?" She leans over to Harper, ducking her head as if she's trying to be discrete, but speaks loud enough for everyone to hear. "Told you she was a *dyke*."

Everyone stops as silence immediately encompasses the room.

One by one, the face of everyone in the locker room turns to look at me, waiting to see my reaction.

I stare at the ground, replaying the scene in my mind. Surely I misunderstood. That's not really what she just said.

I draw my gaze up from the floor, looking Skylar directly in the eye. "What did you just say?"

She doesn't even flinch. "You heard me."

My body goes rigid, my hands clamp into clenched fists as the anger churns within me. In two strides I'm on the other side of the locker room, Skylar's breath hot on my face. She shoves me back. "You got a problem?" she snarls.

I step forward, rage boiling over and press my palms into her chest, driving her back. "Fuck you."

Skylar steps forward, ready to retaliate when Riley and Emily jump in between us. Riley guides me back to my seat, and Emily does the same with Skylar. Her mouth opens like she's going to say something else but she immediately closes it when we hear the brief knock on the door. Coach enters and glances around, instantly aware of the tension enveloping the room.

"What the hell's goin' on in here?" he barks.

Everybody drops their gaze, intentionally avoiding his eye.

Emily speaks up. "Nothing, Coach."

He glances around the room one last time before turning to the board and starting his 'before the game speech'. I don't hear a word he says, my mind still reeling from what just happened.

When I was in the second grade, I got sent to the principal's office for 'fighting'. We were all outside running, screaming, and doing what all seven-year-olds do at recess. Another little boy had just started school that week, Baxter Jenkins. He was one of those kids that was just asking to get picked on. That day he came to school in a ridiculous outfit. He was wearing pink skinny jeans, a tie-dye t-shirt and a matching headband that had cat ears protruding on the outside. Some of the kids thought it would be funny to steal his headband and play monkey-in-the-middle. He was frantically jumping around, trying to get it back. It didn't take long for a crowd to form around them. Kids were laughing and calling him names, happy they weren't the unfortunate soul that was targeted that day. I remember huddling around like everybody else, eager to witness the event.

When it finally dawned on me what they were doing, I snapped. I didn't even realize what I'd done until I was being pulled off one of the boys, blood trickling down my hand as I was led back inside. I got sent to the office and they had to call Nana. To say she was furious is an understatement.

But what she didn't get is that the only reason they were picking on Baxter was that he represented something they didn't even try to understand. He was different from what everyone perceived as 'normal', which meant he was less-than. He never stood a chance.

I haven't thought about that incident in years. But I can see it replaying in my mind like it was just yesterday.

We head out onto the court and begin our usual warm-up routine. I miss every shot I take.

I move off to the side, and stretch out my arms, trying to regain my focus. I finally look into the stands, scanning the crowd. I catch sight of Matty, waving at me from the top of the bleachers. I'm surprised to see Aspen standing next to him. We make eye contact, and she flashes me a smile. I quickly adjust my gaze to the floor, thoughts of what happened in the locker room rip through me. It didn't even occur to me how this might affect Aspen. What if word gets back to her father? What happens then?

"You okay?" Riley asks, redirecting my attention.

I shrug my shoulders, not sure how to answer her question.

"I'm sorry about what happened. I can't believe she said that."

Coach calls us to the bench before I can respond. He gives some last-minute pointers, something about communicating and defense, before we take our spots for tip-off.

The first half ends with a score of twenty-five to twenty-one, Mansfield leading. It's been one helluva first half. Our passes have been sloppy, our communication has been almost nonexistent and we can't get a rebound to save our life.

We head into the locker room with our heads down, bracing for the shit storm that's about to occur when Coach Stewart bursts through the door. One by one, he glares at each of us, his gaze lingering on me. I keep my head down, not wanting to draw attention to myself.

He turns around, grabs a marker from the board and chucks it against the back wall. Pieces of the lid ricochet back towards us.

"What the hell happened out there? That is not the same team that destroyed Crossroads last week." He runs his fingers through his hair, as he paces back and forth. "There's no communication, our passing is atrocious. We're practically giving them the ball." He shakes his head, settling his hands on his hips. "The season is almost over. Is this really how you want to go out? Stop playin' like a bunch of amateurs and go out there and show them we came to play."

"Falcons on three…one…two…three…FALCONS."

The third quarter begins with Riley bringing the ball down the court, her fist in the air, signaling the play. Sara meets her at the top of the key, setting up for a pick-n-roll. Riley passes it to Sara, who fakes to the basket, and passes it to me on the wing. I catch the ball and shoot, watching it soar to the basket as I backpedal towards half-court. It bounces off the rim and Mansfield gets the rebound. I cut them off when they cross half-court, landing me my third foul. Coach calls a timeout and I hang my head as I hustle to the bench.

"Baker, what the hell's the matter with you? It's like you're playing with your eyes closed," he barks. "We still got time to get it back. Now get out there and put the ball in the damn basket."

I get a few pats on the backs as we finish the huddle, but the pit in my stomach just grows deeper.

The third quarter ends with a score of thirty-two to twenty-eight, Mansfield still leading. I skim the crowd, my eyes finding Aspen instantly. She flashes me a smile and winks. She mouths something I don't quite catch, but her smile is just what I needed.

Mansfield has possession of the ball at the beginning of the fourth quarter. We press, pouncing the second the ball is inbounded. I take off, intercepting the pass as soon as it leaves her hands. I push the ball forward and lay it in the hoop.

Mansfield gets another shot off, still leading by two points as the fourth quarter winds down. I glance at the clock, the luminous digits taunting us as the end draws near. Thirteen seconds left. Just enough time for one more play.

The ball is inbounded to Riley. One swift crossover is all it takes for her to throw off her defender and charge down the court. I make a wide cut to the wing, bouncing on the tips of my toes as I anticipate the pass. I catch the ball the same time my defender springs towards me. I pump-fake to the basket, lunging past her and stop just below the three-point line and pull up for a jump shot. The final buzzer bellows through the gym as the ball bounces from the rim and falls to the ground.

Final score, forty to thirty-eight. We lose. Again.

The rest of the Mansfield team sprints to the center of the court, cheering and jumping in the huddle. I hang my head, my feet glued to the floor as the unwanted defeat washes over me. Riley's palm presses on my back, guiding me to our bench to shake the other team's hand. I sulk into the locker room, my gaze still fixed on the floor beneath my feet.

I take my seat, focusing on the splotchy pattern of the locker room floor as Coach barrels in behind us. He stares at us, hands resting on his hips for what feels like hours before finally speaking. "One game left." He holds his index finger in the air. "One game, that's all you got left. For some of you, it'll be the last time you lace up and step foot on a court. For others, it'll just be the end of another season." He glances around the room. "But you owe it to each other, to those people in the stands that come and support you every week, to your parents. But most importantly you owe it to yourself to make it count. But you have to want it. You have to fight for it. You have to go out there and take it, dammit! Don't just roll over and give it to 'em. You're better than that."

"Falcons on three…one…two…three…FALCONS"

The room is unusually silent as everyone ambles to their locker to change out of our jerseys. I remain in my seat, my gaze still centered on the floor, as the hope of receiving a scholarship—my only ticket out of this place—slowly fades from my grasp.

I fucking blew it.

"Looks like we won't be getting celebratory milkshakes tonight," mumbles Harper.

"It's too bad somebody couldn't come through tonight," Skylar says.

"That's enough, Skylar," Riley snaps at her. "We all made mistakes tonight, every single one of us, especially you. So shut your mouth and worry about yourself."

"Well I'm not the one who missed the winning shot. Again," she says, her eyes narrowed at me.

"I'm not talking about what happened in the game."

She huffs, rolling her eyes as she turns back around.

"You okay?" Riley whispers as I finally make my way over to my locker.

"What'd you think?" I hiss at her. "I played like shit tonight and everybody knows it."

"Calm down. It wasn't that bad. You were just a little off tonight. It happens to everybody."

"Easy for you to say. You had how many points? Sixteen? Ms. McCalister is going to watch the first ten minutes of tonight's game and have no trouble deciding who to offer the scholarship to."

"Is that what this is about? The stupid scholarship?"

"You know damn well how much that scholarship means to me. And I fucking blew it tonight."

"You don't know that."

"Well if you were in her shoes, who would you pick? I couldn't make a single shot to save my life out there."

The rest of the team has filed out of the locker room by now, doing their best to avoid awkward eye contact as they shuffle past us.

"Charlie, would it really be the end of the world if she gives the scholarship to me?"

"Oh c'mon, Riley. You have other offers. Why not just tell her you're not interested?"

"Because maybe I am," she snaps.

"Oh."

"Charlie, I—"

I hold my hand up, cutting her off. "It's fine." I throw the last of my gear in my bag and charge out of the locker room without another word.

"Hey, sis. Good game," Matty says when I've made my way over to him and Aspen.

"Yeah. Right."

"Ahh c'mon, Charlie. It's not that bad. You had some nice shots."

"And yet we still lost."

"But you weren't the only one to make mistakes. So you were a little off tonight, it happens to everyone," Aspen says.

"Can we just go?" I say, guiding them towards the exit.

"I'm actually gonna go to Alec's tonight. He had a family thing but I wanted to come to your game. Is it cool if I take the car?"

I nod. "You know one of these days I'm going to stop being so generous."

He smirks. "I'll keep that in mind. See you."

"Bye, Matty," Aspen says before turning to me. "You okay?"

"Let's just get outta here." I open the door and head for her car.

"You wanna tell me what's on your mind, babe?" Aspen says when we've turned onto the road, heading nowhere in particular. She grabs my hand, interlacing her fingers with mine.

I stare out the window, focusing on the trees passing by, trying to wait out the inevitable. There's no sense in avoiding it, she has a right to now, especially if this somehow gets back to her father.

I take a breath, before turning and telling her the details of what occurred before, during and after the game tonight.

Aspen slams on the breaks, pulling the car over to the side of the road. She stares at the road in front of her, her knuckles turning white from gripping the steering wheel. She furrows her eyebrows, pinching her eyes closed like she's about to take the plunge on a roller coaster. Several seconds pass before she turns, eyes watering and lips quivering. "Charlie, do you have any idea how bad this could get?"

I run my fingers through my hair, not sure how to respond. "I—I—I'm sorry, Aspen. I didn't mean for that to happen."

She turns her gaze back to the road, inhaling, big deep breaths. "Oh shit. Oh shit. Oh shit." She leans forward, resting her head against the steering wheel. "Charlie, what if my dad finds out?"

"He might not. Skylar just made a comment. It's not like she painted 'Charlie and Aspen are dating' on the side of the gym," I reply, trying to offer her some sort of comfort.

"Do you know what that word implies, Charlie?"

I sit up, turning towards her. "Yes, I do. But I'm not the one who said it," I snap back.

She raises her head up, reaching over for me. "I know, I'm sorry. I just got scared."

I use my thumb to stroke the back of her hand. "I know, it's okay."

"Do you think the team's gonna say anything?"

"I don't know. I got the impression that some of them were just as angry as me when Skylar said that, except for Harper. But I was also reeling from what came out of her mouth, convinced I'd heard her wrong." I shrug. "So I don't know for sure. And then the conversation got cut short when Coach came in."

She raises an eyebrow at me. "You call that a conversation? You two were ready to rip each other's throats out, not that she didn't deserve it."

I look into her eyes. "I really am sorry."

She brushes the edge of my chin with her fingers. "I'm sorry too. I know that what happened isn't your fault."

"So what happens now?"

She exhales slowly before answering. "Now, we hope he doesn't find out."

I nod. "We'll be careful."

She smiles, rubbing my hand. "I know."

I pull her in, suddenly craving the taste of her lips. I kiss her hard, losing myself in the sweet scent that is her.

We pull back onto the road after our impromptu make-out session and head back into town.

"Are you and Riley going to be okay?"

I shrug. "I guess I didn't realize how much she was considering LittleWood. I really thought she'd pick one of the other schools. But nothing is set in stone yet."

"Well no matter what happens, I'm here for you."

"Thanks, baby."

"I'll pick you up tomorrow?" Aspen says when she pulls over to drop me off.

"Sounds good." I lean over, giving her one more kiss before I climb out of the car.

The sweet aroma of chocolate chip cookies fills my nose the second I step through the door. I head straight for the kitchen and pick up two cookies off the cooling rack, inhaling one in a single bite.

"Hey, Monkey. How was the game tonight?" Gramps asks, helping himself to a cookie as well.

"We lost," I say, my mouth full of cookies.

"Any word from LittleWood?"

"Nope." I turn and head for the stairs before they can hound me with any more questions.

After my shower, I lie in bed scrolling through social media. I go back and forth, looking for any sign that other people know about what happened in the locker room. So far, none of the posts seem to indicate that people know what went down. Hopefully, it'll stay that way.

By the time Saturday morning rolls around, I am more than eager about spending the day with Aspen.

"Hey, baby," she says, grabbing my hand as I slide into the car.

"Hey."

"Did your father say anything when you got home last night? About what happened before the game?" I ask, trying not to sound too concerned.

She shakes her head. "Nope."

"He say anything this morning?"

She shakes her head again. "I didn't really see him this morning, he was up late last night drinking so he was probably sleeping it off."

"Well that's good right? I mean, if he would've heard something you'd probably know by now, right?"

She nods with a feeble smile. "Right."

"So what's the plan for tonight?" I ask.

She turns, biting her lower lip. "I have a few ideas."

I grin. "Oh yeah? Like what?"

"My dad's meeting some of his business pals tonight so I thought we could go back to my place, cook dinner, relax, maybe watch a movie? Or put on a movie while we make out instead," she says with a coy smile.

I look at her, thinking about all the things I'd let her do to me. "Sounds good to me."

We pull into the driveway, shutting off the car. I trail behind her, admiring the way her jeans hug her butt. We stop unexpectedly in the doorway to the kitchen at the sight of her father sitting at the island drinking what looks like whiskey from the bottle.

She takes a cautious step forward. "Uhh…hey, Dad. I thought you were going out tonight?"

He finishes his swig before standing and walking towards us. I can smell the alcohol on his breath as he talks. "Plans changed. Richard's sitter cancelled last minute so we rescheduled for next week." He looks back and forth between the two of us. "I thought you were going on a date with…" He pauses, thinking. "With Andrew from down the street?"

"Right…a date…" she stammers, her enthusiasm quickly deflating as her father continues to bore holes into her.

He tilts his head, raising his eyebrow as he glances between the two of us.

Aspen looks from me to her father. After a moment she says, "Uhh…it's actually a double date. But I forgot my mascara and I wanted to grab it before meeting up with them."

Aspen's father looks at her, considering her response. He swallows another sip of his drink, taking a step closer and turns to me. He gives me a once-over, his eyes darting back to Aspen. "I didn't realize it was a double date. You look beautiful by the way."

"Thanks. We're gonna go now. I'll be back later, bye Dad." We turn, heading straight for the door before he has a chance to respond.

We make it back to the car, and I watch Aspen's face fall as she puts it in reverse to back out.

"Hey, it's okay. We can still have fun. We just have to come up with something else to do."

"I'm so sorry, baby. I really didn't think he was gonna be home tonight."

"It's alright. I just want to be with you."

She grabs my hand, interlacing her fingers with mine.

"Does this Andrew boy know you two are going out? Do I have some competition?" I tease.

She laughs, shaking her head. "I hung out with him a few times when we first moved in. His parents brought us a muffin basket as a housewarming gift and when my father saw they had a son around my age, he insisted we get to know each other."

"Oh yeah? And how'd it go?"

She shrugs. "Turns out I'm not his type, the same way he isn't mine."

"He's gay?"

She nods. "But his parents don't know and I promised not to tell anyone. Now we use each other as a scapegoat so it worked out in the end."

"And he just told you? Just like that? He said, 'Hi, I'm Andrew and I'm gay'?"

"No, silly, but it wasn't that hard to figure out."

"I see. So you tell him you're hanging out with Andrew when you're really hanging out with me?"

She peers over at me, her bottom lip tucked between her teeth. After a moment she says, "Yeah. After everything that happened back home I thought it was easier to let him think I was with a boy. And it seems to have worked. I mean, he still drinks a lot but he doesn't seem as angry, and we've actually been able to have a few decent conversations."

"You realize how messed up that is, don't you? He's nice to you all of a sudden just because he *thinks* you're dating a boy."

"I don't know, Charlie. It's been kind of nice these past couple weeks, like he's back to his old self."

"But it's all a lie. I don't get it. I watch you go from this confident, carefree, vibrant person, to timid and fearful as soon as you're within a hundred feet of your father."

"You remember what happened last time he found out I was dating a girl? You really think he's going to all of a sudden be chill with it?"

"I don't know, people change. Aren't you getting tired of hiding?"

"It's better than the alternative."

"But don't you get annoyed at all the couples holding hands at school and the fact that we can't do that? Is it so wrong of me to want to show you off? To walk down the hall holding your hand."

"No. I would love nothing more than to do that, but you need to look at this from my point of view, Charlie. I don't know what my dad'll do if he finds out." She grabs my hand, the blue hues of her eyes misting over like a storm. "I've never felt this way about anyone before. I know it's not fair, but I can't lose you, Charlie. Please, we don't have that much longer before we graduate and then we can do whatever we want—hold hands in public all the time."

I cradle her head in my hand, lightly stroking her cheek with my thumb. "You're right. I'm sorry. I didn't mean to take it out on you. I guess it's just been bugging me lately. I was fine with keeping it a secret at first, but it just pisses me off that I constantly see other couples being all coupily and shit and we can't do that—whether it's because of your father or the fact that we live in this small town. It's not fair. We have just as much right as they do to be with who we want."

"You're not wrong, Charlie. I know this hasn't been easy for either of us, but I just don't think I want to risk it. Not when we're this close to graduation."

The look in her eyes told me there was no point in trying to argue—her mind was made up. "Okay," I finally say.

She brings my hand up to her lips and lightly kisses the top of it. "Thank you, baby."

I return the smile, unable to resist the shimmer that reaches her eyes.

"So what are we going to do tonight, now that my plan's ruined?"

"I have an idea."

We decide on take-out from the local Chinese restaurant and drive out to the old abandoned park with the lakefront view. We park off to the side, eating, talking, and just enjoying being together. I stare out towards the sky, watching as it turns a darker color, the pigments of the sunset slowly beginning to trace lines across the horizon.

We finish eating, discard the containers, and snuggle close together in the car. I feel the tender touch of her hands stroking my face and neck. "Kiss me," she whispers.

I lift my head up, kissing across her cheek, to the corner of her mouth, and finally edging even closer, setting my mouth over hers. Her lips part and I slip my tongue inside. Her hands trail down my back, her fingers dipping slightly beneath the hem of my pants before flitting back out again like they'd never been there.

I wrap my arms around her, aching to get closer as our kisses deepen. I slide my hand underneath her shirt, conscious of how soft her back feels against my skin. Aspen leans back, her eyes locked with mine as she gently tugs my shirt over my head. I do the same to her before we settle into the backseat.

I watch her, my heart hammering in my chest as she climbs on top. She hovers above me, her eyes slowly sweeping down my body. Very quickly, I feel overexposed. Instinctively, I try to back away, suddenly very much aware of how vulnerable we are right now.

Aspen stops, sensing my hesitation. Her gaze locks with mine as she whispers, "Do you trust me?"

I stare into her eyes; the ocean blue hues radiant despite her darkened irises. And in that moment, it becomes so clear, like the final puzzle piece sliding into place.

"Yes," I murmur. She leans down and I pull her close, kissing her fervently, as her hand slowly descends down my stomach.

Chapter Eight

'm still recuperating from this weekend, thoughts of Aspen tangled in my mind, like little bolts of electricity pinching me to make sure it's not a dream. In fact, I've nearly forgotten about the incident in the locker room on Friday. That is until I get to school Monday morning and it all comes flooding back to me. My first thought is Aspen and what might happen if word gets out. I just got her and I'm not ready to let her go, at least not without a fight.

I decide to avoid nearly everyone on the team, hoping that they all just forgot about what happened.

Yeah, right. Wishful thinking.

I manage to avoid them until lunch. I contemplate skipping but I refuse to give Skylar the satisfaction.

I hop in line beside Riley, feeling the uneasiness snake into my stomach. I haven't talked to her since after the game on Friday and I'm not entirely sure where we stand.

"Hey," I whisper.

She looks over at me and after a moment she smiles, immediately elevating the tension. "Hey."

"I'm sorry about Friday. I was upset and took it out on you and that's not fair."

"It's okay."

"We've been friends for too long to let something like this come between us. I promise to be supportive and happy for you no matter what happens."

"Thanks, Charlie. I promise too."

I glance around the cafeteria, looking for any indication that word has spread about Friday night. But so far no one has taken a second glance in my direction.

"You thinking about what Skylar said on Friday?"

I nod.

"Well I talked to the team after you left. They're not gonna say anything."

"Seriously?"

"Yeah, most of them were just as pissed as I was and agreed not to say anything."

"Most of them?"

"Well there were a few that…" She pauses, searching for the words. "A few that weren't as supportive."

I roll my eyes. "Let me guess, Harper and Skylar?"

She nods, shrugging.

I bump her shoulder with mine. "Thanks, Riley."

She grins. "So what'd you do this weekend?"

"Hung out with Aspen." I smile, thinking back to Saturday night.

Riley nudges me. "What are you so smiley about?"

"Nothin', we just had fun this weekend." I glance down, avoiding Riley's eye as the blush creeps up my neck.

"You know, you really do seem a lot happier since you and Aspen started hanging out."

I smile. "What can I say? She does make me happy." We take our seats, setting our trays down the same time Aspen comes up behind us.

"Hey, Aspen," Riley says to her.

"Hey," she replies.

She looks nervous, her eyes darting back and forth across the table. I want to tell her that everything's fine (I think), but we said we were going to be more careful. And somehow, me leaning over, whispering in her ear doesn't strike me as being more careful. I give her a gentle pat on her knee underneath the table, hoping that might calm her. She flinches at first, not realizing it's me, and then relaxes.

I glance towards Skylar's direction, surprised she hasn't said anything to us, but she's engaged in a conversation with Sara, not paying us any attention. We make it through lunch without any awkwardness, participating in Emily's story about her 'crazy' trip to the store this weekend, before the bell rings. Everybody gathers their things, not pausing to take a second look at Aspen and me. Maybe everything really is fine?

I walk with Aspen down the hall and tell her what Riley told me. She looks relieved and I have the sudden urge to reach out and take her hand. But I don't. We go our separate ways, and head to class.

There's a couple snuggled up against the lockers, kissing and whispering to each other. I glance in their direction, watching the girl dip her head and giggle. The boy smiles and wraps his arm around her waist, pulling her in close to whisper something in her ear. I clutch the straps of my backpack, heat swelling within me as I am reminded yet again that Aspen and I don't have the freedom to do that.

They've stopped, turning to look at me with an expression of annoyance. I realize I'm staring. I duck my head and keep walking.

"You taking notes?" a voice says.

I look over to see Ben leaning against the wall, a smirk playing about his mouth.

I roll my eyes as I walk past him.

He pushes himself off the wall, keeping pace with me. "If you want somebody to show you how it's done, I'd be happy to oblige," he says.

I keep walking, ignoring his comment.

"C'mon, Charlie," he says, grabbing my arm.

I whip my arm back, breaking free from his grasp. "Lay off, Ben. What part of 'I'm not interested' don't you understand?" I snap at him.

"Why?"

I pause, his words taking me by surprise. "Well for starters, maybe try talking to me with a little respect and not like I'm a piece of meat."

"Huh." He raises his eyebrows. "You sure it doesn't have anything to do with what's in between my legs?"

"Oh, I didn't realize there actually was *something* down there." I spit back at him. I turn, continuing to class, leaving him there, speechless.

After practice on Wednesday, Coach calls me into his office.

"It's your lucky day, Baker. Guess who wants you to play basketball for them next year?"

"Are you serious?"

"Yep. I got the call this weekend. Ms. McCalister wanted me to tell you she'll be by later this week to get all the paperwork sorted out."

I stand there, my mouth hanging open in a small *O* as I slowly comprehend the words he just said. They want me. They actually want me. I might be getting out of this town after all.

"Wait. What about Riley?"

"She didn't tell you?"

"Tell me what?"

"New Mexico University called last week. They officially want to offer her a scholarship. She called Ms. McCalister to let her know that she was going to accept. Which is great because they were going to go with you anyways."

I can't help the smile spreading across my face as it finally sets in that I actually have my ticket out. "Thanks, Coach."

"Why didn't you tell me?" I say to Riley as soon as I walk into the locker room.

"I didn't want to say anything until I knew for sure."

I give her a playful shove. "You asshole. I'm so happy for you."

"Thanks. Any word on LittleWood?"

"Yep. They want me."

Riley pulls me into a bear hug before I can stop her. "I knew it. I'm so happy for you, Charlie."

"Thanks. I'll see you later."

I meet Aspen at her car, aching to tell her the good news. It takes everything in me to not pull her in for a kiss as soon as she's within arm's reach.

"So Coach told me LittleWood's made a decision."

She hesitates for a minute before saying, "And?"

"They want me."

"No way." A smile spreads across her face. "I'm so proud of you, baby."

"Thanks."

I wait till we're safely out of the parking lot, away from the school before I make her stop down a back road so I can feel her lips on mine.

I nudge her backward, adjusting the seat to give us more room. I climb over the center console, my legs straddling her lap. I cradle her head in my hands, pulling her in for a long, luscious kiss. Her hands slide down my back, lingering just below my hips. Just when I think I can't breathe, her mouth trickles off mine. She kisses my neck, burning my skin with the touch of her lips.

She pulls back, biting her lower lip. "What's gotten into you?"

Before I can answer Aspen kisses me so hard and so quickly that I lose all sense of reality, unable to focus on anything but her tongue in my mouth and her body pressed into mine.

After our unplanned make out session, I lean back in my seat, still giddy as we drive back into town. I reach over, intertwining her hand with mine.

"That was unexpected," she says.

"I missed you. And I'm really happy."

She pulls my hand up to her mouth, giving me a tender kiss on my knuckles.

She pulls over a couple driveways down. "Will you help me with my art? I need to submit my portfolio by Monday and I can't decide which pieces to choose."

"Sure. I should get out of practice early on Thursday. I could help you then."

"Perfect," she leans over, kissing me before I get out of the car and head into the house.

I walk into the house, surprised to find it empty. I head to the kitchen, hunger gnawing at my stomach. I'm rummaging through the fridge and nearly drop the container in my hands when Matty comes up behind me.

I turn, giving him a playful shove. "You almost made me drop the spaghetti."

He chuckles, reaching past me to get a soda. "It's not my fault you're such a spaz."

I roll my eyes. "Where are Gramps and Nana?"

"They had some church thing. Said they would be back later." He glances at the clock on the over. "Although, you seem to be getting home pretty late."

"Practice ran long," I say, removing the container of spaghetti from the microwave.

He raises his eyebrow at me. "I stayed late to work on a project for class and you left right before I did. Strange how I got home before you."

My ears begin to turn red. I was so focused on Aspen, I didn't even notice the car was still in the parking lot. I shrug my shoulders, trying to play it off.

"You've been spending a lot of time with Aspen recently, I've noticed."

"She's fun to hang out with," I mumble with my mouth full. I turn my attention to my food in front of me, wondering why Matty is so curious all of a sudden. Does he know? Would I really be upset if he did?

"Charlie, can I ask you something?" he says, interrupting my thoughts.

"What's up?"

"Are you and Aspen like, I don't know, a thing?"

"Yes." I'm surprised with my immediate response but I look up at him smiling. I had no idea how good that would feel to say out loud.

He nods, dropping his gaze to the floor as he takes a drink of soda.

I drum my fingers on the table for a few moments before I ask the question I'm not sure I want to know the answer to. "Do Gramps and Nana know?"

He shakes his head, "I don't think so. They're pretty oblivious to everything." He tosses his can in the trash with a very deliberate *thud* and breezes past me up the stairs without another word. I turn, watching as he takes the step two at a time. I finish the last of the spaghetti and trail after him.

I lightly tap on his door before barging in. He looks up from the magazine in his hands and rolls eyes.

"Did I do something?" I ask.

He drops his gaze back to the page in front of him and doesn't answer me. I walk over, snatch the magazine from his hands, and toss it on his desk. "Why are you all of a sudden pissed at me?"

He sits up and lets out an exasperated breath. "Why didn't you tell me?"

"What'd you mean?"

"Why didn't you tell me about you and Aspen?"

"I'm not sure exactly," I whisper. "We needed to keep it quiet."

"Did you really think I would compromise that? C'mon, Charlie it's me. Did you think I would care if you're gay? After everything we've been through, is that really what you think of me?"

"No, not at all. I—I—I'm sorry. I knew you wouldn't care, but—"

"So why'd you wait until I brought it up to tell me?"

I glance down at the floor. "I don't know. I'm sorry."

"It's fine." He grabs the magazine off his desk and lays back down on his bed.

"Matty—"

"It's fine, Charlie. Just go."

I nod, shuffling my feet as I quietly close the door behind me. It's not until I get to my bedroom that I realize I forgot to tell him about LittleWood.

Practice on Thursday ends earlier than expected. I meet Aspen at her car, eager to have some extra time with her.

"You sure your dad's not home?" I ask as we head west toward her house.

"Yes, he's got some business dinner and won't be home till late."

I follow her into the kitchen, nearly trampling her when she stops dead in her tracks. I turn to see what made her stop so abruptly.

The kitchen counter is littered with beer bottles, whiskey bottles, and several paper bags discarded off to the side.

"Shit," Aspen says. "I'm sorry."

"It's okay, let me help." I trail behind her, helping her gather the empty bottles and throw them into the recycling bin out in the garage. She picks up the last few bottles, and I grab a paper towel and wipe down the counter.

"See, good as new," I say, trying to get her to smile.

She grabs my hand. "Let's just go upstairs."

"You wanna show me what pieces to choose from for your portfolio?" I ask when we enter her bedroom, hoping changing the subject will put her at ease.

She nods, walking over to her desk and lays out several photos on her bed. "We have to include pieces that fit into certain categories for the portfolio. I have everything except some sketches. I've narrowed it down to these." She gestures towards the bed. "But I can only pick two."

I peer down at the bed, studying the pages. There's a drawing of an outdoor landscape, shaded very precisely. There's a bookstore, the shelves displayed aimlessly throughout the page. One's a picture of the school, the colors blended to highlight the different features around the outside. The last one is a drawing of a basketball court, but it takes me a minute to realize it's not what you would normally see in a typical basketball game. The court has been sketched in a way that resembles a stage, the edges curved, spotlights shining on the players below. The bleachers surrounding it are replaced with curtains, parted so that the audience can see the action. There is meticulous detail in the drawing of the players, all the way down to the logo on the shoes.

"It's incredible." It's only after I've picked up the paper, that I realize I've said that out loud.

Aspen steps closer to me, her face inches from mine, and stares at the drawing. "You're part of the reason I drew that piece. It reminds me of you."

I turn towards her, handing her the picture. "You have to include this one. The detail is unbelievable."

She nods, taking the paper. "What'd you think for the other one?"

I glance back down at the bed, pick up the bookstore drawing, and hand it to her. "This one."

She smiles. "I drew this after you took me to *The Book Worm*. That was such a good day." She gathers the rest of the papers, putting them back in the folder.

I lie down on the bed. "So what you're saying is I'm basically your muse?"

A soft laugh bubbles out as she lays on the bed next to me. "Something like that."

"I can't wait to see all the amazing art you create when you get in."

"Let's just hope I do get in."

I shift my body, adjusting so Aspen can snuggle up to me. I run my fingers through her hair. "You're going to get in, baby. I just know it."

"I'm just so ready to get away from this place, finally be free. Finally have a little control over my life and have the freedom to live it how I want to live it. "

I kiss her on the top of her head. "I know, just a little while longer and then we graduate. We'll go off to college, where we can get a fresh start. And we'll only be a train ride away from each other."

"You really think we can make it work?"

"Hell yeah. You'll be doing your art, making masterpieces. I'll be playing ball. We can see each other on the weekends, talk on the phone. Before you know it, four years will just fly by."

She lifts her head, a tender kiss dots my lips. "You make me so happy."

I nestle her head in my palm, pulling her in for a long, slow kiss. Her hand trickles down to my hips, tightening as I feel a slight nudge backward. She gently slides her fingers down my midriff, her hands finding their way underneath my shirt. I roll over, pinning her beneath me as I tug at the hem of her shirt. It's not enough that I'm kissing her, I don't just want to taste her, I want to feel her, all of her. I can't get enough. Both of us frantically explore each other, touching and tasting, our limbs crashing together, writhing for the perfect angle, only to move on to the next.

Slam

The sound of the front door is all it takes for us to stop. Our heads immediately turn in the direction of her door. We untangle ourselves, giving Aspen enough time to toss open a random textbook in the middle of the bed before a woman I've never seen before comes into view.

She stops in the doorway, leaning against it. She's got short brown hair, similar to Aspen's except her's is cut into a pixie style, and curly. She's wearing jeans with rips down the thighs, a red fitted top with a black leather jacket, and white vans.

"Aunt Beth," Aspen sputters. "What are you doing here?"

She glances between the two of us, surveying the scene, her brow rising slightly. "Your dad called and wanted me to check in on you. He told me you knew I was coming by."

I'm surprised, she and Aspen's father look nothing alike. She's petite, compared to his burly build and her style is so different from how Aspen's father dresses. I would've never guessed they were related.

"Oh, must've slipped his mind. Charlie was just helping me pick out some pieces for my portfolio." She gestures toward me.

She walks towards me, reaching out her hand. "Hi, Charlie. I'm Beth, Aspen's aunt. It's nice to meet you."

I extend my hand to shake hers. "Hello, nice to meet you."

Her eyes peer around the room, shifting between me and Aspen, before she turns back towards the door. "You ready?" she asks.

"Ready for what?" says Aspen.

Aunt Beth leans back against the door frame, "I guess he also forgot to tell you I'm treating you to dinner tonight."

Aspen gives her a sheepish smile. "Yeah I guess he did, but that's okay."

I stand up. "I should probably go." I glance around the room, trying to remember where I tossed my shoes.

"Why don't you join us?" says Aunt Beth.

I pause, looking up at her. "That's okay, I wouldn't want to impose."

"Nonsense, I'd love for you to join us. As long as that's okay with you, Aspen?"

Aspen nods her head, smiling. "That'd be great."

"Okay."

I have to admit I was extremely nervous about hanging out with Aspen and her Aunt Beth. It's not like her father has made much of an effort to get to know me, so I wasn't sure how dinner was going to go.

We went to a steakhouse not too far from her neighborhood. Ten minutes into dinner, I could tell that Aunt Beth was nothing like Aspen's father.

"So Charlie, have you lived in BluHaven your whole life?" Aunt Beth asks after the waiter takes our order.

"Since I was seven."

"And what do your parents do?"

Almost instinctively, Aspen grabs my hand underneath the table. I see her giving Aunt Beth a look that says *sensitive subject*. I gently squeeze Aspen's hand, giving her a reassuring smile before turning back to Aunt Beth, "I live with my grandparents, actually."

Her face softens, "Oh I see. I'm sorry, I didn't realize—"

"It's okay," I say, cutting her off. "My grandparents are retired. Nana used to teach at the community college and Gramps was a police officer. But now they like to volunteer."

She nods. "And you play basketball?"

"Charlie's probably the best one on the team, she even got a scholarship to LittleWood University in the fall," Aspen says.

Aunt Beth leans back, smiling. "I had no idea you were such a big sports fan now, Aspen."

Aspen shrugs, trying to hide the blush displaying on her cheeks. "I wanted to show my school spirit."

"I see. Well congratulations, Charlie. I'm sure your family is very proud."

"Thank you. It actually worked out pretty well since Aspen will be going to that art school that's also in Arizona, so at least we'll both know one person."

"How lovely," Aunt Beth chimes as the waiter sets our meals down. "Maybe we can come watch you play sometime when I visit Aspen?"

"I'd like that."

"I'd like that too," Aspen says. "Especially since I doubt dad's going to be thrilled if I get in. It'd be nice to have a friendly face to come visit me."

"Your father still isn't happy about you wanting to study art?" Aunt Beth asks, her tone soothing.

"Not at all," Aspen mutters as she twirls some noodles onto her fork.

"Well, you need to do what makes you happy and if that's studying art at a college many miles away from here, then so be it. This is your life to live, not your fathers, remember that."

"That's easy for you to say. You don't live with him."

"I think you're forgetting that I grew up with your father. I know exactly how he can be, especially when he sets his mind on something. He can be so stubborn, just like our father."

"So why are you so cool? I mean you guys grew up in the same household, but you two seem...uh very different." I glance down at my plate, realizing how that sounds. "I'm sorry, I—"

"It's okay," she says cutting me off. "You're not wrong. Sometimes I wonder how I turned out the way I did. Our parents were very strict, still are. They're also very religious. They've attended the same church since we were kids and they're convinced that Pastor John walks on water."

I tilt my head, cocking an eyebrow. "But not you?"

She shakes her head. "No. Ever since we were kids, I've always marched to the beat of my own drum so to speak. Whereas Brian believed every word that came out of that man's mouth, without question; I didn't. I wanted to figure things out for myself. I would read the same scripture he would preach on, yet we never interpreted it the same way. He used it as a way to camouflage hate and I just couldn't get behind that. Don't get me wrong, not everything he said was hateful. But I couldn't sit there and listen to him preach about how the world is full of horrible people just because they don't have the same beliefs as him."

"I take it that didn't go over well with your parents?"

"No, it did not. But it's gotten better over the years. I can't say my parents are happy I don't attend that church anymore, but they have stopped pestering me about it."

"Maybe you can convince my dad to stop making me go," Aspen mutters.

"I tried but he wasn't havin' it."

"So why does he let me hang out with you then? I mean you guys clearly have very different beliefs."

"We're family. He moved back here for a fresh start, and be surrounded by his family. I know you two have gone through a lot recently. And I know we may not agree on everything, but at the end of the day, we're family."

"I'm glad we're family, Aunt B."

"Me too, kiddo."

When I get home, Gramps and Nana are watching some Law & Order show on TV. I still haven't had a chance to tell them about LittleWood and now is the perfect opportunity.

"Where's Matty? There's something I need to tell you all."

Nana turns in my direction as I enter the living room. "What is it, dear?"

"Matty," I holler. "Come here for a second." It's still a little awkward between us ever since he confronted me about dating Aspen but I'm hoping that when he hears the good news, it'll put him in a better mood.

A few moments later, he comes barreling down the stairs. "What?"

I raise my hands high above my head. "Guess who's going to LittleWood in the fall?"

Nana rises from the couch. "Oh, Charlie. That's terrific news."

Gramps stands up and wraps me in a hug, followed by Matty. "I'm happy for you, sis."

"Thanks."

"Now Charlie, tell me a little more about this school," says Nana.

"It's a good school. They offer a variety of programs and majors. I was looking over their website and the campus is beautiful. There seems to be a lot of things to do there, other than going to practice and class. There are some neat hiking trails, a massive mall with over fifty stores, and a lake that's not too far away. I think it's a good fit for me."

"But is this a good Christian school?"

I shrug. "I don't know. I don't think so. Why does that matter? It's a full ride, they have a great business program, and it's a great opportunity. What more could I want?"

"Well I just want to make sure you're going someplace where you'll be surrounded by good Christian folks. I don't want to see you go off to college and fall into the wrong crowd."

I roll my eyes. "Just because some people might not go to church doesn't mean they're not good people. Look at Emily. Her family doesn't go to church and she is one of the best people I know. She's a good friend, has a full ride to Texas Tech, and her family has always been welcoming."

Nana stares at me with her hands resting on her hips.

I turn towards Matty, wanting someone to back me up. "Matty, tell her she's being ridiculous. She's acting like I'm joining a cult."

He shrugs. "Nana, she does have a point."

"It's a good school, Nana. Why can't you just be happy for me?"

"I am happy for you, dear. I just don't want to see you fall into the wrong crowd, that's all."

"Well I've managed to make it this far without doing something to end up in jail."

"But college is different, honey. Young ladies such as yourself, need to be careful. You don't want to be getting tangled into something you can't handle."

"Why? Because I'm a girl?"

"I didn't say that."

"You didn't have to. Gah! You think that just because I'm a girl, I'm incapable of surviving without a man."

"Well look how that turned out for you mother. Once your father left, she couldn't take care of herself, let alone either of you."

"That's not fair. She tried," I whisper, forcing away the tears that are brimming the surface. I look at Matty. "Tell her that's not fair. Mom was sick. She couldn't help it."

Matty glances up from the floor. "Oh c'mon Charlie. Don't you remember what it was like? We were miserable."

"Not all the time."

"She nearly killed us. Why are you acting like she was some kind of saint?" he spits, his voice beginning to rise.

"I'm not. But you're not being fair. It wasn't her fault."

"Wasn't her fault? Are you kidding me? I don't remember either of us forcing her to go out and get so high she didn't know what day it was. We're lucky we got out when we did."

"That's enough," Gramps snaps.

Matty shakes his head, brushing past me as he heads upstairs without another word.

Gramps looks at me. "Charlie, we're all very happy for you. We just want what's best for you."

"Whatever," I huff, sulking up the stairs. I close the door a little too hard before burying my face in a pillow. I know Matty has every right to be upset, especially after everything that happened when we were still living with mom. I'm not trying to make excuses for her but she had an addiction—a disease—and that's what nearly killed us.

But when you really think about it, the world has such a messed-up notion of what is perceived as "normal." She had the type of illness that you couldn't see on the outside; the type where society thinks that if you pretend it's not there, it'll simply go away on its own. She was doomed from the beginning; she never stood a chance.

I'd like to think that if she knew about my scholarship to LittleWood, she'd be proud of me.

Chapter Nine

O ur last game is against Holden. It's a bittersweet feeling, as I lace up my shoes for the last time of my high school career. It's ironic, we spend all this time dreaming about the day we'll graduate, move away to college and start our life outside of high school. It's something everyone looks forward to, this idea of freedom that awaits us on the other side. But no one prepares you for the overwhelming emotion when you realize that everything you've worked towards these past four years all comes to an end in ninety minutes. It doesn't matter if you continue to play in college or just on the side for fun. When the final buzzer goes off, it's over, for everyone.

As we sit, waiting for Coach to come in and give us his before-the-game speech for the last time, I glance around the locker room, taking it all in. The laughter from a couple of girls, the same lockers we've had the past four years; the stain on the floor from when Sara got sick in the middle of practice and couldn't make it to the bathroom in time. The smudges on the wall, the smell of perfume, hairspray, and sweat all mixed into one stale scent, and the people I've met along the way.

My mind drifts back to the times we spent laughing and crying in here. The wins, we celebrated by jumping up and down, huddled in a circle, cheering and patting each other on the back. The losses we endured. Each game bringing us closer to where we are now.

I'm proud of the team I'm a part of, proud to call each one of these girls friends, teammates, and proud that the last game of my high school career will be with the same girls I started with.

There's a gentle tap on the door before Coach Stewart comes waltzing in with a smile on his face. He claps his hands slowly, looking around the room at each of us. "This is a big day. For some of you, it'll be the very last time you put on your basketball shoes to play. For others, it's just the beginning of your basketball career. But for all of you, it'll be the very last time you play together as a team. I want you to enjoy this," He pinches his thumb and fingers together, bringing it up under his chin, "Savor the moment, because it all ends here." He looks at us once more. "Take it all in, the gym, your teammates, the crowd cheering you on, even the refs. This is it, ladies. Now let's go out there and end this season on a win."

"Falcons on three…one…two…three…FALCONS."

Our last game is a blowout, final score forty-seven to twenty-one. When the final buzzer echoes through the arena, we all run into the middle of the court to celebrate, the crowd erupting with applause around us. This is a feeling I'll never get tired of and one that I'm going to miss.

We make our way back into the locker room, still celebrating as the realizations of our season officially ending settles upon us. We take one last group photo, everybody smiling from ear to ear, before we head to our lockers and change out of our uniforms for the last time.

It doesn't take long for the conversation to turn to the end-of-season party tomorrow night. It's practically been the main topic of conversation the past three weeks. Skylar rambles on about the logistics and minor details she's told us multiple times already. I say my goodbyes, tell Riley I'll see her tomorrow and head out the door.

"Baker," Coach hollers from his office. "Come in here."

"Charlie, nice to see you again," says Ms. McCalister as I enter the office. She reaches out her hand and I shake it. "I'm sure Coach Stewart mentioned this to you, but we would like to officially offer you a scholarship to play basketball next fall at LittleWood University. How does that sound?"

"That sounds incredible. When can I sign?"

She cracks a smile. "I love the enthusiasm. I've got some papers for you to sign now and I'll be in contact regarding the logistics of everything else, summer program, dorm rooms, registration, stuff like that."

"Sounds good to me." I take a step forward, grab the pen from her outstretched arm, and scribble my names on the designated line.

"Congratulations, Charlie." She hands me a manilla folder. "This will give you and your family more information about the area, campus, programs, and the likes. I'll be in touch with the other matters at a later date. Do you have any questions before I go?"

"Will I be able to visit the campus before school starts?"

She nods. "You'll be coming up at the end of July for the summer program. Classes don't start till mid-August so you'll have plenty of time to get settled in before then. Since you'll be living in the dorms, your roommate will be another freshman from the team. I'll get her contact info for you before you move in. That way you have a chance to get to know one another first."

"Alright, cool. I can't wait."

"Anything else?"

"No ma'am."

"Well feel free to contact me if you have any other questions."

"I will. Thank you again."

I head for the exit, my stomach tingling as I see Aspen waiting for me.

"Where's Matty?" I ask when I've reached the other end.

"He left right after the game ended. He said something about needing to finish up a project."

"Oh," I say, trying to hide the hurt in my voice.

"You two okay?"

"We kinda got into a fight last night about my mom." I shrug.

"You wanna talk about it?"

"Not really. I'd rather just try to forget about it."

"Alright, but I'm here if you want to talk."

"I know. So, did your Aunt Beth say anything about us after she dropped me off last night?" I ask as we head towards the car.

"She said she likes you and that she was happy that she got to meet one of my close friends," Aspen says, emphasizing the word close.

"You think she knows?"

"That we're together or that we were making out seconds before she walked into my room?"

"Both?"

She lets out a breath. "I don't know. She didn't say anything other than when she emphasized the words close friend."

"You think she'll tell your father?"

"I don't think so. Not after everything she told us last night."

"I had no idea how intense your grandparents were."

"Me either. They didn't really seem that strict when I've been with them. But I guess that explains why my father reacted the way he did about me being gay. He's completely convinced I'm going to hell."

"You really think that?"

She shrugs. "I don't know. But I've been to that church a couple times now and Aunt B wasn't lying when she said he preaches a lot of hate. And if you're told something enough times—whether it's morally right or not—you end up believing it."

"So how did he and your mom stay together if they have such different views like that?"

"I know it sounds hard to believe but we really didn't go to church that much when we were in Texas. My mom's side of the family isn't religious, and I don't think the issue of LGBTQ people ever came up until my parents found out about me and that girl."

"Maybe he'll come around. I mean look how cool your Aunt Beth turned out."

"I think Aunt Beth was the odd man out."

"Still, you never know."

We park our normal distance away from my house, kissing goodbye before I get out and head inside.

That night, as I'm lying in bed replaying the events of the past couple weeks in my mind, it dawns on me how *right* it feels when I'm with Aspen. Every time we're together I find a peacefulness that consumes me, uncovering a truth about myself that I didn't even know I was hiding.

I slide into the backseat of Riley's car Saturday evening for the party, saying hello to Tyler as I do.

"I still think Aspen should've tagged along with us," says Riley once I'm settled in.

"Why didn't she?" asks Tyler.

"It's not a big deal. She's coming later," I mutter.

Tyler looks over to Riley, resting his hand on her thigh, his question unanswered. She gives him a look that says *you know why.*

I never explicitly told Riley not to tell Tyler, but I'm not surprised that he knows. They've been dating for over two years so there's very little that isn't shared between the two of them.

"It's bullshit, Charlie, and you know it. All the girls are bringing their boyfriends, you should be able to bring your, uh," she looks at me, her brows furrowed.

"You can say girlfriend, Riley. It's not like it's a secret from either of you."

"I agree with Riley," says Tyler, turning his head to look at me. "Who cares what other people think."

I give him a soft smile. "Thanks, Tyler but it's just easier if we don't make it a big charade. That's the last thing Aspen wants."

"Alright. You have our support, just so you know."

"Thanks."

"So do Skylar's parents know what kind of get together she's throwing tonight?" Tyler asks. "Considering how religious her family is, I find it hard to believe they're okay with what's going on tonight."

Riley shrugs. "That hasn't stopped her before. And her parents like to think that if they ignore the problem long enough, it will go away on its own."

A few minutes later, we pull into Skylar's driveway and park next to the row of cars in the grass. Her house is nearly twice the size of Aspen's. The external structure is made up of solid brick, except for the entryway jutting out, made of stone. We climb out of the car and head to the front of the house. The inside is just as exquisite as the outside. The artwork on the walls reminds me of Aspen's house, except this art is more flamboyant. There's a massive flat-screen TV in the living room playing a rerun of an old basketball game. The kitchen's marble countertops are covered with chips, pretzels, sliders, dip, wings, pizza, even a veggie tray, and every bottle of alcohol that you could possibly think of.

We stroll through the house, getting the lay of the land. When we make it to the backyard, we find two kegs sitting on the patio. We seem to be the last of the team to arrive. When Skylar notices our presence, she calls for everybody to come to the kitchen. We gather around the island in the middle and she begins passing out shot glasses. Once everyone's shot glass is full, she holds hers in the air.

"A toast," she says, raising her glass higher, "To the end of a season, and the beginning of a new journey."

I roll my eyes as we all raise our glass and drain the shot. We take a few more shots, remembering our highs and lows from the season. Once everyone's said their piece, Skylar glances at her phone. "Let the party begin, bitches!" she yells.

Twenty minutes later, the sun has completely set, the music's been turned all the way up, more people have arrived, drinks are being passed around, kids are dancing, making out, and somebody's doing a keg stand in the backyard; the party is officially in full swing.

I wander aimlessly through the house, talking to a couple people here and there. I pull my phone out just in time to see a text from Aspen.

Just pulled in. :)

I slide my phone in my pocket, and head for the door. "Hey you," I say. My eyes follow the slender outline of her body, lingering on her lips.

"Hey," she says, glancing around. "Damn, you weren't lying when you said Skylar's family has a mansion."

I chuckle, "Nope. Can I get you a drink?"

"Sure."

She follows me into the kitchen where I grab the first bottle I see and pour some into a red cup and hand it to her.

"Thanks," she says. "How was the team bonding thing earlier?"

I roll my eyes and shrug. "Same thing every year. We take a bunch of shots, reliving the glory days." I lift my cup in the air like a toast. "And that's about it."

"Oh yeah, I can totally see why you wouldn't want an outsider crashing that sacred tradition."

I laugh. "There's nothing sacred about it. Skylar just likes to do things her way."

"Yeah, I kinda picked up on that."

We spend the next twenty minutes wandering around the house. The smell of beer permeates the room, the temperature rising with all the bodies filing inside. Several times I have to stop myself from reaching out and taking her hand.

As we head out of the kitchen, Will and Trey cut us off, the smell of beer and cigarette wafting from their lips. Trey's eyes dart between Aspen and me, struggling to stay focused on either of us.

"Hey, you two," Trey says, slurring his words.

I open my mouth to respond but Will cuts in. "You two wanna get out of here? Go someplace a little quieter?"

"No thanks," I say, trying to move past him.

"Ahh, c'mon now, don't be like that. We're just trying to have some fun." Trey twirls a piece of my hair between his fingers.

I swat his hand away, ready to tell him to fuck off, when Riley grabs my arm, stepping in between Trey and me.

"Charlie," she says, her tone rising an octave. "I've been looking all over for you. Let's go dance."

Before I can protest, she's pulling me towards the crowd of people dancing and grinding in the middle of the room. I grab Aspen's hand, taking her with us.

Riley spins around, facing me, her body swaying to the beat. "Saw you two over there, thought you might need some saving." She gives us a wink.

Tyler appears behind her, drinks in hand. He gives one to me, Riley, and Aspen. I take a sip and glance around. Everybody's dancing and laughing, not taking a second look in our direction.

Relax, Charlie. It's just a party, everybody dances at parties.

I bring my eyes up, meeting Aspen's. I watch her as she takes a sip of her drink, her hips starting to move along with the music.

She shuffles closer to me, her eyes locked on mine. I glance around one more time, checking to see if anyone's focused on us. Although, Aspen doesn't seem to be too concerned, maybe I should stop being overly cautious.

The song changes to something that's a mix between techno and dubstep. Everybody starts jumping up and down to the beat, I join in. Riley notices, her face lighting up. When we all get tired of jumping, I find my body moving along to the beat with everyone else. Riley pulls us closer, practically dancing on top of us.

Aspen moves in behind me, her hand touching my hip, pulling me towards her. My backside connects with her, my heart race increasing as she begins grinding with me, my body reflexively following along. I catch a whiff of her coconut scented perfume as she leans into me.

I turn around, admiring the way her slender curves sway back and forth. She looks sexy as hell, and all I want to do is pull her lips to mine. Instead, I place my hands on her hips, drawing her towards me. She runs her tongue over her bottom lip, her eyes studying me. The air is hot and sticky with sweat. The bodies all around constantly bump into us but I don't care. The only person I'm focused on is Aspen. We continue to dance with the music, her body pressed so close to mine, it sends a shiver down my back.

I'm seconds away from running my hands through her hair when I feel the pressure of someone behind me pulling me backward. My butt now pressed against someone else. I look up and see Trey doing the same thing to Aspen. It doesn't take me long to figure out that Will is behind me. I try to wiggle away from him, but he places one hand on my hips and wraps the other one around me.

He leans forward, whispering in my ear, "C'mon, Charlie. We saw how you two were dancing. We just want in on the action." His words slur together into one long sentence.

"Get off." I manage to squirm out of his grasp. I grab Aspen's hand, pulling her away from Trey, and lead her outside.

The cool evening air is soothing as we step out to the back patio. We make our way to the cooler. I lift the lid, looking for some water; there's none.

"No water, just more beer."

"Wanna go back to the kitchen? I'm pretty sure I saw some when I first arrived," says Aspen.

"Yeah, but let's go this way," I gesture towards the door on the other side of the patio. "I don't wanna run into Trey and Will again."

She nods and we head back to the kitchen. I locate two water bottles in the fridge, hand one to Aspen, and open one for myself. I drink over half of the water in one gulp. I lean on the counter, very much aware of how close my body is to hers.

Aspen leans in. "Let's go exploring," she whispers. She grabs my hand and leads me through the living room, past the couples and dance floor. We come around the corner and head upstairs. My heart skips a beat as we climb the stairs, hand in hand.

Aspen giggles. "Damn, Charlie. How many bedrooms does this place have?"

"I know right? But you're the spoiled rich kid."

She turns, a sly grin tugging at the edge of her mouth. She opens the first door, immediately closing it when somebody yells at us to 'fuck off'.

She opens the next door, finding the room empty. Aspen turns, tugging at her bottom lip, and pulls me towards the bed. I close the door behind us and grab her waist, steadying her when she nearly trips. She giggles, her hands finding my hips.

"Thanks, baby," she says, her words slurring slightly. She tilts her hand, pulling me in for a kiss.

My grip tightens around her, pressing her body to mine. My hands caress her cheek, as she slips her tongue in my mouth.

"I've wanted to do that all night," I say.

She plants another kiss on my lips and whispers, "I've been thinking about kissing you since the minute I walked through the door."

There's a faint inkling in the back of my mind that's telling me this is a terrible idea. Aspen wraps her arms around my waist, pressing against me as the heat radiates off her. Her hands glide up and down my back, as the last trace of worry drizzles away.

She runs her tongue along my bottom lip, begging for entry. I open my mouth to hers, allowing her tongue to slip inside. She spins me around, nudging me to a sitting position on the bed. Our eyes lock as her fingers comb through my hair. Her eyes are so wide I feel like I could fall in, lost in the presence of her. She climbs on top, her legs straddling my lap, pulling me in for another kiss. My hands slide up and down her back, slipping underneath her shirt. The feel of her skin is warm and soft.

Bam!

The sound of the door slamming open is so loud it causes both of us to jump. I jerk my head around, my eyes squinting, adjusting to the light that was just switched on. The first thing I notice is the phone dangling in the air. Several *click click click* sounds echo through the room before I realize that they're taking pictures. I shift my gaze past the phone, and standing in the doorway, bright-eyed and smirking is Skylar.

Chapter Ten

The warm grip on my shoulders anchors me back to the present. Aspen squirms in my lap, writhing free from my grasp, before turning on her heels and charging out the door.

"Aspen, wait," I pant as I lift myself up off the bed and hurry after her. I manage to grab her arm, swinging her around as we make it to the living room. "Aspen, stop. Let's talk about this."

She winces, immediately taking a step back as her lips begin to quiver. Her eyes dance around me, refusing to meet my gaze. It doesn't take long for the house to become eerily silent, the rambunctious crowd now a captivated audience, eager to observe the spectacle.

"I can't," she sputters. She turns, heading through the front door, without looking back.

I follow.

"Are you gonna hide who you are for the rest of your life?" I fire at her.

She stops, one foot still slightly raised in the air, before turning to face me. The pitter-patter of footsteps reverberates in the distance as the swarm of kids make their way outside.

I meet her eyes, my heart thrumming erratically in my chest. "Aren't you tired of it? Tired of pretending? Tired of trying to be somebody you're not?"

"You don't understand, Charlie. You have no idea how hard this is for me."

"You don't think this isn't just as hard for me? Constantly lying to everyone, pretending to be something I'm not? It's not just about you."

"You don't know what my dad'll do," she mutters in a voice barely above a whisper.

I spin around, my arms spread wide, gesturing to everything around us. "Look around, it's only a matter of time. It's out there." I turn back to face her, heat rising in my stomach. "You're eighteen, we graduate in less than two months, you're practically an adult." My voice rises an octave as the anger continues to build. "Don't you think it's time to be honest with your father? To be honest with yourself?"

She steps forward, her forehead creasing like it always does when she's upset. "You don't understand, Charlie. But I wouldn't expect you to. It's not like you have parents of your own to worry about, do you?"

I stop, my breath catching as the sound of her words resonate in my ear.

I shake my head, the sting of her words visible on my face. "That's not fair."

She lifts her hand in the air and drops them back to her side. "Fair? Who said any of this was fair?" She shifts her gaze to the ground, shaking her head. "I can't do it anymore. Goodbye, Charlie." And she walks away.

I stand there, rooted to the ground as my eyes cling to her fading silhouette.

When my alarm echoes throughout my room Sunday morning, I make no effort to get up out of bed. The incident from last night replays in my head over and over, like it's on a never-ending time loop. I bury my face in my sheets, willing myself to go back to sleep.

There's a soft knock at the door. I mumble 'go away' from under the covers, but it didn't carry because I hear the latch of my door opening. It's Gramps.

"Hey, Monkey. Are you feeling alright? Didn't even see you come in last night." He sits down on the edge of my bed.

I called Matty to come pick me up after Aspen left and everyone went back inside last night. I almost thought he wasn't gonna come because he was still pissed at me, but he was there ten minutes later.

As soon as we pulled in the driveway, I raced up the stairs and locked myself in my room, not even bothering to say hi to Gramps or Nana. Matty tried to ask me what happened, but when he saw the look on my face, he thought better of it.

I remove the comforter from my head but turn so I'm facing the wall, away from him. "I've got really bad cramps," I whimper, knowing that'll shut him up.

"Alright, well why don't you stay home and rest and we'll check on you after church?"

I nod my head, afraid if I say anything else, I'll just start crying. After my door closes, I reach to the bedside table, grabbing my phone. I slide it open, hoping to see a message from Aspen but I don't. I shouldn't be surprised but I can't help but feel a twinge of sadness when my hunch is confirmed. There is a text from Riley though. I open it.

R u okay? Call me when u get this.

I close out of it, ignoring it for now. I know she's worried about me but I just don't feel like talking right now.

I've been putting off looking at social media, knowing that photo probably already went viral. I know I shouldn't give in, that I should just ignore it, but I can't help myself.

I open the app and thumb through my newsfeed. The first thing that pops up is the picture Skylar took of me and Aspen kissing. That bitch. I wonder if she followed us up there, waiting to make her move. I wrack my brain, trying to remember if we were being followed but everything is so fuzzy. My attention was focused so on Aspen, everything else was just a blur.

The photo's been seen by over two hundred people and counting. There's no telling how many people are going to see it by Monday morning. I read through the comments, the knot in my stomach tightening. There are several comments that include the word 'lezbos' or 'dyke', several comments of people expressing their lack of surprise, mainly about me, and a few comments of support that catch me off guard.

I toss my phone to the side and lay back, my eyes fixed on the ceiling, wondering how everything went so wrong, so fast.

My door opens and Matty steps into the room.

"Thought you're still pissed at me?" I ask him.

He shrugs. "After seeing you last night, I figured you have more important things to worry about."

"I'm sorry about getting into it with you the other night."

"I'm sorry too."

"Wait a second, why aren't you at church?"

"I convinced them that I should stay here in case you need anything." He gives me a sheepish smile.

I sit up, making room for him to sit on the end of the bed.

"I saw the picture. It's all over Facebook and Instagram. I tried reporting it to get them to take it down but it didn't work. Are you okay?"

I shrug my shoulders.

"What happened?"

"I don't really know. One minute we were at the party, having a good time. The next minute, I see Skylar with a phone in her hand taking pictures of us."

"What'd you do?"

"It took me a minute to realize what was happening. Then chased after Aspen." Hot tears begin rolling down my cheeks and drip onto the comforter. "I chased her into the yard and we just started yelling at each other. I'm so tired of hiding who I am. It's not fair. I don't care if people know I'm gay, I'm not ashamed of who I am. I just don't get why she can't get past it." I wipe the tears from my eyes. "I just feel like it shouldn't matter at this point. We graduate soon and we'll be going off to college, why do we have to keep hiding?"

Matty reaches forward, patting my knee. "It's not fair, Charlie. I'm sorry."

We sit in silence for a minute. "Have you talked to her since then?" Matty asks.

I shake my head.

"You think you should try to call her?"

I shrug my shoulders. "I don't even know what I would say."

"Maybe you should tell her how you feel?"

"I tried, it didn't end very well."

"I just think it's worth fighting for. I've never seen someone make you this happy."

I run my tongue along the back of my teeth, considering his words. He's not wrong, but after what happened last night, I just don't know where that leaves us.

"Well whatever happens, just know I'm here for you."

I smile at him, wiping the tears from my eyes. "Thanks, Matty."

We spend the next hour sitting on the couch, watching TV. After checking my phone for the fifth time, I decide to give in and text Aspen first.

Hey, can we talk?

I check my phone every five minutes, knowing damn well I would've heard it ring if she responds. The credits roll at the end of the show and I glance down at my phone one more time, still nothing.

When Gramps and Nana get home, she makes lunch and has us eat at the kitchen table, convinced I'm feeling better since I'm downstairs watching TV and not laying underneath the covers in bed.

I stare at my plate, not bothering to say 'Amen' when Gramps finishes the blessing. I eat in silence, thankful that Matty is doing most of the talking. We're in the middle of cleaning up when the doorbell rings.

"Are we expecting company?" says Nana.

"I didn't think so. I'll get it," says Gramps.

I turn as the door opens, curious to see who it is. I recognize the beefy build and slicked back hair instantly. The plate drops from my hands, shattering on the floor when I realize that Mr. Sullivan is standing on our front porch.

What the hell is he doing here?

"Charlie Marie, watch what you're doing," Nana snaps.

I mumble 'sorry' and quickly sweep up the broken pieces with a dishtowel. I glance back up, only to see Gramps motioning for him to come inside. The knot in my stomach tightens when I see Aspen trailing in behind him. I'm so thrown off and focused on getting her attention that the towel slips from my grasp, causing the ceramic pieces to scatter back onto the floor.

"Charlie, c'mon dear. Stop messin' around and clean that up," Nana says.

I drop my gaze back to the floor, picking up the broken pieces and wondering why can't it be this easy to pick up the broken parts of myself.

Nana scurries to the living room, leaving me in the kitchen. What the hell are Aspen and her father doing here on a Sunday afternoon? Gramps hollers for me come to the living room when it dawns on me.

He knows.

I toss what's left of the plate into the trash can, and walk into the living room. Matty follows me but hangs back and leans against the wall.

"Charlie, honey. Mr. Sullivan says there's something he wants to talk to us about," says Nana. She turns back to Aspen's father, eyebrows raised and curiosity written all over her face.

"Mr. and Mrs. Baker, I thought it was only fair that you know what exactly your granddaughter has been up to these past couple weeks." He extends his arm, gesturing to me. "She has been influencing my daughter to partake in homosexual acts. Did you have any idea that your granddaughter is a lesbian?" He stops, but not long enough for them to answer.

I'm speechless, my mouth hanging open in a small *O*.

This can't be happening.

He continues, "I assumed good Christian folk like you should know what your granddaughter has been doing behind your back." He turns, eyes narrowed on me. He takes a step closer. "Now Charlie, I don't know what's going on in that little head of yours. Whether you're just confused or something is mentally off, I can't decide which. But you will not have any more contact with my daughter. She will no longer be influenced by your *disease*. Is that understood?"

A disease?

Mentally off?

We weren't doing anything wrong.

I look over to Aspen, she's staring at the floor. I silently plead for her to lift her head, look at me in the eye, give me a sign, a gesture, anything to tell me that she's not okay with this, that she doesn't agree with what he's saying. Mr. Sullivan steps in front of me, blocking my view.

Gramps speaks for the first time since I entered the living room. "Charlie, honey, tell me this isn't true?"

I stare at the floor, my lips pulled tight, trying to force the lump rising in my throat back down.

Nana steps in front of me, forcing me to look her in the eye. "Charlotte Marie Baker, answer your grandfather. Tell us this isn't true."

I shake my head. "I can't," I murmur.

Nana waves her hand back and forth in front of her. "No, no, no, this cannot be." She turns to Mr. Sullivan. "There must be some mistake. What you're describing does not sound like something Charlie would do."

Mr. Sullivan pulls out his phone. "I'm afraid there's been no mistake, Mrs. Baker." He flips his phone around, the photo of Aspen and I kissing displayed on his screen.

The knot in my stomach continues to grow as each agonizing second ticks by.

Gramps squints, stepping closer to get a better look. "No, that can't be," he whispers, gasping when he realizes that the girl in the photo is me. "Oh dear."

Nana moves in closer to the phone, her reaction no better than Gramps. "I don't believe this," she mumbles. She raises her head. "Mr. Sullivan, I am terribly sorry for any trouble Charlie may have caused. I can assure you that we will get to the bottom of this and it will not happen again." She turns to me, her lips pressed in a taut smile. "Charlie, apologize to Mr. Sullivan and his daughter."

I look up, my eyes burning with tears. "But I didn't do anything wrong."

The look on my grandmother's face is one I've only seen a handful of times; when my mother almost burned down our apartment complex, when I punched that boy in second grade, and when Matty accidentally broke her antique vase when he was playing superheroes inside the house. It's such a drastic contrast from her typical, chipper appearance, I nearly choke.

She steps closer to me, her expression fierce and tense. Her voice is low and firm. "Charlotte Marie Baker," she hisses, "You will not continue to embarrass this family. Now apologize this once."

I turn, meeting her eyes. "But we didn't do anything wrong, Nana. I…I *love* her," I whisper. As soon as the words are out of my mouth, I see Aspen take a slight step forward out of the corner of my eyes. My heart skips it a beat and I know she believes me. Every fiber in my body is screaming, begging to run across the living room and wrap her in my arms.

I turn my body to face her and Mr. Sullivan steps forward, his hand raised in the air as if he's signaling 'stop'. "Mrs. Baker, clearly there are some things Charlie needs to work through, before she can admit her wrong doings. I have no doubt that you will get her the help she needs." He turns towards the door. "We should be going now, we've already taken up too much of your time."

I chance another look at Aspen. She glances up, meeting my eye for the first time since she entered the house. She holds my gaze, as she takes a small step forward and reaches out her hand. "Charlie, I—"

Mr. Sullivan grabs hold of Aspen's arm and escorts her to the door before she can finish. Nana mutters another apology as she ushers them out. I close my eyes, letting the tears roll down my cheeks and plunge to the floor.

Nana comes charging back into the living room. "What on Earth has gotten into you?"

Matty walks up behind her. "Nana, take it easy. It's not that big of a deal."

She whips her head around, her forefinger extended. "Not that big of a deal? Do you have any idea how this looks on our family?"

"But, Nana, don't you want Charlie to be happy?" he pleads.

She turns back to me, her voice soothing. "Charlie, my dear, you're just confused is all. You don't actually have feelings for that girl. I mean, you just can't."

I look back and forth between Gramps and Nana, not recognizing the two people standing in front of me. My sweet, sweet grandparents, who took us in and gave us everything we ever wanted. My grandparents who showed Matty and me what it meant to be a parent, what it meant to be there for the people you love. Who threw us birthday parties, took us out for ice cream, read us bedtime stories, taught us how to ride a bike. How could they've raised me to be who I am today, and look at me like I'm a stranger? How can the same people that taught me right from wrong, to be kind, and brave, to believe in myself, stand here and tell me that what I am is *unacceptable*?

I look up at her, my voice trembling. "But I do, Nana. I love her."

She shakes her head. "No, I will not stand for this. It's unacceptable, Charlie."

"Why? Because she's a girl and not a guy?"

"Charlie," Nana says calmly. "This is just a phase. It'll pass."

"That's bullshit and you know it. I didn't ask for any of this to happen, it just did." I take a step forward, my voice rising as the anger builds. "We don't get to choose who we love, Nana. What I feel for Aspen isn't confusion or some phase I have to get out of my system, it's real. She makes me happy. Can't you see that? I'm still the same person I've always been. Why does me being gay have to change anything?"

Nana recoils when I mention the word gay, as if I just slapped her. She lifts her head up, indignation and sorrow glisten in her eyes before she turns away. She takes a moment to compose herself before looking me directly in the eyes. "Charlie Marie Baker, you will not use that kind of language in this household. This is exactly what I was worried about when you go off to college. It's why I wanted you to go someplace closer, find a nice young man to settle down with. I—"

"Just stop, Nana," I snap. "It doesn't matter where I go. I was never going to end up with a man anyways."

She flinches, taking half a step back.

"Think about it Nana," I plead. "When was the last time I went on a date with a boy? Or even talked about one? My entire life I thought there was something wrong with me. I thought that I was broken because being around guys never affected me the same way it did Riley or other girls on the team. Aspen was the one who showed me there was nothing wrong with me in the first place. Can't you see how much happier I am now? Don't you want me to be happy?"

Nana turns to Matty acting as if I hadn't spoken. "Did you know about this, Matty?"

He glances from me to the floor, avoiding Nana's eyes. "Yes."

"And you didn't think to tell us?"

I step forward, the anger beginning to boil over. "It wasn't his business to tell. It wasn't anybody's business but mine."

"Then why didn't you tell us? We could've gotten you some help. We still can."

"I don't need any help because there's nothing wrong with me."

She tilts her head, sighing as she lightly pats her hand on her chest. "I tried to do everything right," she whispers. "Tried to undo the damage your mother did. I took you to church, gave you a nice home, tried to raise you to be a good Christian woman. How could something like this happen, Charlie?"

"This isn't your fault, Nana. Nothing you could've said or done would've changed me being gay."

"I failed your mother, but I will not fail you."

"But Nana—"

Gramps steps between us, like he's a referee separating two opponents in a boxing match. "Let's all just calm down. We don't have to figure everything out right this instant. Charlie, why don't you go upstairs so your grandmother and I can talk." He glances at Matty. "Matty, why don't you go too."

I turn without another word and walk upstairs. Matty grabs my arm before I can enter the bathroom. "Charlie, cut her some slack. This is all new to her."

I spin around to face him, shrugging his arm off. "Cut her some slack? Were you in the same room I was just in?"

"Just give her some time, she'll come around."

I scoff. "You really think so? Matty, she thinks I'm broken, that there's something wrong with me."

"I don't think she really thinks that. It's a lot to take in. She just needs some more time."

"I can't believe this. Of all people, I thought you'd be on my side."

"I am on your side. I'm just trying to help you see it from her point of view."

"Her point of view is wrong. Why aren't you downstairs trying to get her to see it from my point of view?" I turn, slamming the bathroom door before he's able to respond.

I strip down and step into the shower, turning the water on high and letting it beat over my head in tiny rivulets. I close my eyes to the water as the heat seeps into my skin. I rest my head against the cool ceramic tiles, letting my mind fade into dullness where everything is a foggy illusion.

I climb out of the shower and check my phone as I'm drying off. There are two more texts from Riley. I open them up, already having an idea as to what they'll probably say.

R u ok? Call me

I'm worried so I'm coming over. B there in 20.

I check the time and see that she sent her last text fifteen minutes ago. I scramble around my room, throwing on an old pair of sweats, a long-sleeve shirt and tennis shoes. I sling my backpack over my shoulder and rush downstairs, grateful to be given an escape, even if it's only for a short time.

Gramps and Nana are still in the living room, their voices low as they talk. I'm sure they're still trying to figure out what to do about their current 'situation'. I mumble something about studying with Riley and walk out the door before I hear their response.

I toss my bag in the backseat and climb into the car. Riley's wearing a pair of leggings and an oversized t-shirt. Her long blonde hair is thrown up in a messy bun and I'm surprised at how together she seems considering how much she had to drink the night before. She gives me a gentle smile before she backs out of the driveway and heads towards town.

We ride in silence for a few minutes before she looks over at me and says, "You wanna talk about it?"

It doesn't take but a few seconds for me to open my mouth and recount everything that's happened the past sixteen hours. She's patient, nodding her head as I speak. Her eyes soft and soothing as she waits for me to get my voice under control when I start sobbing.

When I finish, my eyes feel raw, my cheeks thick with salt from my tears, and the rest of my body numb.

"Want me to go egg her house for you?" Riley says.

I let out a soft laugh. "I don't think that would be very helpful." I grab another napkin from the glove box and blow my nose. "It's all over the internet. I don't even wanna know how many more people have seen it since this morning."

"I can't believe Skylar did that. What a bitch."

I shrug my shoulders. "We should've been more careful. I'm really not that upset that the world knows I'm gay; now I can stop pretending. I just hate what it did to Aspen. I just wish I could talk to her."

"Even after what she said to you last night? And what happened this morning? You still wanna talk to her?"

"I don't think she meant what she said last night. We were drinking, she was scared and felt alone. It's easy to lash out the people that are closest to you. And then when she came over, she didn't look angry or sad, just empty." I pick at a hangnail on my pinky. "And when I said I love her, she looked over at me for half a second and said my name before her dad practically pushed her out the door. But that was just enough time for me to know that she feels the same way. I'm still angry about how everything went down and how my grandparents reacted but at the same time, I'm lucky. I have you and Matty on my side. And I know you both have my back. I don't think she has anyone, except her father who is hateful and cruel. It's not fair. I just wish I could be there for her."

"You've got such a big heart, Charlie. That's one of the things I love most about you. And you're right, you have me and Matty and I think most of the girls on the team too. They're not okay with what Skylar did."

I close my eyes. "Oh god. I don't even want to think about what it's going to be like at school."

Riley nudges my shoulder. "Hey, it'll be okay. Just take it one day at a time. And besides, I'll kick anyone's ass who tries to mess with you."

I smile. "Thanks, Riley. But it's not really me I'm worried about."

"It'll be okay. Are you going to try to talk to her at school?"

I run my fingers through my hair. "I don't know. She might not even want to talk to me.""You think her dad is gonna move somewhere else again?"

I shake my head. "I don't know. I don't think so. This is where his family is. But who knows? After what I heard him say today, I wouldn't be surprised if he tried to ship me off to a mental institute."

"Matty wouldn't let that happen. And neither would I."

"Thanks, Riley."

She smiles. "That's what best friends are for." We ride in silence for several minutes before she opens her mouth to speak again. "You think you and Nana are gonna be okay?"

I run my hand over my face, considering her question. "I don't know. I mean, I knew a part of her blamed herself for what happened with my mother, and that she still sees it as a betrayal to some extent. I guess I just never thought she'd see me being gay as another betrayal."

"Oh, Charlie. I'm sure that's not what she thinks."

"I don't know, Riley. She asked me where she went wrong, like she could've done something to prevent me from being gay."

"Maybe you just need to give her some time? I'm sure she'll come around."

"Yeah, maybe."

We spend another half hour or so driving around before she drops me back off at my house. I go upstairs and do my best to avoid everyone. When Nana calls for dinner, I begrudgingly make my way to the table.

We eat in silence, nobody expressing any interest in having a conversation. After ten minutes of cutlery clattering on plates, Gramps clears his throat.

"Charlie, your grandmother and I were talking and we think it's best…" He pauses, looking over to Nana. "We think it's best if you do not see Aspen anymore."

I stare at my plate, refusing to make eye contact with either one of them.

Nana sets her fork down and leans forward. "We think some time apart will help you sort through these—these feelings that you're having right now."

I look up, my eyes glancing back and forth between the two of them. "These feelings aren't just gonna magically go away, no matter how hard you try to push me. It's not gonna happen."

Nana tilts her head, her voice is calm and even. "Well, we'll see about that. We're not going to discuss the matter further right now." She interlaces her fingers together, placing them in front of her. "You will not see Aspen, is that understood?"

I stare at my Nana, letting my fork clatter on the plate below me. I push my chair out from underneath the table and march upstairs.

I lean against my bedroom wall, my feet sliding out from under me as the weight of everything comes crashing down. I've read books, seen countless movies and tv shows where people describe the moment everything changes, the moment where everything they believed in turns out to be a lie. As the events replay in my mind and the tears stream down my face, I realize that none of those descriptions were anywhere close to accurate. How the sporadic *thump thump* of my heart continues to beat even after it's been broken in two. How thoughts of Aspen and what we had together tumble through my mind like an accelerating train, with no intention of stopping.

Chapter Eleven

can't fight the impeding day any more than the beat of my own heart as it pounds miserably against the cage of bone and cartilage. I aimlessly grab a pair of jeans and a t-shirt, the lump in my throat sinking lower with each step as I stumble downstairs. I mumble a 'good morning' to my grandparents who give me a patronizing smile.

"You sure you're up for this?" Matty says as we pull out of the driveway.

"Do I have a choice?" I shake my head as if I could easily shake away the anxiety that's creeping into the back of my throat. I fake a smile and look over at Matty. "I'll be fine."

He doesn't look convinced but he nods anyway.

Walking in from the parking lot is uneventful. It's when I get inside that I get the first inkling that I'm the big news story of the day. A group of girls off to my right stare at me and then whisper, not even trying to be discreet.

I continue towards my locker, doing my best to ignore the incessant eyes that turn in my direction. Although I expect it, my stomach sinks when I turn the corner and Aspen is nowhere to be seen. I scan the entire area, looking for any sign of her.

I turn, exchanging my books from my locker when I feel a hand on my shoulder. I flinch, ready to shove past them. I relax slightly when I realize it's Riley.

She gives me a feeble smile. "Hey."

I do my best to return her smile, but I can feel my eyes brimming with tears.

She squeezes my forearm. "C'mon, get your books and I'll walk you to class."

I nod, too afraid to say anything that might cause me to burst into tears.

We walk down the hall towards first period. People turn and whisper, pointing and snickering, like I'm a part of a one-man show putting on a performance.

We get to the classroom; Riley watches as I quietly enter and find my seat. I stare at my desk, my eyes focused on a chip in the top right corner. If I thought I was distracted by Aspen in class before this, I'm completely disconnected now. Mrs. Arden's voice is nothing but a dull drone in the background. I can't even pull my notebook out and pretend I'm even trying to pay attention.

I shift my attention to my leg bouncing beneath my desk, counting the seconds as they pass by, focusing on anything other than what is going on around me. The perpetual stares from the kids behind me bore holes into my back. I duck my head lower as a prickle shivers down my spine. The bell rings and I make a beeline for the hall.

Where the hell is Aspen?

The rest of the morning drags on, each class consisting of the same stares, and the teachers' monotone voice in the background. When lunch rolls around, I take my time heading to the cafeteria. My appetite is pretty much non-existent but I'm desperate to see Aspen, and I'm hoping I'll be able to sneak a peek of her at lunch.

Riley falls into step beside me, her tone gentle as she says, "How are you?"

I shrug my shoulders, my gaze scanning the kids scattered throughout the lunchroom. We get in line, but so far there's no sign of her.

"I've heard some of the things people are saying. I had no idea they could be so cruel," Riley says.

"Now I know why Aspen was so adamant about keeping it a secret." I take a long breath. "I should've been more careful. Now look where it's gotten us."

Riley squeezes my forearm. "This isn't your fault. You weren't the one who posted that photo and outed you two."

"Well it probably didn't help that I made a big scene about it on Saturday."

"You have every right to be with someone who makes you happy. I'm sorry some people can't get past their insecurities and get with the twenty-first century."

I give her a soft smile. "Me too." We make our way inside and grab a slice of pizza. "Have you talked to anyone else from the team?" I ask.

Riley nods her head. "Most of 'em are pretty upset about everything that happened."

I keep my eyes trained on the ground until we come to our table and sit down.

"Eat," Riley says.

I push my tray back, looking up for the first time since we sat down. "I'm not hungry."

"I'm sorry about what happened. That was so not cool." Emily says.

"Me too," says Sara.

"Yeah, Charlie," Tyler chimes in. "If Skylar wasn't a girl, I'd totally kick her ass for you."

I smile at Tyler's comment. "Thanks, guys."

The low thrum of footsteps approaching forces my eyes upward, my pulse quickening at the thought that it might be Aspen. My stomach drops when I realize it's Skylar. Our eyes meet and something flickers behind her eyes—something that was there and gone too quickly for me to identify.

"What do you think you're doing?" Emily snaps at her.

Skylar tilts her head, eyebrow cocked. "What?"

"You really think we're going to let you sit with us after what you did this weekend?"

Skylar huffs, her expression showing genuine surprise. "Oh come on, it was just a joke."

"You call that a joke?" Riley hisses. "Do you have any idea the kind of backlash you caused?"

"It's not like it wasn't obvious." Skylar smirks, turning to me, her face a mixture of annoyance and arrogance. "It sure didn't seem like you two were trying to hide it."

I glance back down at the table, trying to mask the misery I'm feeling right now.

"What the hell, Skylar? I knew you could be a bitch most of the time but I didn't realize how vindictive and cruel you are. Are you jealous or something? Is that why you couldn't leave Charlie alone? What has she done to you to justify outing her like that?"

"Whatever, Riley. I did her a favor. Now she can stop pretending to be something she's not."

"Are you fucking kidding me? Is that what you're telling yourself to feel better about what you've done?" Riley's tone rises and I glance around the cafeteria. Multiple tables have gone quiet as their eyes wander in our direction.

"Riley," I whisper as the heat rushes to my face. "Leave it alone."

"No," she snaps before turning her attention back to Skylar. "Did you even think about what might happen once you posted that photo? What could you possibly gain from outing them like that?"

"Oh my god, Riley. It's not like it was a secret. We may live in a small town but we're not blind. I felt like the student body deserved to know what kind of people they were associating with."

"But that wasn't your business to tell. You act like Charlie and Aspen are bad people because your church tells you so. Yet, the book they use to justify their reasoning also tells you to treat your neighbor as yourself, to be kind, to love one another. How can you stand there and—"

"Riley, please," I beg, grabbing her arm. She stops mid-sentence and looks at me. "I appreciate you standing up for me, but I don't need any more attention drawn to me."

Riley glances around me, scanning the now quiet cafeteria. She pivots back to Skylar, who's still standing there with her head cocked to one side. "You've done enough, Skylar. Go find someplace else to sit."

"Whatever." She rolls her eyes before grabbing her tray and heading towards the opposite end of the cafeteria.

"Remind me never to piss you off like that," Tyler says, giving her a kiss on the cheek.

"Yeah, that was pretty intense," says Emily.

Riley glances at me. "Sorry, Charlie. I didn't mean to cause a scene but she just made me so mad."

"It's okay." I bump her shoulder with mine. "I'm lucky to have a friend like you."

She grins. "Yeah, you are."

"Don't worry about everyone else. We'll be done with school soon and you'll be off to college where you can be whoever you want to be," says Emily.

The crushing weight that's been slowly building—with each glare, each comment about my sexuality, each point and whisper—alleviates slightly, giving me the chance to take a breath.

I'm not alone.

I manage to sit up a little straighter, taking a couple bites of pizza and engaging in the conversation at lunch.

I glance around the cafeteria one more time, recognizing the wavy brunette hair instantly. I spot Aspen in the back corner, walking with a boy whose back is turned to me. Riley turns to see what I'm looking at, her face stiff with irritation when she realizes who it is.

"You okay?" Riley whispers.

"Who's that boy she's with?" I ask.

"What? Oh I think that's Brandon."

"Seriously? What's she doing with him?"

Riley shrugs. "I heard they're kind of a thing."

I whip my head back around towards Riley. "No way."

"I don't know that's just what I heard. Maybe he's just a cover?"

The lunch bell rings before I have time to respond and I hastily gather my things, rushing after her.

"Aspen, hey," I say when I've caught up to her.

A look of surprise flashes behind her eyes before she regains her composure. She stares at me, her lips parted as if she's going to say something, then snaps them close.

I glance at Brandon, his mouth pulled into an amusing smirk.

"Can we talk?" I ask her.

"This isn't really a good time," she says, trying to shuffle past me.

I step in front, cutting her off. "Please."

She turns to Brandon. "I'll see you later."

He looks back at me, his gaze lingering on my face. "You sure you don't want me to walk you to class?" She nods, giving him a smile that makes the knot in my stomach feel like it's contorting my insides. When she looks back at me her expression is blank, almost bored. "What?" she snaps.

"I just wanted to see how you're doing?"

She crosses her arms. "How do you think I'm doing, Charlie?"

I turn my body towards Brandon's direction watching him saunter down the hallway. "He seems to think you're doing just fine."

Her back stiffens as she crosses her arms over her chest. "Is that what you came over here for? Who I hang out with is not really any of your business anymore, is it?"

I look up to her face, our eyes meeting. "So that's it? After everything that's happened, this is how it ends?"

She drops her arms to her sides and for a moment there's a hint of the old Aspen in her eyes, the one I fell in love with. And just as quickly as it was there, it vanishes and the cold, hard stare returns. She shrugs. "I don't know what you want me to say, Charlie?"

"I want you to talk to me. I want you to finish what you were going to say yesterday."

Her head snaps up, our eyes meeting. I take a small step forward, aching to be closer to her before continuing. "I know you feel the same."

"So what if I do, Charlie? You think we're going to ride off into the sunset together? Do you have any idea what my dad'll do to me if he finds out I'm talking to you right now?"

"So that's it? You're just going to throw it all away. Isn't it worth fighting for?" I reach out and take her hand in mine. "Aren't *we* worth fighting for?"

She slowly shakes her head, her gaze locked onto the floor. "No."

"Why not? You haven't even given it a chance?"

She lifts her head, meeting my eyes. "Because it never works out in the end." She removes her hand from my grasp and brushes past me down the hallway.

I stand there, anchored to the tile beneath me as I watch her walk away, the weight of her words settling over me like a blanket.

I don't know how I manage to make it through the last of my classes but I do. Because our season is over, there's no need for me to skip study hall and go to the gym but I do it anyway. I'll at least be able to hide out in the locker room until school is over and I can leave.

Since we're seniors we don't have to partake in offseason practice but that doesn't mean we get a free pass to leave school early. We still have to hang around until the final bell rings.

I pull my phone out of my bag, checking it for the first time today. I thumb through social media, no longer surprised at the hostile comments from several different kids. I get a notification that I have a Facebook message. I almost ignore it, expecting it to be just another hateful message about me being gay. But the thought that it might be Aspen reaching out, causes me to open it. It's a message from Makenzie Forester. I've had several classes with her but would never have really considered us friends.

What the hell? It can't get any worse than it already is. I open it.

Hey. Sorry about everything going on. I'm here if u need someone to talk to.

I stare at the screen, rereading the message. I debate what I should say or if I should respond at all. What if it's a trap?

I settle with a simple response:

Thanks.

I put my phone away and spend the rest of sixth period reading a random book I found in my backpack with my feet propped up on one of the chairs. The rest of the team make their way into the locker room. I do my best to ignore them and focus on the words on the page. They end up blurring together and it takes me five minutes to realize I've been rereading the same sentence over and over, without having any comprehension of what it says.

Riley strolls in and takes the seat next to me. She glances around before leaning over and whispering, "How'd your talk with Aspen go?"

I open my mouth to respond but Emily walks over. "Charlie, Coach wants to see you."

I give Riley a wary look before tucking my book away and heading to his office. I pass Skylar on the way out, a sneer etched across her face.

I ignore her, turning to knock on Coach's office. "You wanted to see me?"

He waves me in, closing the door behind me. "Have a seat." He gestures to the empty chairs in his office.

I sit, bouncing my leg repeatedly as I wait for him to speak.

"I understand there's a photo of you and another student going around school."

I swallow the lump in my throat, not sure if that was a question or a statement.

He shakes his head. "I'm very disappointed in you, Charlie. This is not what you need when you're about to go to LittleWood on a scholarship. They want players who are exemplary, not someone who's going to cause trouble."

I stare at him, unable to respond.

"What's the matter with you? You've worked so hard to get where you are today, to secure this scholarship. Don't throw it all away because of some confused feelings for a—for a girl."

He knows? Of course he knows; gossip spreads faster than wildfire here.

Could this really cost me my scholarship?

"But I've been emailing and talking to Ms. McCalister. She's already sent me the rest of the information," I stutter.

"That may be true but if they get wind of what you've been up to, if they see that photo, they may rethink their offer."

"But that doesn't make any sense. I didn't do anything wrong," I say, my voice rising an octave.

"I'm not sure that's what they're going to think." He sits down, meeting my eye level. "Charlie, you've come so far. I've had several conversations with Brian Sullivan. And the things I've been hearing, it doesn't sound like either of you. I've known your grandparents for years, I went to school with Brian and his sister. I think you're just confused, Charlie." ."

I stare at him, wanting nothing more than to jump up and scream at him.

But I don't.

I take a breath before opening my mouth. "With all due respect sir, you have no idea what I'm going through right now. I'll call Ms. McCalister, and get everything taken care of. Being gay has nothing to do with my ability to play ball, and if you can't see that then that's on you. It's not my job to make sure everyone else is comfortable." I turn and walk out of his office.

"What was all that about?" Riley says, handing me my bag so we can leave.

"Coach said that if LittleWood gets wind of that picture, they'll revoke my scholarship."

"They can't do that. That's completely unfair."

"I'm gonna call Ms. McCalister and sort it all out."

"Let me know how it goes."

"Sure."

We exit the gym and walk through the parking lot to Riley's car. Will and Trey step in front of us just as we're getting to the parking lot, causing us to nearly knock into them.

"We heard about you and Aspen," Will says, gesturing to Trey. "We had feeling you two were fuckin' each other. Turns out we were correct. It's a shame, really. Aspen looks like a nice piece of ass." He leans in closer, a sneer tugging at the edge of his mouth. "Tell me Charlie, was she as good in bed as everyone said she was?"

In that frozen second, the words hung in the air like daggers. It's like all the emotion that's been boiling inside of me all day long, finally made its way to the surface. I rear my arm, throwing my body weight behind the fist that connects with Will's face. I hit his jaw with such force that he bends over, spitting blood onto the ground. I am incredibly surprised at the pain that blazes up my arm but I don't care.

I take a step closer to him. "Fuck you," I grit through my teeth.

Riley grabs my arm, pulling me to the car before Will and Trey have a chance to retaliate. I throw my bag in the back and climb into the passenger seat.

"I did not expect that," says Riley.

"He had it coming. Asshole."

She nods to my lap. "How's your hand?"

It hurts like a bitch but I shake my head, trying to brush it off. "I'll be fine."

"I don't encourage violence but as your best friend I must say, that was awesome."

I grin.

We ride the rest of the way in silence. When she drops me off at home, I grab an ice pack from the freezer and head straight for my room. I scroll through my contacts till I come to Ms. McCalister.

I take a breath and press *call*.

She picks up after the third ring. "Hello."

"Hello, Ms. McCalister, it's Charlie Baker."

"Ahh, Charlie. What can I do for you? Did you not get the rest of the information regarding your scholarship?"

"No I did, I was calling about something else." I stand up and begin pacing back and forth around my room.

"What's up?"

"There's uhm—there's something I need to tell you. Um, well you see, uhm. I'm gay," I mumble.

There's silence and I'm afraid that the call disconnected for some reason. I pull the phone off of my ear and see that the call is still going.

"I see, well thank you for sharing that with me."

I pause, waiting for her to go on. When I realize she's done speaking, I ask, "So I get to keep my scholarship?"

I hear a muffled laugh, "Of course, why wouldn't you?'

"Well it's just that, um, well there's a photo of me and my girl—, uhm someone took a picture of me and another girl and it's all over school." I move the phone away from my mouth as I sniff, tears beginning to streak down my face. "And Coach Stewart said that if you got wind of it, you might revoke my scholarship," I sputter.

Her tone is soothing as she says, "I see. What kind of picture is this?"

"Just some stupid photo somebody took of me and a girl kissing."

"Mhmm. And where was this photo taken?"

"At a friend's house," I whisper. I take several deep breaths as I try to swallow the lump that's slowly building in my throat.

"And what were you all doing at this friend's house? Was it a small social gathering? A party?"

I drop my head as I whisper, "A party."

"Was there alcohol present?"

"Not that you can see in the photo."

"I see." After a beat, she says, "Listen, Charlie, I appreciate you being honest with me about this situation but I need to talk to my colleagues and get back to you. My concern is the effect a compromising photo like this might have on you and the university—regardless of whether it was with a girl or a guy."

"Yes ma'am, I understand."

"I'll get back to you when we've reached a decision."

"Okay."

I hang up the phone; the lump in my throat no smaller than it was this morning. If anything, it's only gotten worse. I sulk to my bed, curling into a ball underneath my covers as I try to forget about today's events.

An hour and a half later, Matty is leaning over the bed, shaking me to wake up. It takes me a few minutes before I'm able to orient myself and realize where I'm at.

"What?" I say harsher than I intended.

"It's time for dinner."

"Tell Nana I'm not hungry."

"Tell her yourself. I'm not a fucking telephone service."

I sit up, tossing the covers off. "Who pissed in your cereal bowl today?"

"Just get up and come downstairs. Nana said to hurry."

"Matty, wait."

"What?" he snaps.

"Why are you mad at me all of a sudden?"

"Just drop it. It's not a big deal."

"Then tell me what the issue is."

"It's nothing. Leave it alone."

I climb out of bed and grab his arm before he can open the door all the way. "Just talk to me. Did I do something?"

"Not intentionally," he mutters.

"So what's the issue then?"

"People were just talking shit but it's not a big deal."

"Saying stuff about me?"

He nods.

"Oh. What'd you do?"

"Told 'em to shut the fuck up. Mrs. Walker wasn't exactly thrilled I chose the middle of class to tell them that. So she gave me detention."

"Damn, Matty. I'm sorry."

He shrugs. "It's whatever."

"What'd Gramps and Nana say?"

"Well Nana put on her 'teacher voice' and laid into me and Gramps just shook his head and told me I knew better."

"I'm sorry, Matty. This is all my fault."

"It's fine. Let's just get downstairs before Nana finds another reason to ground me." I follow him down the stairs and slump into my normal seat at the table.

"How was school?" Gramps asks like he does every night.

"It was fine." Matty shrugs, avoiding their eyes.

Gramps turns to me. "And Charlie how are things for you?"

"Other than being the butt of everyone's joke and everyone constantly staring and whispering about me, things are just peachy," I say sarcastically.

Gramps raises his eyebrows in confusion. "What do you mean, sweetie?"

"I haven't exactly gotten the warmest welcome from everyone after Skylar outed me and Aspen."

Nana clears her throat at the mention of Aspen's name. "I thought we agreed it was best if you no longer saw Aspen."

Gramps sets his fork down and raises his hand in the air. "Now wait a second, Lydia." He turns his attention back to me. "Charlie, what's been going on at school?"

I drop my gaze to my plate, considering how I should answer. When I bring my head back up, Gramp's eyes are still locked on mine. "They mainly just point and whisper when I walk by, not trying to hide their look of disgust. A couple kids have said some ugly things but I just try to ignore it. Riley and most of the team have been supportive, so it could be worse."

"I'm sorry, sweetie. I had no idea."

"It's okay," I say, glancing back and forth between Gramps and Nana. I sit up a little straighter, feeling a strength inside me now—one I didn't have a couple months ago. And with it comes the realization that this is my life and I have control of it.

"Some people just don't like what they can't understand. I shouldn't have to hide who I am to make people more comfortable. I may not like how everything went down, but at least I don't have to pretend to be somebody I'm not."

I turn towards Nana, trying to take advantage of my unexpected confidence boost. "I know you may not approve of me being gay, but sooner or later you're going to realize that I'm still the same girl you raised and love. I'm not ashamed of who I am, Nana. And I'm going to be with somebody who makes me happy, regardless of how it affects those around me."

Several moments of silence tick by as we all sit and stare at each other. Finally, Nana opens her mouth. "Can't you at least *try* to be straight? Did you even give those boys a chance?"

I let out a long, slow breath, "It doesn't work like that, Nana. And I tried, trust me."

"Charlie Marie—"

"Lydia, please," Gramps says, cutting her off. "I know this is hard for both of us to wrap our minds around but we are not turning the rest of dinner into an interrogation."

Nana huffs, scooting her chair back and retreating to the bedroom. A moment later, Gramps gets up and follows after her. Matty and I finish the rest of our dinner in silence.

The rest of the week passes by in a blur. I make my way from class to class, doing my best to ignore the continuous stares and whispers. Riley meets me every morning, making sure I get where I need to be. Her being there helps, but I'm struggling to ignore the constant pit in my stomach from my expectation that Aspen will be waiting for me. I make a few more attempts to talk to her but she shoves past me each time, leaving me to stare after her as she walks away.

I can't help but survey the lunchroom each day looking for Aspen. She's eaten lunch with Brandon each day, laughing like nothing's out of the ordinary. It's infuriating. But I don't know what else to do. She won't return my calls or texts. She won't even look in my direction. After everything we've been through, how can she just act like nothing happened?

"Why aren't people giving Aspen crap the way they are me?" I ask Riley at lunch that day.

Riley shrugs. "Well I don't exactly think they're giving her the royal treatment, Charlie."

"But look at her, acting like everything's fine. Just because she's pretending to date a boy, kids will leave her alone? Like she wasn't just as much in that picture as I was?"

"People know you, Charlie. Aspen came here a couple months ago. She doesn't have the same social standing that you do," Emily says.

"It's not fair," I mutter.

Riley gives me a sheepish smile. "I know, but people are already starting to forget about it. Pretty soon it'll be old news and they'll have something else to gossip about."

I take one last look over at her table and see Brandon, tucking a strand of hair out of Aspen's face. The corners of her mouth crinkle as she laughs, her head tipping back as she settles her hand on top of his forearm.

That's it. Now I'm really pissed.

The lunch bell rings and I rush to the other side of the cafeteria, determined to make her stop and talk to me.

I step in front of her just as she rises from the table. "Can we talk?" I ask.

She stops, startled by my sudden appearance. Agitation flutters across her face. In the next moment, her expression is impassive.

Brandon steps in between us, leaning towards me "I don't think she really wants to talk to you."

"This doesn't concern you, Brandon." I turn back towards her. "Please."

She brushes past me. "There's not much else to say, Charlie."

I grab her arm, forcing her to look at me. "You don't just get to run away, Aspen."

Brandon takes another step towards me, his hips knocking into my arm. "She said she doesn't want to talk to you, *dyke*." He inches forward, his index finger jamming into my shoulder, pushing me back.

I slap his hand away. "Don't touch me," I snap.

The conversations cease to continue as the cafeteria stills, wide eyes turning in our direction.

He moves closer, this time using the palm of his hand to propel me backward. He cocks his head to the side. "Or what? You act like a guy, dress like a guy. Thought it was time somebody started treating you like one." His hands deliberately push me back, until I'm pinned against the wall. The iciness of the tiles seeps through my shirt as I try to flatten myself against it.

Aspen grabs his arm, attempting to haul him back, but he easily wrangles out of her grip. He places his palms on either side, making a cage around me. He leans in, his breath hot on my face. "Not so tough now, are ya?" he whispers. "I think it's time somebody taught you a lesson about being a homo in this town. I oughta get a couple of guys to *make* you straight. Then beat—"

Before he can finish, somebody clutches the collar of his shirt, thrusting him backwards and into the mass of chairs and tables. My hands flatten against the wall, my breath catching as I stand frozen in place. Several seconds tick by before I ease my body forward only to see Brandon pinning someone on the ground beneath him.

We've drawn a crowd. Students continue to file in, gathering around us as they chant, "Fight, fight, fight!"

It isn't until Brandon leans back, rearing his arm above his head, fist clenched, that I realize it's *Matty*.

I lunge forward, using both hands to grasp the fabric of his shirt and yank him back. The unexpectedness of my actions is enough to throw Brandon off balance, sending him tumbling backward.

The crowd becomes a hushed audience as the kids shuffle sideways, creating just enough of an opening for Mr. Rodriguez and Principal Lynch to step forward, their eyes narrowed on the three of us.

Chapter Twelve

Matty holds ice wrapped in a towel against his face as we sit outside Principal Lynch's office, waiting to be called in.

"Are you okay?" he asks.

"Shouldn't I be asking you that?"

He shrugs his shoulders. "I'll be fine, it's just a scratch."

"He gave you a bloody nose and probably a black eye. I'd say that's a little more than just a scratch." I bump his knee with mine. "You didn't have to do that, you know."

He rolls his eyes at me. "Charlie, you're my sister. I'm not just gonna stand around and watch some guy treat you the way he did."

I duck my head, trying to hide my smile. "Thanks. I'm really lucky to have you as a brother."

"Let's just hope Gramps and Nana see it that way, because this on top of my detention…" He shakes his head. "If I'm not careful they're going to ship me off to military school."

The lump in my throat plummets at the mention of their name. I haven't even thought about how they're going to react to this. The door creaks open and Brandon comes waltzing out of Principal Lynch's office, a heavy smirk etched across his face.

Reluctantly, I stand and follow Matty into his office. Principal Lynch takes a seat behind his desk, interlaces his fingers and sets them gently on the space in front of him. His office is impeccably tidy. There's not an ounce of clutter atop his desk. His bookshelves are lined with various textbooks, all in alphabetical order. And his diplomas from colleges all over the state are hung neatly on the wall directly behind him.

"We've called your grandparents, they're on their way," he says. His voice is deep and husky. It reminds me of my gym teacher from middle school, who always sat on his ass yelling at us from the sidelines. Except my gym teacher was heavy and had a musty smell that followed him everywhere. Principal Lynch is tall and brawny, his hair is combed off to one side with gel.

He leans forward in his chair, clearing his throat. "I'm very disappointed that you two were engaged in this kind of behavior. We teach better values than that. I can only imagine how disappointed your grandparents are going to be when they get here."

Matty sits up, removing the ice from his face. "But he started it. I just pulled him off before he went after Charlie."

Principal Lynch shakes his head. "That's not what it sounded like to me. Mr. Lewis said that Charlie was bothering him and another female student. When she wouldn't let him leave, you stepped in. He was just defending himself."

His words completely knock me off-center. "Th-that's not what happened, sir."

He opens his mouth to respond but closes it when there's a knock at the door. He hurries around his desk, the potent scent of cologne following in his wake.

It's Gramps and Nana. Nana plasters a smile on her face when she enters, and Gramps quietly shuffles to the bookshelf, as if he is admiring the selection. Principal Lynch grabs two more chairs from the meeting room across the hall and motions for them to sit down. Once seated, he returns to his spot behind the desk.

"Mr. and Mrs. Baker, I'm sure you're wondering why we called you in today," he says.

"Yes, is everything alright?" says Nana.

"Well, you see, Matty was involved in an altercation with another student."

She tilts her head, looking from me to Matty. "What does Charlie have to do with this?"

"Well she seems to be the reason there was an altercation to begin with."

"I don't understand," she says.

"Well from what I have gathered, Charlie was arguing with another student and instead of continuing on to class, they wouldn't let it go, and that's when Matty stepped in and it escalated to the point of physical contact."

Nana slowly shakes her head. "Are you sure this is not one big misunderstanding?"

I turn in my chair, to face her, my head spinning. "That's not what happened."

"Charlie Marie Baker I—"

I cut her off before she can continue. "Don't you at least want to hear my side of the story. What Brandon told you was a lie," I say to Principal Lynch. "That's not what happened."

Principal Lynch lets out an exasperated breath, motioning his hand face up in the air, indicating *go on.*

I begin my detailed explanation, explaining what happened from the minute I walked over to the other side of the cafeteria, to the minute that Matty was pinned underneath Brandon. "He wasn't defending himself, he started it," I say gesturing to the door as if Brandon was standing just behind me. "Matty was just trying to protect me."

I slump back down in my seat, my body suddenly exhausted as Nana, Gramps and Principal Lynch look back and forth at each other. Why can't they understand that I haven't done anything wrong? That the real issue is guys like Brandon who think they can walk all over people like me, or think that because I am gay somehow makes me less-than.

I look between my grandparents, Nana's face is full of bewilderment and Gramps looks pensive. "Did you not hear what he said to me?" I whisper.

Gramps leans forward. "I heard you." He turns to Principal Lynch. "I believe Charlie. I know my grandkids and neither one of them have even gotten into an altercation like this. They're good kids. I think Matty was just trying to look out for his sister."

"That may be Mr. Baker, but I can't ignore the fact that your grandson was in a fight with another student."

"You call that a fight? Did you not hear what Charlie said? The other boy had him pinned to the ground."

"Can't you go back and look at the cameras? You'll see how it happened," I say.

"I already looked and unfortunately where you three were standing, was out of view of the camera."

"So what happens now, Mr. Lynch?" asks Nana.

"Well given the circumstance of the situation, and the fact that this is Charlie and Matty's first major offense, we are going to let them off with a warning." He turns towards me. "But let me be very clear, if another incident like this occurs, you will face severe consequences, is that understood?"

"Yes sir," I mumble.

He stands. "Mr. and Mrs. Baker, thank you for taking the time to come down here."

"Of course. Thank you for being so generous," Nana says.

I roll my eyes, standing to follow Matty and them out of the office.

"We will discuss this more at home," Nana says. "But right now you two need to hurry up and get to class."

I turn and head down the hallway without another word. Matty mutters a 'good-bye' and then rushes to catch up with me.

"You okay?" he asks.

"What do you think?" I snap at him.

He holds his hands up in front of his chest. "Jeeze, I was just trying to help."

I lean against the wall and shut my eyes. After a moment I say,. "You're right, I'm sorry. I'm just tired of everyone treating me like I have some disease."

"Not everyone," Matty mumbles.

I look over at him, his bright green eyes meeting mine. "I know, but some days, it still doesn't make it any easier. It's not like one big wound you can stitch up and call it good. It's like a million little paper cuts over and over, every day. The looks in the halls from other kids, the whispers behind my back, the way Nana looks at me now. People like Brandon who think they can treat me like garbage because being gay somehow makes me different. I know I have people on my side, but sometimes it doesn't seem to help much when it feels like so many people are against me."

Matty steps forward, wrapping an arm around my shoulder to pull me in for a hug. "I know it's not fair. But schools almost out, and pretty soon this'll all be behind you. Until then, you have me to look out for you."

"Thanks, Matty."

"C'mon, we better get to class before we give Lynch another reason to hate us."

I nod, following behind Matty before we head in separate directions. I round the corner, nearly running into Will who's leaning up against the wall with a grimace stretched across his face.

"Heard what happened at lunch today," he says.

I ignore him and instead debate my best escape route. He propels himself off the wall and in two quick steps he's inches from my face.

"It's about time somebody put you in your place. I just wish I could've been there to see it."

"Screw you."

"You know, Charlie, now that I think back to middle school, it makes sense why you hung out with the boys more than the girls." He ducks his head closer. "I'm just glad we weren't friends long enough to be contaminated by your disease," he whispers. He takes another step forward as he lifts both hands and pushes me backward with such force I stumble into the trash can behind me. He turns around, chuckling to himself and walks away.

It takes me a few moments to gather myself before I make a beeline to the girls' bathroom. I duck into the first stall, relieved to finally have some privacy. I take my time, having no desire to resume the role of being the center of attention any time soon.

When I open the stall door, I stop dead in my tracks. Aspen's leaning up against the bathroom sinks, her expression unreadable.

We make eye contact for a moment, before I look away, turning my focus to the faucet in front of me.

"I'm sorry about what happened at lunch," she says.

I ignore her, vigorously scrubbing my hands as if it would be this easy to wash away everything else I'm feeling.

"Charlie, I'm...I—"

"What, Aspen?" I snap.

She looks down at her hands, her lips quivering, "I'm sorry. I didn't know Brandon was going to do that," she whispers.

"Whatever." I reach around her, ripping a paper towel from the dispenser.

"Are you okay?"

"What do you think? You have no idea what I've been going through. And now you're all of a sudden talking to me after dodging me this whole time?" I let out a sigh. "I just don't get it."

She takes a step closer, reaches her arm out and then drops it back down to her side. "I'm sorry, I thought if I ignored you, it would make everything easier." She sniffs, wiping the right side of her face, "But it isn't." She looks up, her eyes brimming with tears.

"That's not what it seems like considering you've been snuggled up next to Brandon all week long."

"That's not fair."

"Fair? You wanna talk about fair?" The anger continues to rise and this time, I don't force it back down. "How about when your dad came over and outed me to my grandparents? Or how about the constant looks and whispers I get when I walk down the hall? Or my personal favorite, how about guys like Brandon and Will who think they can say whatever they want and treat me like a piece of garbage because they think they're better than me? I don't see you having to deal with any of that stuff."

"I'm sorry, Charlie. I don't know what else to do," she mutters in a voice barely above a whisper.

"Fight for what you want. Stand up for yourself, Aspen."

"I can't. I'm not strong like you are."

I shake my head. "The Aspen I knew, the one I fell in love with, was ready to conquer the world. And I know that deep down, she's still in there."

"I wish I believed you."

"Me too."

Saturday is bleak and lifeless. This normally would've been a day I'd spend with Aspen but it's one o'clock in the afternoon and I'm still in bed. I have no energy at all and would be completely content with laying in my nest of blankets and sheets until graduation rolls around.

Last night was fairly calm considering everything that's happened in the past week. We ate dinner in silence and then I retreated to my room and haven't left since.

I finish another episode of *House Hunters* the same time my phone rings. I glance at the screen, immediately recognizing Ms. McCalister's number.

"Hello?" I say, trying to mask the wariness in my voice.

"Charlie, it's Juliet McCalister. Is this a bad time?"

"No ma'am."

"Well I'm calling about the incident we discussed previously."

I swallow the lump in my throat. "Yes?"

"I've talked with my colleagues and we've taken everything into consideration…"

The thrum of my pulse beats in uneven intervals, the anticipation of hearing the words that are going to make or break my future is almost unbearable. I close my eyes, bracing myself for what comes next.

"…And we've decided to allow you to keep your scholarship with the understanding that if something like this happens again we will take disciplinary action. Is that understood?"

"Yes ma'am. Thank you. Thank you so much."

"You're welcome, Charlie. Enjoy the rest of your day."

"You too." I flop back in on my pillows feeling the weight that's been anchoring me to this place for so long slowly dissipate with each passing second.

I'm in the middle of texting Riley the good news when there's a knock at the door. I hit send as Matty shuffles into the room and gives me a feeble smile. There's a purple bruise underneath his eye and his lower lip is swollen.

"How are you?" he asks.

"Tired. But the good news is I get to keep my scholarship."

"That's awesome, Charlie. I'm happy for you."

"Thanks. What's up?"

"Nana needs you downstairs. She sent me up here to get you."

I exhale slowly. "Can't you just tell her I'm not feeling well? I don't want her to ruin my good mood."

"No can do. She explicitly told me that you need to come downstairs."

"Do you know what she wants?"

"No idea."

I huff, throwing my covers off and slump out of bed. I throw on a pair of sweats and an old t-shirt. My hair is a tangled mess, so I finger-comb it before descending the staircase. It doesn't take long for the dread to snake into my stomach.

When I step off the stairs, the first thing I notice is Reverend Charles sitting on the far side of the couch, smiling up at me. Gramps is seated in his recliner, his expression placid, and Nana is seated on the other side of the couch, smiling. There's a lady sitting in between them, who looks vaguely familiar. She's wearing a floral dress that looks like a cheap tablecloth, a hideous pair of brown clogs, and her hair is pulled up in a tight bun.

Here we go again.

I take a deep breath, wishing I was anywhere else but here right now.

He stands up, the smile still plastered on his face. "Hello, Charlie."

He reminds me of a used-car salesman, one that's desperate to close a sale to give purpose to his small, miserable life. He's wearing navy slacks, a plain white button-up, patent-leather dress shoes, and his hair is combed backed perfectly, not a strand out of place. He has a Bible in his right hand and gestures for me to come into the living room.

"Charlie, I'd like you to meet someone," he says, turning to the woman to his right. "This is my friend, Jennifer."

She stands up, reaching out her arm to me. "Hello, Charlie. It's nice to meet you."

I return the gesture, giving her a nod and a mumbled, "Hello."

Reverend Charles sits back down, resting his elbows on his knees, and leans forward. "Charlie, do you know why I'm here?"

I lean against the banister, crossing my arms over my chest. "No."

"Charlie, your grandmother asked me to come speak to you about some issues you've been going through recently, specifically involving a girl named Aspen, I believe?"

Nana pipes in, "Yes, Reverend, that's her name."

His presence and words confirm that my family thinks I'm in need of repair, that I need someone like him to 'fix' me. I might laugh if I didn't feel like crying. I've had one helluva a week but a man who barely knows anything about me or what I'm going through thinks he knows what's best for me. Maybe if his God wasn't so busy paying attention to the lives of people like me, the world might be a better place, a kinder place.

But life isn't fair. It's why some people can't stay clean long enough to take care of their children. It's why kids like Baxter Jenkins get harassed for being different. It's why people like Reverend Charles and my grandmother think they can tell me who to love, as if it were as simple as picking out a new car.

He gives me a gentle nod, straining to make the smile on his face seem natural. "Charlie, I'm here to tell you that God loves you, He always has, always will. And He just wants what is best for you. We don't want to see you go down this path of destruction. A path that leads you away from God instead of towards him. He'll help you through this confusing time, if you just let Him…" He pauses, giving me another forced smile as he waits for me to respond. I keep my expression even despite the agitation growing inside me.

After another beat, he continues. "Charlie, I brought Jennifer with me, hoping that she may be able to shine a light on what you're going through right now. The feelings you're experiencing right now can be resolved if you just try. I've seen it happened."

That got my attention.

Jennifer jumps in, picking up right where he left off. "Charlie, I too was like you once. Confused, scared, angry, damaged. I had all these emotions going on inside me and didn't know how to deal with them. I became involved with somebody of the same-sex and it got to a point where I just lost myself completely. But then I let Jesus into my heart and realized that He was what was missing the entire time. I wasn't a lesbian, Charlie, I just had a lesbian *problem*, most likely rooted in the traumatic experiences I endured as a child. And I believe that's what's happening to you right now."

I stare at her, speechless.

A *lesbian problem?* Are you fucking kidding me?

She takes my silence as an invitation to keep going. "Charlie, I know exactly what you're going through. I can assure you, you're not alone. You have a whole group of people that want to help you get through this, to turn your sinful desires into something fruitful. You just have—"

"Stop. Just stop," I snap. I've had enough of this. I lean away from the banister, my back straightening with the rage slowly making its way to the surface. "I'm not sick, or have some disease that I need to be cured of. There's nothing wrong with me."

Jennifer stands up, a bright smile spread across her face. "Charlie, it's okay. Denial is normal. Why don't you come over here and we can pray for you?"

Reverend Charles stands, nodding his head. "Yes, I think that's a good idea." He waves me over. "Come, let us pray that our almighty God takes these sinful thoughts and feelings away and cleanse you of your inner demons."

I wince, taking a step back. "No."

Nana stands up, her eyebrows furrowed as she narrows her eyes at me.. "Charlie, dear, let us pray for you. We just want to help you, sweetheart."

Matty steps forward, his tone calm. "She said no, Nana. Why can't you see this isn't what she wants?"

"You don't know what she wants, she's just confused, that's all." She turns towards me, her arm out gesturing for me to come closer.

I look at her, my eyes welling with tears. I choke back a sob before I open my mouth to speak again. "There's nothing wrong with me. I'm still the same person I've always been, can't you see that?"

Gramps stands up, stepping into the middle of the room between me, Reverend Charles, Jennifer, and Nana. "I think that's enough."

We all stare at him as he turns towards the Reverend. "I think it's time for you to leave."

Nana steps forward, shaking her head. "James, what are you doing? He's not finished yet."

Gramps' tone is firm and gentle. "Oh but I think he is. Look at Charlie, dear. Can't you see what we're doing to her? This isn't helping her. It's making it worse. The God I believe in made her just the way she is, and the last time I checked, He doesn't make mistakes. She doesn't need to be fixed, honey, she needs our support."

Nana takes a step back, looking as if he just slapped her across the face. "She was fine until she got involved with that *girl*." She says the word 'girl' like she just spit out something foul and sour.

"Lydia, please darling." Gramps places his hands soothingly on her shoulders. "Charlie's right. She's still the same wonderful girl we've always loved. How can we tell her it's okay to be who she is and when she does, we treat her like she has a disease?"

Nana shakes her head, covering her mouth with her hand and turning away from Gramps' grasp.

Reverend Charles's steps forward. "It looks like you all have some things to discuss and work through. We'll see ourselves out. But please call me if there is anything I can do." He turns to me, "And Charlie, the same goes for you, we'll be praying for you."

Gramps ushers them out, while Nana still stares at the floor, her face a mixture of betrayal and confusion.

I let out a breath I didn't realize I was holding. I take two long strides across the living room and fold myself into my grandfather's arms.

"I love you," I murmur into his shirt. He smells of lotion and aftershave, a scent that always reminds me of home.

"I love you too, Monkey," he says, gingerly rubbing my back.

When he releases me, I turn to look at Nana. Her gaze traces over my body, her demeanor rigid and perturbed.

After a beat she says, "How could you do that, James? Embarrass us in front of the Reverend like that?"

Gramps opens his mouth to respond, but she waves him off, turning to look at me. "I will *not* make the same mistake twice." She settles a hand on her hip and waves the other one in the air. "I'm just trying to do right by you, Charlie. Can't you understand that?"

"But none of this is your fault, Nana. Why do you keep blaming yourself for things that are out of your control? I didn't choose to be gay, I just am. Can't you see that this," I flail my hands in front of me, "isn't helping? That me being gay has nothing to do with how you raised me? I finally feel like myself; that I'm growing into the person I'm supposed to be. Don't you want that for me? Don't you want me to be happy?"

She deflates, her shoulders sagging as she exhales a long, slow breath. "I do want you to be happy, Sweetheart."

"So *let* me be happy, Nana," I plead. "Stop trying to force me to be someone I'm not."

She opens her mouth to speak, then abruptly closes it before storming out of the living room.

Gramps glances at me and Matty before following after her.

I mumble a 'see you later' to Matty and stumble out of the house, desperate to breathe some fresh air.

When I make it to the driveway, I pull my phone out of my pocket and call Riley, she picks up on the first ring.

"What's up?" she says.

"You busy?"

"Not really, just helping my mom out back. Everything okay?"

"Could you come get me? I just really need a break from this place."

"Sure, I'm on my way." I hear her muffled voice as she says goodbye to her mom and grabs her keys. "What's going on, Charlie?"

"I'll explain when you get here."

"Alright." She hangs up and I sit on the hard concrete, waiting for her.

Five minutes later, she pulls into the driveway and I half-slump into her passenger seat.

"Hey," she says gently. "Where are we going?"

I shake my head. "I don't care, anywhere but here."

She nods, putting the car in reverse and slowly backing out of the driveway. We ride in silence for a few minutes, maundering around town, no particular destination in mind.

Riley breaks the silence. "You wanna tell me what's up?"

"My grandmother thinks I'm going to hell."

She creases her brows and tilts her head at me, so I elaborate, recounting the events that occurred this morning at my house.

"According to Reverend Charles and the ex-homosexual that came over, I'm not actually gay, I just have a lesbian problem that's rooted in the trauma I went through as a child."

"Holy crap, Charlie. I had no idea. What did you do?"

I finish telling her the rest of the story. By the time I get to the part where Gramps basically threw the Reverend out, I'm crying.

I wipe the tears from my face, my voice coming out in choked sobs. "I'm just so tired of everything. I'm so ready to be out of this small close-minded town and somewhere else where people don't take one look at me and think I'm a defect."

Riley grasps my forearm, her touch comforting. "I don't think you're a defect."

"That's because you're my best friend."

"Charlie, you have people on your side. I know it might not seem like much, especially after everything you've been through recently, but you're not alone. You have people that care about you."

"I know," I mumble. "I just can't help but wonder if everything I'm going through right now, and everything she's dealing with right now, might be a little more bearable if we were dealing with it *together*, instead of having to face everything by ourselves."

"You mean Aspen? Seriously?"

"Yeah, I'm serious."

"After everything she's put you through, the way she's ignored you and then everything that happened at lunch, you still feel this way?"

"I ran into her in the bathroom after I left Principal Lynch's office, and you didn't see the look on her face. She apologized and I know deep down she feels the same way I do." I look over at Riley. "I think she's just trying to get through everything, hoping she's going to make it to the other side."

"Wow. I'm sorry, Charlie. I didn't know."

"It's okay, I know most people don't understand what we had, even you. And I get it, I didn't even understand what we had until it was gone. But I've never met somebody that made me feel the way I felt when I was with her. She's the first person who's ever made me feel so... so *alive*. Like I had been sleepwalking before, and I needed someone like her to wake me up, show me everything that

I was missing. It felt like I had breathed my last breath until I had the opportunity to be with her again, just be in the presence of her." I shake my head, staring out through the windshield as my mind indulges in the memory of her.

"Have you told her all this?" Riley asks.

"I never really got the chance."

"Maybe you just need to put it behind you and try to move on," she whispers.

"I don't think I can. At least not until she tells me that's what *she* wants. School is almost over, and maybe it's naive of me but I'm still hanging on to a small sliver of the possibility that she didn't mean all those things she's said and done. That deep down she still feels the same way I do. I mean, it's not like a light switch you can turn on and off. She can't go from what we had last week to suddenly having no feelings for me whatsoever. It just doesn't make any sense."

Riley gives me a languid smile, "I hope you're right. I just don't want to see you get hurt."

"Thanks, Riley but I don't know if things can get much worse than they already are."

We drive around for about another hour or so until Riley suggests that we get dinner somewhere. The mention of food makes my stomach rumble. I had forgotten I hadn't eaten anything all day. We pull into a burger joint and make our way to a booth in the back corner.

We both order a burger and fries and end up combining the fries into a single pile on the tray and douse them in ketchup.

We're in the middle of a discussion about Riley's mom's plant situation when a familiar voice says my name. I look to my right and see Aunt Beth standing next to our booth.

"I thought that was you," she says. Her hair is shorter since the last time I saw her, the color still the same as Aspen's. She's wearing black skinny-jeans, a red tank-top and the same leather jacket I saw when I first met her.

I'm completely caught off guard but I manage to push out a, "Hello."

She glances at Riley then back to me. "My bad, Riley, this is Beth, Aspen's aunt. Beth, this is Riley. We play ball together."

She smiles, reaching out her hand towards Riley to shake it. "It's nice to meet you. Are you playing ball at LittleWood University with Charlie next fall?"

I'm surprised she remembered.

Riley returns the handshake, "No, I'm actually playing at a university in New Mexico."

"Ahh I see." She turns back towards me. "I was over at Brian's yesterday. I heard you and Aspen had a falling out. I'm sorry."

I swallow, my mouth all of a sudden dry as a desert. "Yeah, me too."

"I'll let you two get back to dinner." She turns towards the door and then pivots back to us. "I know my brother can be an ass and he's only gotten worse since his wife died. But Aspen's the best thing he ever did. I hope you two can work it out. She seemed really upset when I was over there, but she wouldn't go into detail about it." She stops, like she's contemplating saying something else. "All I'm saying is that I know how much you mean to her, even if she doesn't know how to say it. I just hope you two can get past whatever happened."

I nod, struggling to form a coherent reply. "Me too," I mumble.

She smiles as she lightly squeezes my shoulder. "I'll see you around. It was nice to meet you, Riley." And walks out of the restaurant.

"She seems cool," says Riley the moment the door *dings* closed behind her.

"Yeah. I was shocked when she said that she was related to Aspen's father. I mean they are literally complete opposites."

"You think she realizes you two were more than just friends?"

I mull over her question. "I don't know. I only met her once and I couldn't figure out if she knew and didn't want to say anything or didn't have a clue."

Riley's eyebrows rise. "Oh she knew."

"How do you know?"

"Did you not hear what she said? And it's not like you two did a great job of being discreet. Everyone saw the way you two looked at each other."

I shrug my shoulders. "I don't know what I'm supposed to do, Riley. It's not like her dad will let her within fifty feet of me. And what if I'm wrong? What if she really doesn't have feelings for me anymore and just wants to move on?"

"Charlie, c'mon. You heard her aunt. She's devastated." She plucks a fry from the pile and pops it into her mouth, licking her fingers. "There's no way she would be acting like that if she didn't have feelings for you and wanted to move on."

"So what am I supposed to do? She's barely speaking to me. She won't even text me back."

"Do you want to be with her? Like, really want to be with her, Charlie?"

"Yes. I do."

"Then maybe you need to try harder. Tell her how you feel, how you really feel and make her listen. And then it's up to her. The ball will be in her court."

"Only you could find a basketball analogy to incorporate into this conversation," I say, flicking a fry at her.

She catches the fry and shoves it in her mouth. "I'm your best friend, it's my job."

We finish the last of our meal and then Riley drives me back home. When I crawl back into bed, I don't have the same heart-wrenching feeling I did when I woke up this morning. Instead, the feeling that transcends is something I've been too afraid to admit to myself: hope.

Chapter Thirteen

The next couple of weeks pass by in a clouded trance. Things have finally started to calm down at school. I still get the occasional side-eye but I'm no longer the current topic of everyone's conversation. I've slowly started to focus more in class but with graduation right around the corner, schoolwork is the last thing on anyone's mind right now.

I've been in contact with Ms. McCalister pretty regularly. The last of the paperwork was finally sent off, which means I'm officially a LittleWood Tiger. She sent me the information about the summer program and moving into the dorms. A couple of the girls from the team have reached out to me on social media. We've been talking a couple times a week, getting to know each other, and solidifying the idea that I'm finally getting out of this small town.

I've made a few more attempts at talking to Aspen, but each time I get shut down. She's stopped hanging out with Brandon every day, but she still won't even look in my direction. Matty thinks I need to cut my losses and move on but I just can't. There's a part of me that's still clinging to the idea that deep down, she still has feelings for me. And I am determined to figure it out for myself.

I decide to stay after school today and see if Aspen still hangs around to work on her art. Maybe she'll talk to me if there's nobody else around? After the final bell rings, I explain my plan to Riley just outside the locker room.

"You sure this is a good idea?" she asks, her mouth pulled in a taut grin.

"No, but I'm running out of options. I need to know how she really feels before I can move on."

She exhales a slow breath. "Okay. But call me if you need me."

I nod, before heading back up towards the main building. I wander aimlessly around the hallways, trying to wait out the kids that are still here. After about fifteen minutes, I head towards the art room.

I peer through the open door. Aspen's back is to me. I take a moment to admire her, knowing this might be the last chance I can. Her hair has gotten longer since the last time I'd seen it. She's wearing a pair of jean shorts that hug her hips perfectly and a white fitted t-shirt. She's sitting on top of a stool, hunched over what looks like a sketch pad. I lightly knock on the door with my knuckle.

She turns, startled. For a second her mask drops, giving me a glimpse of the real Aspen. But just as quickly as it went away, it returns.

"You have a minute?" I ask.

She hesitates and I brace myself in anticipation of her kicking me out. I let out a breath when she nods her head. I shuffle inside and take a seat on the stool that's at the other end of the table. We're only a few feet apart but it feels as if an inexpressible gulf lies between us.

"What are you working on?" I ask gently.

She shrugs her shoulders. "Nothing really. I've been staying here after school to avoid having to go home. I told my dad it was for an art project but I finished it last week."

I glance down at the sketch pad in her hand. It's a drawing of two silhouettes. One looks like a child, the other an adult. They're sitting on a park bench in a storm but instead of rain, it's books with the pages ripped out, fluttering around them, creating a sort of dome.

"I like it. Did you hear back from The Waltson Institute?" I ask.

She nods, a soft smile tugging at the edge of her mouth. "Yeah, I got in."

"That's great, I'm really happy for you."

"Thanks. My dad wasn't too pleased but Aunt Beth was excited."

"Well, you're gonna do great up there."

"Yeah, maybe." She peers back down to the pad in her lap.

Several moments pass and I let my eyes linger on her face, studying the features I'd become so familiar with. She looks exhausted and I have the sudden urge to take her in my arms and run my fingers through her hair.

But I don't.

"How're you?" I ask.

"Okay, I guess."

I fidget with my hands in my lap, my tongue suddenly feeling like sandpaper. I've spent a lot of time thinking about everything I'd say to her if we just got the chance to be alone. I'd thought about it so often that my imaginings had taken on the quality of a photograph, one that had become faded from being taken out and looked at too many times. And now that I'm sitting six feet away, in an empty art room, my mind is blank.

"I'm so sorry, Charlie," she says, breaking the silence. It's not until I look up that I realize there are tears streaming down her face. I watch one roll off her cheek and plunge to the tiles below.

She wipes the side of her face with the back of her hand. "I never meant for any of this to happen and I hate what it's doing to me, to both of us. All the shit you've gone through." She shakes her head, the tears continuing to fall. "It's all my fault. I never wanted to hurt you like that. My dad just lost it and I didn't know what else to do. I thought being around all those guys would get him off my back and take my mind of things but it didn't. And I couldn't take it anymore, pretending to be something I'm not." She's sobbing now, her words jumbling out in between shallow breaths. "I'm just so tired of everything."

Without thinking, I stand up and pull her into my arms. I wrap myself around her, gently stroking her back as she cries into my shoulder. Her tears soak through my shirt but I don't care. I hold her tight, our bodies pressed together as I tenderly kiss her temple.

I cradle her in my arms until her breathing settles. She steps backward, our faces still inches apart and I lean down, pressing my lips to hers. It's gentle at first, almost hesitant. Then her lips part, deepening the kiss, and all of my fears and worries about what's going to happen next fades away. The taste of Aspen on my tongue is the only thing I can focus on right now, anchoring me to this moment I so desperately needed.

Her arms slide down my side, tightening around my hips. I press my body closer to hers, aching to feel the warmth from her skin. I let my hands drift down her lower back, wanting nothing more than to rip her clothes off.

She steps back, disentangling herself from my grasp. "I'm sorry, Charlie. I can't."

"Why not? I know you feel it too."

She shakes her head, her voice sounding like a distant drone. "I just can't."

"I love you, Aspen," I haven't even registered what I said until I see a ripple of surprise flutter across her face. Before she can respond, I take a step forward, grasping her hand, pulling her closer. "I mean it, and I know you do too." I force my eyes to meet hers and my pulse leaps forward, like a horse charging out of the starting gate at a race. "I've never met someone that made me feel this way. For the longest time I thought I was broken. You made me realize I wasn't. I know this has been hard, and I know this hasn't gone the way we wanted it to. But I want to be with you and I'm tired of hoping these feelings are just going to disappear because they're not. And if I'm being honest I don't want them to.'"

I take another gradual step closer and when she doesn't pull away, I continue. "I know that there's a part of you that feels the same way. What we had together, you can't fake that, Aspen."

She stares at the floor for what feels like an eternity. I keep my gaze locked on her, searching for the answers I hopelessly wanted to hear. She brings her hand up to her hair, almost without realizing it, and twirls the ends around her fingers. I recognize the reflex immediately, it's what she always does when she's nervous.

"Tell me you don't feel the same way," I plead. "Tell me this isn't what you want." I move in front of her, forcing her to look at me. "Tell me you don't *love* me too."

Her eyes dance around my face as if the answers are written on the walls behind us. She holds my gaze for a moment, an expression of what can only be described as hope flickers behind her eyes, before she whispers, "I don't, Charlie," and walks out of the room.

My plan is to spend the entire weekend snuggled in my bed with a tub of *Ben & Jerry's* while I watch reruns of *CSI* on my laptop. I'm hoping the blood and gore of the crime show will help take my mind off things. I poured my heart out to her, I let it all out, everything that's been building these past couple weeks and it felt like she ran over me with a semi-truck. I don't even have the energy to cry anymore; I just feel empty.

I'm in the middle of shoveling another spoonful of ice cream and when there's a knock at the door. I throw the extra pillow across the room, mumbling, "Go away." The pillow falls to the ground with a soft thud as the door cracks open. I slump back down in the bed, too defeated to say anything else. I set the ice cream down and pull the blanket up over my head as Riley shuffles into the room and takes a seat on the end of my bed.

She sits for a minute, glancing around my room, taking in the disaster that is me. "I take it your talk with Aspen didn't go so well?" she says.

"I don't wanna talk about it," I mutter from underneath the covers.

She yanks the comforter from my face, "I can't hear you. I tried calling and texting and when you didn't respond I thought I should just come over and check on you."

I give her a sheepish smile. "I'm fine."

She cocks her head. "You don't look fine." She stands up and walks to the end of my bed, pulling back to the covers to slide in next to me. "Do you wanna talk about it?"

I shake my head, feeling the tears well up. My eyes are red and irritated from the crying I already did and I force the sob back down. "I told her how I feel." I pull at a loose thread on top of the covers and tell Riley the rest of what happened. I turn towards her. "She said she doesn't love me," I whisper. "I just don't get it. I know she felt it too, it's not something you can just fake." Riley shifts closer, gently wrapping her arm around me as I sob into her shoulder. "It's not fair."

We sit in silence for a few minutes. Riley continues to hold on to me, softly massaging my arms, while I try to get myself under control.

"I'm so sorry, Charlie," she whispers.

I sit up and use the sheets to wipe my face. "I just want to forget about everything."

Riley leans back, her eyebrows raising slightly. "C'mon, get up."

I pull the covers under my chin. "What? Why? I don't want to."

She stands up and tugs at the blankets. "I'm not going to let you sit around and mope all weekend."

I give her a smug look. "Why? I'm perfectly fine with spending the weekend with my two best pals, Ben and Jerry," I say, motioning to the pint of ice cream.

She shakes her head, successfully removing the covers from my grasp. "Nope. Get up, take a shower and get dressed. There's a party at Lucas' house tonight and you're coming with me and Tyler."

I slump back down, pulling my knees up to rest under my chin. "Do you remember what happened the last time I went to a party? I would prefer not to make the same mistake twice."

She waves off my comment, "That's not going to happen. Skylar isn't invited and you'll be getting drunk with me."

"I don't know. I'm not really in the mood for socializing. And besides, wasn't there a party a couple weeks ago that got busted? I don't need to give LittleWood another reason to potentially revoke my scholarship."

"That was because some idiots thought it was a good idea to have a car race in the open field behind the house. That's not gonna happen tonight. It'll be chill."

"I don't know, Riley. I'm not really feeling a party."

"I don't care. You can't just sulk forever. You need to get up and have some fun." She clutches my arm and pulls, forcing me to stand up or risk tumbling off the bed.

"You're not going to leave unless I come with you, are you?"

She grabs a magazine and plops down on my desk chair. "Nope. Now go get ready. I'll be waiting right here so you can't bail on me."

"Fine," I huff, heading to the bathroom.

A shower and change of clothes later, I'm sitting in the passenger seat of Riley's car on our way to Lucas's.

I watch the sunset as we drive towards town, painting the sky in hues of red blended with orange, purple, and crimson. It reminds me of the book I lent Aspen, *Bellow From Beneath*. There's a part where he spends his days talking to the sky, thinking it's the only thing that'll listen. But then he realizes that no matter what he says or how many times he says it, he's never going to get a response. Because in the end all we're left with is ourselves. Once he figures this out, he decides he's going to do whatever it takes to get off that island. That's when he discovers the group of people that already live there, and finally understands that he was never really alone after all.

"We gotta make a pitstop to get Tyler," Riley says, interrupting my thoughts.

When we pull up to Tyler's house, he's waiting out front for us. He walks to the driver's side door and gives Riley a kiss through the window before sliding into the back seat. "This party is going to be sick," he says.

Riley lets out a soft laugh in response and I turn my gaze back to the window.

"Riley told me what happened with Will and Trey, how you punched Will in the face. The guy's a total douchebag and he had it comin'. I just wish I could've been there to see it."

I shrug my shoulders. "It wasn't that great. It hurt like hell."

"Still, he deserved it." His voice softens, "I'm sorry about you and Aspen. I was really rooting for you two."

"Thanks."

Riley cuts in, "But that's not what we're dwelling on tonight. We're gonna go get drunk and have some fun," she cheers.

"Whatever you say, babe," Tyler says, smiling.

The party is in full swing when we arrive. The aroma of beer, sweat, and pizza fills the air as soon as we step through the door. There's music blaring in the background, a football game playing on the TV, and a makeshift dance floor in the den.

I follow Tyler and Riley into the kitchen to get a drink and when nobody does a double-take or makes a snarky comment, I start to relax. Tyler hands me a cup, the liquid burns the back of my throat as I swallow it all in one big gulp. I set the empty cup on the counter, my body beginning to loosen up.

I get another cup and let Riley drag me out to the dance floor without protest. I sip on my drink and let the music drown out the world around me.

Several drinks and upbeat songs later, I'm feeling really good, probably a little too good. I stumble out of the crowd of sweaty bodies and rummage through the kitchen till I locate some water. I take a long swallow, letting the hydration set in. I refill my water, gesture to Riley that I'm okay, and lean against the counter to take a breather.

"Hey, Charlie," a voice says.

I turn to my right to see Makenzie Forester standing next to me. She's wearing a pair of skinny jeans, a blue short-sleeve button-down shirt, and her hair is in a long braid off to the side. I catch a whiff of vanilla and lavender as she leans past me to grab a cup.

"Hey," I say.

She inches closer, nearly shouting over the music as she says, "You enjoying the party?"

"It's alright. How 'bout you?"

She shrugs, flashing me a gentle smile. "They've got alcohol and decent music."

I respond with a half-smile. I glance down at my water, my fingers tapping the edge of the cup, not sure what to say or do next.

There's a loud crash coming from the living room, startling us both. We turn, craning our necks to see the commotion. A couple of guys decided to play football in the living room, knocking over a vase and two paintings. There's some shouting before the music picks back up and everyone resumes whatever they were doing.

"It's getting kind of crazy in here, you wanna go outside where it's a little calmer?" she asks.

"Sure."

We weave around the crowd of kids huddling inside, making our way to the back patio which is much larger than I originally thought. I trail half a step behind Makenzie as we walk along the border, stopping at the edge of the grass. I lean against the railing, breathing in the crisp evening air.

"How are you?" she asks, bringing her cup up to her lips to take a drink. Her emerald green eyes glisten in the moonlight as her eyes find mine.

"I'm okay."

"I'm sorry about everything that's happened. Some people can be so heartless."

I shrug, my gaze shifting to my water. "It's alright."

"I must admit I'm a little surprised to see you at a party so soon."

"You and me both. But Riley wouldn't take no for an answer. And then I thought, what the hell, school's almost over so I might as well enjoy the last days of being in high school while I can."

A shy smile tugs at the edge of her mouth. "Well I'm glad you decided to come."

"Yeah, me too."

We stand there for a few more minutes, talking about the colleges we're going to in the fall and what we hope to gain from getting out of this small town. Turns out Makenzie is going to film school all the way in California.

"I'm gonna go grab another drink, can I get you one?" she asks after she finishes her story about the horrid application processes.

"Sure, why not."

When she returns with our drinks we continue along the edge of the grassy area. I inhale another whiff of her vanilla scent as she moves in closer, our arms inches apart. When we stop moving, I realize were alone on the far side of the backyard. It's darker over here, the light from the moon silvering the planes of her face.

I sip on my drink, feeling the warmth from the alcohol rush throughout my body. After a few minutes she says, "I bet being outed like that makes you feel super alone, huh?"

I nod. "I did at first, but I know I've got people on my side," I say, twisting my head towards the party, thinking of Riley. "And I know I'm not the only person at BluHaven who's gay. But we live in a small town and I wouldn't be surprised if there wasn't a surge of people coming out, especially after what happened to me."

Makenzie laughs, her dimples peeking out. "Well would it make you feel better if I told you I'm also gay, along with a couple other girls from school?"

I nearly spit out my drink. "No way."

She nods. "We're a close-knit group which isn't all that surprising. It's the only place we can truly be ourselves."

"Makes sense. Does anybody outside of the group know?" I ask, completely intrigued.

"Not really, and after seeing what happened to you and Aspen getting outed like that, none of us are saying anything until we go off to college."

"Understandable but I'll be honest, part of me is happy I'm finally out."

She looks at me, her eyebrows raised. "Even after everything that happened? The way people treated you?"

"Don't get me wrong, I hate how everything went down. But now I don't have to keep hiding anymore and pretend that I'm somebody I'm not. In a way it feels like I'm finally free."

"I get that. How'd your family take it?"

"My brother was supportive, my grandfather is getting there and my Nana thinks I'm going to hell."

"Shit, that sucks."

I shrug. "It's not all bad. It could be a lot worse. They could've shipped me off to therapy or something."

"True." She takes another sip before continuing, "I must admit, I wasn't all that surprised to learn that you're a lesbian."

I laugh. "And you're probably not the only one."

"So are you and Aspen still…" She pauses, raising an eyebrow.

I shake my head. "No. Not anymore."

"I'm sorry."

I shrug, trying to brush it off. "It is what it is."

"Well for what it's worth, I think she really missed out on you."

I stay silent, taking another sip as the heat rises in my cheeks. I set my cup back down as she shuffles closer, our bodies barely two inches apart. She shifts her torso, letting her palm settle on my forearm. Her touch is tender, her skin surprisingly warm. She tilts her head, her eyes lingering on my lips. Slowly, she brings her gaze up. When our eyes lock, she leans forward, her lips parting slightly as I feel the pressure of her mouth on mine.

Her lips are soft and wet. I open my mouth to hers, feeling my head starting to spin, not sure if it's because of the liquor or the fact that we're kissing right now. She moves her hand from my arm to my hips as her tongue slips into my mouth. Her grip on my waist tightens, pulling me closer as she runs her fingers through my hair.

The head-spinning that had surged up recedes with a sharp recoil, like an elastic band springing back. I go numb, even as Makenzie's tongue continues to explore my mouth. The numbness washes over me with an icy shock of realization. Something felt wrong, even more so than the hopelessness of longing for someone I couldn't have. This was something else, a sudden jolt of terror as if I'd taken a confident step forward and instantly plummeted into a black void.

I gasp and jerk away from Makenzie with such force I nearly stumble. I grab ahold of the railing beside us, willing my body to settle.

"I'm sorry, Charlie. I didn't mean to—"

I hold my hand up, cutting her off. I turn, flashing her a shy smile. "I'm sorry. It's just... I...I think it's just a little too soon."

She nods, her expression sincere. "It's okay. I understand. I shouldn't have pushed you like that."

"It's okay. I'm just not ready yet."

"No worries." She reaches her hand out, lightly patting my arm. "Why don't we just stick to being friends for now?"

I nod. "Sounds good."

We spend some more time talking as we wander aimlessly around the backyard. Riley comes staggering out of the house, practically crashing into us.

"I've been looking all over for you," she mutters, making it all come out like one long word. She grabs my arm for support, her breath hot with the smell of beer. "What've you been doing?"

I grasp her arm, holding her steady. "Nothing, we were just talking," I say.

She turns to Makenzie, opens her mouth like she's about to speak, then pivots back to me, "You sure that's all you were doing?" she mumbles, her eyebrows raised.

"Yes." I say, thankful that it's too dark for Riley to see my face blush.

She turns back to Makenzie, eyeing her up and down, before she rotates back to me, clutching my arm for support. "I think it's time for another drink."

"I think you've had enough." I tighten my grip so she can't walk away. I turn my attention back to Makenzie, "I think it's time for us to go."

Makenzie smiles. "I'll see you around, Charlie." She places her hand on my lower back as she maneuvers around us and heads back inside.

Tyler and I manage to get Riley home without incident. When he drops me off I head upstairs. It's not until I'm lying under the covers, staring at the ceiling that I recognize why I stopped kissing Makenzie. It felt like a betrayal.

Chapter Fourteen

The last couple weeks of school seem to fly by. Everybody's bustling around with end-of-the-year projects, finals, last-minute applications, and nobody takes a second glance at me anymore. I rarely see Aspen, which makes it easier to push thoughts of her from my mind. At lunch, the whole table's talking about the notice of graduation rehearsal we all received in the mail.

This is it.

There's hardly any time left. Graduation's right around the corner and before I know it, I'll be heading to Arizona for the summer program in July. It's time to face it: the reality of graduation confirms that Aspen, along with this town, will soon be behind me. I'll have a chance to start over. A fresh start.

I've hung out with Makenzie a few times since the party. She's introduced me to a few of her friends that are also like us. I have to admit, it feels great being surrounded by people who understand and know exactly what I'm going through.

On Saturday, I spend the morning playing pickup games with Riley and several other girls from the team.

That night, I go over to Makenzie's and we spend the evening watching some independent films that she saw at a film festival last summer. It's after dodging two kisses that she lands the third. I don't freak out like I did at the party and I'm not surprised to learn that she's a pretty good kisser.

It's on the way home that I recognize that the knot in my stomach is because I still feel guilty about kissing Makenzie. But that doesn't stop me from doing it again the very next weekend. People keep telling me I need to move on, maybe this is how I do it.

Saturday is graduation rehearsal. I arrive with Riley and we make our way through the crowd of seniors to Emily and Sara. The place is buzzing with conversations about summer plans, college, vacations, and anything else that signals the end of our high school journey.

Emily got accepted to Texas Tech and is planning on majoring in creative writing. Sara has a long line of military personnel in her family and is planning to follow in their footsteps. It's almost surreal; that in the next few weeks, the people I've grown up with will be branching off in separate directions, starting their own lives.

We're shuffling down the aisle two-by-two to our assigned seats when I spot Aspen. I choke down the familiar lump in my throat, doing my best to avoid staring at her. She ends up sitting a few rows ahead of me to the right and I can't help but steal a few glances while Mrs. Burns, our school counselor, rants about the expectations.

When Aspen's row stands up to exit, we make direct eye contact as she turns to walk up the aisle. Her demeanor is flat and impassive as if she's just the shell of a person going through the motions of life, just trying to get by. She's far from the girl who turned every head in the cafeteria several months ago; the one who made my heart pound sporadically with just a fleeting touch.

After everyone gathers their cap and gown, we're dismissed. Riley comes barreling out of the doors, a bright smile spread across her face. She slings her arm around me, pulling me in for a side hug that causes me to stumble.

"Can you believe it, Charlie? We're about to be high school graduates," she says, her voice rising, making it come out as more of a squeal.

"I know," I say once I regain my footing. "I never thought this day would come."

She suddenly stops, sticking her arm out against my torso so I don't have any other choice but to stop beside her. "We need to take a picture and document this moment." She pulls out her phone and opens it to the camera.

"Aren't we supposed to take pictures on the actual day of graduation?"

She holds it up in the air above our heads. "Say 'college here we come'," she says and snaps a picture. She brings the phone down, turning the screen out to show me. I wasn't ready so my expression's awkward and we both start laughing. She makes me take one more serious one before we head for her car.

I promised Matty I would spend the rest of the day with him. The reality of me leaving for college very soon is starting to sink in for him and I can tell that he has some reservations, although he would never admit that to me.

Things are still a little tense between me and Nana so I suggest we do something that'll get us out of the house.

"What'd you have in mind?" he asks after we're in the car and are pulling out of the driveway.

"I thought we could go to the mall. I want to get a new graduation outfit."

"I thought you and Nana already picked one out?"

I shake my head. "That's what Nana wants me to wear but I want something else. Something that feels more like me."

"Okay."

BluHaven Mall contains about thirty stores, spread out along four different alley-type pathways. We cruise down the center of one of the paths, window shopping at a few stores before we enter, *Pinnacle Clothing*. There's a look of confusion of Matty's face when I head for the men's section instead of the women's.

"I don't think Nana's going to be too happy with you picking something out from the men's clothes."

"Well it's a good thing Nana isn't the one wearing them."

I gather several different button-downs and pants before heading to the dressing room. When I try on the first shirt and pants, I step out to show Matty.

"Wow," he says. "That actually looks really good on you."

I smile, turning to see myself from every angle.

"You're not worried somebody will say something?" he asks.

I shrug. "I mean at this point it's not like it's a secret that I'm gay. So why shouldn't I wear what I wanna wear?'

Matty continues to stare at me, crinkling his brows.

"Think about it," I say. "When have I ever been ecstatic about wearing a dress or a sweater or a blouse with a ridiculous pattern on it that always reminds me of a tablecloth?"

Matty shrugs, holding his hands up. "Never, now that I'm really thinking about it."

"I've always thought I would feel more comfortable in men's clothing, but was too scared to actually wear it. But I thought having you here with me would help." I turn back to the mirror, admiring my outfit. "And I was right," I say, smiling.

"Then I say go for it; you look great, Charlie."

"You really think so?"

Matty looks me up and down before answering. "Yes I do. It looks more like you, like you're finally growing into the person you're meant to be."

"Thanks, Matty. That means a lot."

"You wanna get a bite to eat? Gramps and Nana said something to me about having a church thing tonight so we're on our own for dinner."

"Sure."

The food court is a few stores down from the shop we were just in so it only takes a few minutes to get there. We're welcomed by the scent of Chinese and pizza. The restaurants are spread out along the outside of the area, and there's a variety of tables and booths scattered throughout the center. I get in line to order some pizza while Matty finds us a table and gets the drinks.

Someone nudges me from behind and I turn to see Makenzie and two other girls, whose names I don't remember, standing next to me.

"Hey stranger," she says with a coy smile.

"Hey, what are you doing here?" I smile in return.

She gives a slight tilt with her head, motioning to the girls standing behind her. "Wren and Zoe dragged me along because of some makeup sale. Makeup isn't really my thing but I thought why not. What about you?"

I nod my head toward Matty. "I'm here with my brother. We just wanted to get out of the house."

"Ahh, the one who gave Brandon a little taste of his own medicine?"

A soft laugh bubbles out. "I wouldn't go that far."

"I don't know. Everyone was talking about what happened. I have to admit, I was impressed. Must be nice to have someone to look out for you like that."

I nod. "Yeah, it is. I know he'll always have my back."

We've made it to the front of the line and I order three slices for Matty and two for me.

"Mind if we join you?" Makenzie asks, after ordering. "I could use a break from the never-ending conversation about eyeshadow."

"Sure." I lead them over to the table Matty grabbed, pull up a table next to it, and introduce Matty to the other girls.

We're in the middle of a conversation about Matty's favorite TV show, *Robot Wars*—who knew Makenzie was a sucker for robot battles—when I catch sight of Aspen and her Aunt Beth walking on the other side of the food court. Their heads are turned, talking to each other and I drop the pizza on my plate, dipping my shoulders low to try and hide behind Matty.

He gives me a puzzled look, turning from his discussion with Makenzie. "What are you doing?" he asks.

I shake my head, trying to play it cool. "Nothing."

He turns around and from the look on his face it's obvious he saw her too. "Do you wanna leave?" he asks, his tone genuine.

Makenzie's gaze follows Matty's, her expression impassive. "You okay?" she asks.

I take a deep breath, annoyed with myself that even after all this time she still has the ability to cause a reaction like this.

"No," I say, shakier than I intend. "I'm fine."

He looks as if he's about to argue and instead shrugs and inhales another bite of pizza. "So when exactly do you leave for Arizona?" he asks, his mouth full.

"I've heard there are some really awesome places to hike. You should check out Seven Falls. My cousin hiked up there and said the waterfalls were breathtaking," Makenzie chimes in.

"There's a summer program Ms. McCalister said I could attend at the end of July. They've worked it out with the campus so we can move into the dorms early. So I'll be leaving the second week of July." I turn towards Makenzie. "I'll be sure to add it to my list of things to do while I'm there. In between practice, class, studying, and more practice."

"Do you know who you're rooming with?" Matty asks.

I nod. "Yeah. It's another freshman who's also on the team. Her name's Niko and we've been talking quite a bit. She seems really cool."

"Niko? That's an interesting name. I wonder where she's from," says Makenzie.

"Maybe I can meet her when I come visit you," says Matty.

I smile. "Yeah, I'd like that."

I pop the last bit of the crust into my mouth when a familiar voice says, "Hey, Charlie."

I turn to the left, not surprised to see Aunt Beth standing beside us. I glance around, Aspen is nowhere in sight.

I finish chewing before I return the gesture.

"Congratulations. I hear graduation is not too far away."

"Thanks." I gesture to Matty and the rest of the table, introducing her to everyone.

"It's nice to meet you all," she says with a smile plastered on her face. She glances around like she's searching for something, "I'm not sure where Aspen went, we came out here so I could take her shopping for a new graduation outfit."

"Charlie found a new outfit too. So much better than the old one," Matty says.

"That's great. Aspen wanted a new dress. Ah, there she is," she says, waving Aspen over. "Aspen, look who I ran into."

She wraps her arms around her torso like she's trying to fold herself in. "Hey," she says tepidly.

"Hey," I say. Matty gives her a head-nod and pushes the last of the crust in his mouth. Makenzie lightly waves and the other two are so deep in a discussion about mascara that they don't even register what's going on.

Aunt Beth glances back and forth between us, sensing the tension. Her gaze falls back to Aspen. "Well we better get going. It was good to see you, Charlie. Best of luck to you this fall. It was nice to meet you all."

"Thanks," I manage to say with a halfhearted smile. Like a magnet, my gaze finds Aspen. A hint of sorrow flutters behind her eyes before she waves softly and trails behind her Aunt.

"Well that was…interesting," Matty says, after a beat.

I shrug my shoulders, feigning indifference. We spend another twenty minutes chatting with Makenzie before we say our goodbyes and head for the car.

"You sure you're okay?" Matty asks once we've pulled out onto the main road.

"Yeah." I turn, facing him as we come to a stop at a red light. "I'm good. I promise."

He holds my stare. After a beat he says, he says, "Did you see the look on Aspen's face when she realized it was you? It looked like she'd seen a ghost. She just seemed sad. I felt kind of bad for her."

"Me too," I mumble, not surprised he picked up on something so subtle. I keep my eyes on the road ahead, trying to ignore the inkling that maybe she still feels something for me.

The last week of high school comes and goes without a hitch. When Saturday rolls around, I'm met with smiles and the smell of pancakes as I venture into the kitchen in my cap and gown.

Gramps steps over, embracing me in a bear hug. "I'm so proud of you, Monkey." I inhale the familiar scent that is him and muffle a 'thank you' into his shoulder.

Nana sets down my plate, her mouth pulled into a cheerful smile. "We are so proud. Graduating high school is a big deal."

Matty is the last to say something, shuffling over to fold me into a hug. "Proud of you, sis."

"Thank you," I say to all of them.

After we finish breakfast and clean up, we pile into the car and head for the local university for the ceremony. We finally find a parking spot after circling the lot four times, and I race ahead of them to meet up with Riley before everything starts.

The arena is a gymnasium that they converted to accommodate our graduation. They brought in a stage, lined up numerous rows of chairs, and the teachers and staff are scattered about in their college caps and gowns, guiding us to the correct area.

I slowly look around, taking everything in—the teachers, my classmates, the parents, grandparents, aunts, uncles, and friends that came to watch and celebrate—and it occurs to me how much I've grown. I'm not the same person I was a few short months ago. I feel confident, happy, excited for what's next, but most importantly, I feel proud—proud of who I am, and all that I've accomplished.

Makenzie waltzes towards me, her long dark hair dangling beneath her cap. "Hey," she says with a smile.

"Hey." My eyes trail the outline of her body. She's wearing a sleek, black dress, accented by a deep V-neck, underneath her unzipped gown, and red heels.

"There's a small get together at Tyler's. You coming?"

"Yeah," I say as Riley catches my eye and heads my direction.

"I guess I'll see you there."

"See you tonight."

She shuffles past me, heading to another group of girls and I catch the familiar whiff of vanilla and lavender.

"Hey, girl," Riley says beaming. "You look great. I'm diggin' the new shirt. It's different, I like it." She waves her fingers up and down, motioning to my attire. I'm wearing a navy-blue button-down with tiny white roses, a pair of khakis and a new pair of dress shoes.

"Thanks. I thought I'd change it up a bit."

"Saw you talking to Makenzie. You seem to be hanging out with her more often."

I shrug my shoulders. "We're just friends. And I've only hung out with her a few times."

"Hey, all I'm sayin' is that if you're ready to get back out there, I think you should. Whether that's with her or somebody else. You still coming tonight?"

"Yes, around seven, right?"

"Yeah, just wanted to make sure you weren't going to bail on me."

Before I can respond, Mrs. Burns calls over the microphone for us to take our seats. We file into the rows two-by-two like we rehearsed, while the audience quiets down around us. Mrs. Burns begins her opening speech, welcoming everyone to the ceremony, her eyes shine with the hint of tears as she tells us how proud she is of everything we've accomplished.

After Mrs. Burns finishes, Principal Lynch takes his place in front of the podium. He seems much smaller behind the podium compared to how he looked in his office all those weeks ago. He's wearing a plain black suit, his forehead shiny with sweat. He begins his speech similar to Mrs. Burns; congratulating us and thanking the parents for their support

He directs his attention back to us. "Seniors, I know you've waited a long time for this day. You're eager to walk across this stage, get your diploma, and begin the next chapter in your life. You've accomplished quite a bit and you should feel proud of yourselves. Making it this far wasn't easy but you did it anyway. You overcame the obstacles, the setbacks, the disadvantages."

He continues but I only hear bits and pieces, my mind reminiscing over the past school year. I wanted nothing more than to rush through senior year, so I could move away from here and start over somewhere new. I didn't think I'd find something that would truly make me happy in a town like BluHaven.

I was wrong. I found Aspen.

She helped me discover a new part of myself, a part that makes me feel whole. She gave me the confidence I needed to be myself, to be proud of the person I am.

We were supposed to be celebrating this day together, supposed to be looking forward to moving away together, to starting the next chapter of our life, together. I don't regret anything I've done this past year, I just wish I could've given her the confidence to stand up for herself like she did with me.

When Principal Lynch finishes his speech, our valedictorian, Keshawn Thomas moves in front of the podium. I had several classes with Keshawn and he was always really sweet. He delivers a beautiful speech and finishes by thanking those that helped us along the way.

Finally, the time comes for our names to be called. You can hear the pride radiating from the stands as students walk across the stage to receive their diploma. I watch Riley walk across, her picture-perfect smile out, ready for the photo-op at the end. When Aspen walks across, she's smiling, still stunning. I watch Skylar walk across the stage, no longer having to choke back the resentment. When it's my turn, I can't stop the delighted grin that spreads across my face. I shake Principal Lynch's hand, still smiling as he hands me the diploma. It feels pretty damn good to finally have it in my hands.

When the last of the names are called, Principal Lynch gives us one last note of congratulations and then we launch our caps into the air, celebrating our official high school graduation. The people in the stands rise to their feet, the gymnasium erupting with applause. We spend a few more minutes, hugging and waving before we slowly start to fizzle out.

I weave through the horde of family members and classmates, trying to locate my own family. I spot Aunt Beth standing off to the side. I slow my pace, surprised to see Aspen's father nowhere in sight.

Aunt Beth catches my eye and gives me a gentle smile and a wave. I return the gesture as Aspen walks over and Aunt Beth wraps her in a bear hug, mumbling something in her ear that I'm too far away to hear. I watch as they walk towards the exit, Aunt Beth's arm still firmly around her.

I bring my gaze back toward the crowd and head towards the left when I spot Matty and my grandparents. Matty pulls me in for a hug, squeezing me so tight it's like he's trying to break me in half.

"Congratulations, Charlie. I'm so proud of you."

"Thanks," I say when I've caught my breath.

Gramps steps forward next, bringing his arms around me. "Congratulations, Monkey."

"Thanks, Gramps."

Nana steps around Gramps and cups my face in her hands. "I'm so proud of you, sweetheart."

"Thanks."

She keeps her hands on my face, her eyes brimming with tears. "I know we haven't seen eye to eye on everything. And I know I haven't made these past months easy on you but that doesn't mean I don't love you and I'm not proud of you. I've spent a lot of time blaming myself for what happened to your mother—thinking I wasn't on top of her like I should've been and that's why things played out the way they did. I thought I could make up for that with you and your brother—that I could somehow right those wrongs. But you're not your mother. You're strong, independent, brave, determined. And the same sweet girl you've always been, even if we don't agree on who you choose to date. I'm sorry I couldn't see that sooner. I love you so much, Charlie."

I wrap my arms around her, my eyes filling with tears hearing the words I've been desperately waiting for. "I love you so much, Nana."

We take several photos, some of all of us and a couple of just Matty and me. I find Riley so we can take some pictures as well. Her parents both give me a hug and congratulate me. My mouth starts to ache from all the smiling but I don't care. I want to savor this moment.

When we get home, I change clothes, grab a bite to eat, kiss my grandparents goodbye, and tell them I'll be back later. The drive over to Tyler's is short. He lives in a subdivision that isn't too far from my neighborhood. I park in the grass next to the other cars and head inside. There's already a crowd of about thirty-five people. I maneuver through the house, grab a drink from the kitchen, and meet up with Riley in the living room. She's standing by a table where Tyler and John are playing beer pong against Jamal and Darius.

"I thought you said this was supposed to be a small get together?" I say.

She shrugs. "That's what I thought but people just keep showing up."

The living room erupts with cheer when John nails the last shot of his game. Tyler stumbles over, clearly enjoying himself, and drapes his arm around Riley. "Did you see how good we did, babe?" he says.

"Oh yeah, you did so good," she says with a hint of sarcasm.

"Tyler, you up for a rematch?" Darius says.

"Hell yeah," Tyler says. He turns back to the table. "Where'd John go?"

Darius raises his hands, "Hell if I know. Find somebody else."

Tyler turns to Riley, a drunken smile on his face. She immediately starts shaking her head. "No way. The last time we played beer pong together, it ended in an argument."

He turns his attention to me. "Charlie. You and me, what'd you say? I've seen you on the court. Darius and Jamal don't stand a chance."

I shrug. "Alright."

Tyler throws his hands in the air like he'd just scored a touchdown.

After my third shot, the faint flush I was feeling at the beginning of the night is now in full effect. I'm not sure how, but Tyler and I manage to come out on top.

About an hour later, there's a crowd of about fifty people. I amble around the house, mingling with people. Tyler and I dominate in another game of beer pong, him doing most of the drinking, the music's on point and everybody's celebrating the fact that we are no longer high school students. I'm foraging in the kitchen for some water when I turn and see Makenzie standing next to me.

"Hey, I was wondering where you were."

She smiles. "Took longer than I thought to get away from my parents."

"Can I get you a drink?"

"Sure."

I grab one of the bottles, pour some into a cup, and hand it to her. "You don't want any?"

"I had plenty earlier, I think I'll just stick with water for now."

"You enjoying yourself?" she asks.

"Probably more than I should be."

She glances around the house before she turns back to me. Her eyes linger on my lips. "You wanna go somewhere that's not so loud?" she asks, bringing her gaze back to my eyes.

"Sure."

We head outside to the backyard where we can talk without having to shout over the music. "Wanna keep going?" she asks.

"Okay."

We walk down the path, further away from everything. She intertwines her hand with mine, sending a small shiver rippling through my body. She stops walking and turns to face me. She tilts her head slightly, her eyes locked with mine, and leans forward. She presses her lips to mine, gentle at first and when I don't pull away she parts her lips, teasing me with her tongue. I bring my hand up to her face, caressing her cheek as I slide my tongue inside her mouth.

She slides her hands down my side, stopping at my waist. She leans back, her lips pulled into a sly smile. Her grip on my hips tightens as she goes in for another kiss. My hands drift down her back, slowly inching my way underneath her shirt. Her skin is soft and warm against my fingers. Her lips trickle off mine as she kisses my neck. She tugs at my shirt, slips her hand beneath it, and runs her fingers underneath the hem of my pants.

When we come up for air, my phone rings. I take a step back and reach in my pocket to pull it out. "It's probably just my grandparents checking in. They freak if I don't answer," I say.

She nods as I unlock my phone to answer without even looking at the screen.

"Hello," I say.

"Hey," a soft voice says. "Do you have a minute? I'd really like to talk."

Chapter Fifteen

A spen's voice is all it takes to be knocked off-center. My mind races in a million different directions. I run my fingers through my hair, trying to get a grip. I'm very much aware that I'm at a party making out with another girl. I glance to Makenzie who raises a questioning eyebrow.

"Charlie? You still there?" Aspen says quietly.

"Yeah, one sec," I mumble. I hold up an index finger and walk further down the path, glancing back to see if I'm out of earshot. "What do you want?" I say, a little harsher than I intend to.

Her voice is shaky like she's been crying. "I know I'm probably the last person you want to be talking to right now…" She pauses and I wait for her to continue. "I just…I would really like to see you."

I let out an exasperated breath. "I'm kind of in the middle of something right now."

"I…I'm sorry, I know you probably hate me." Her voice is weak and traffic echoes in the background.

"*Hate* you?"

"After everything I put you through, I didn't think you would actually pick up."

I take a breath. "Aspen, I don't hate you. And a lot of what happened wasn't your fault." The sound of a car horn resonates through the phone. "Where are you anyways?"

"I…I went for a walk. I really screwed up, Charlie." Her breathing turns into shallow gasps.

I stand there, with the phone pressed to my ear, debating what I should do. I toy with the idea of just hanging up the phone but I can't bring myself to do it. Part of me wants to drop everything and rush over to her, but it felt like I was finally moving on. Wouldn't running right back to her be like taking one step forward and three steps back?

"I lied to you," she chokes out.

"What are you talking about?"

"What I told you that day in the art room after school. I didn't mean it."

The hairs on the back of my neck stand up at the crunch of leaves and sticks. I exhale slowly, trying to force my emotions back down. "Look, I can't do this right now. I gotta go." I hang up the phone, taking a few moments before I turn back to Makenzie.

Her expression's genuine. "Everything okay?"

I nod. "Yeah." I smile but she sees right through it.

"That was Aspen wasn't it?"

"Is it that obvious?"

"Yeah," she sighs. "But it's okay. I knew what I was getting myself into."

I look up at her. "I'm sorry. I didn't think she would still have this effect on me."

Makenzie walks over to me, gently grabbing my elbow. "It's okay. It's late anyways and it seems like you need to figure some things out."

"No, I just need a minute—"

"Charlie," she says, cutting me off. "It's okay. I'm not upset or anything." Her smile is sincere and I produce a feeble one in return.

"I'm going to head back to the house but I hope you figure everything out, Charlie."

I nod. "Me too. Thanks, Makenzie."

She turns and heads back to the house. I rush out of the house without a second thought. I climb into my car and rest my hands on the steering wheel, trying to catch my breath.

I call Aspen back and she picks up on the first ring. "Charlie?"

"Hey," I whisper.

"Hey."

"Where are you?"

"By that steakhouse we went to with Aunt Beth."

"Stay there, I'm coming to you."

"Really?"

"Yeah, be there soon."

It takes me eight minutes to drive to *The Wild Bites*. I spot Aspen and pull up next to her on the side of the road. I roll down the passenger side window. "Get in."

She slides into the passenger seat, running her hands through her hair trying to tame it. She's wearing a pair of yoga pants, an oversized long-sleeve shirt and there are dark circles under her eyes. She still looks beautiful.

"What are you doing out here?" I ask.

"I needed some fresh air, and I really wanted to talk to you."

"Why now?"

She fidgets with her hands in her lap and I can see her eyes brimming with tears. "I'm sorry, I don't even know what you might think of me. Maybe I shouldn't have called you."

I sigh loudly. "I thought I was over you, had finally moved on, and then you just call me out of the blue and it's like I'm right back to square one."

"I'm sorry. I know I wasn't fair to you. I can't blame you for being angry with me."

"I'm not angry. Okay, maybe I was a little angry, but mainly I was just hurt. I poured my heart out to you and you didn't care. You just stood there watching me bleed."

She shakes her head, tears streaming down her face. "That's not true."

"What do you mean?" I snap as the anger rises. "I told you I loved you and that I wanted to be with you and you just walked away. You couldn't even say it back."

"I care about you, I still do. I never stopped. But when my dad found out about us and saw that picture…" She pauses, wiping her face with the back of her hand. "He was so angry and I just didn't know what else to do. I tried to stand up to him. I told him he couldn't control who I dated. But it just made him angrier. He just kept saying that it was all in my head; that me being with you was wrong. He was relentless. I was scared, Charlie and part of me was ashamed—not about being with you but about not fighting for you more. And there was still the part of me that wanted to please my father. I know how fucked-up that sounds. But at the end of the day, he's still my dad. And then I saw what he did at your grandparents and I was afraid of what else he might do. I thought cutting you out of my life would be easier on both of us, but it wasn't." She's sobbing now, her breathing raspy. "I thought pretending to date Brandon would get him off my back but I just couldn't keep up the charade anymore. It wasn't worth it."

"I had…I had no idea, Aspen. I'm sorry. But why now? What happened?"

"Aunt Beth," she whispers. Her face is flushed, eyes reddened as the tears continue to fall.

"What about her?"

"I started spending more time with her. I didn't really want to be home and I didn't have anyone else, so I hung out with her. After a while I finally broke down and told her what happened. I told her about us, the party, my father's reaction, everything." She lifts her head, meeting my gaze. "I even told her you said you loved me and that I was a coward and couldn't say it back. After I spilled my guts to her she said I could stay with her as long as I needed. She went with me to get some of my things and I've been with her the past couple weeks."

"How'd your father take it?"

"He was pretty upset at first and I have to admit I was more than willing to let Aunt Beth handle him. But then I thought about you and what you said. Honestly, I haven't stopped thinking about it since you said it. And you were right, Charlie. This, us…" She gestures between the two of us. "Is real. It's worth fighting for. So I told him that if he wants to be a part of my life then he has to love me for me, all of me. He doesn't get to pick and choose what he deems acceptable. I reminded him of the love he and my mom shared. How happy they were together; how you could see it written across their face, clear as day. I told him that's how I felt about you. How my days seemed to get just a little bit brighter with you around; how I felt whole and complete whenever you were with me; that I should be proud of myself, regardless of what other people think. I'm a better person because of you, Charlie."

I stare at her, my eyes wide. "Wow," is all I can manage to croak out.

She nods, her breathing beginning to steady. "Surprisingly, he took it a lot better than I thought he would. Although, he didn't say much after I finished. He just kind of stared at me with an expression that can only be described as shock. Aunt Beth and I agreed that it was best if I continued to stay with her to give both of us time to process everything."

"Shit, Aspen. I—I had no idea. Have you talked to your father since?"

"A few times but he usually just asks how I'm doing."

"I see. So why are you telling me all of this now?"

Her gaze drops to her lap as she fidgets with her hands. "I thought about just leaving you alone and trying to move on with my life. But I couldn't stop thinking about you. I know it's not really fair of me to spill on this on you now, especially after everything you've gone through. But I had to tell you how I felt. Being with you made me feel so alive, like I could conquer anything knowing I have you by my side. I'd never felt that way with anyone. I didn't even realize you *could* feel that way about someone. Until I met you. And I know I probably don't deserve someone like you but that doesn't stop me from wanting you. I love you, Charlie. I never stopped."

I stilled, my mind reeling as I try to comprehend the words that just came out of her mouth.

She looks up, her gaze meeting mine. "I want you, to be with you, Charlie. That's all that matters to me right now. I know I fucked up but please, just give me a chance to show you I mean what I say."

I stare at her, digesting everything I've heard the past hour. If I go running back to the girl that broke my heart, am I being brave or stupid? But that's the thing about love, right? You meet someone who shows you the beauty in the world when all you've ever seen was the outline on the surface. It's like you've been going through life in a desolate illusion until she opens your eyes to everything you've been missing.

I lean over, cradling her face in my hands. There's no hesitation as our lips crash into each other. The familiar feel of her mouth on mine sends rippling shivers from end to end. Every nerve in my body comes alive with sensation. I melt into her as the kiss deepens, feeling the tightness in my chest slowly dissipate.

We break apart, our foreheads pressed together. "I love you," she whispers. "I love you so much, Charlie Baker. And I never want to stop loving you."

I answer her with a kiss, hungry for another taste of her lips. "I love you too. I always will."

I feel so alive with electricity it's hard to contain my excitement when I get home. All the lights are off except for the lamp in the hallway and I quietly slip through the living room and up to my bedroom.

I know it's late but as my best friend, it's only right that Riley's the first person I tell. She picks up after the third ring, her voice groggy. "Hello?"

"Riley, it's me."

"Charlie?" She fumbles with something, her voice somewhat muffled as she says, "Is everything okay? Where did you go? You just left."

"I'm sorry I bailed out like that." I pause, suddenly afraid that speaking it out loud will make it too real, that I'll be waking up from a dream. After a moment I say, "Aspen called me."

"Really? Why?"

I take a breath and then tell her everything that happened tonight, leaving out the intimate details about our make-out session.

"Holy shit, Charlie."

"I know."

"You sure about this?"

"What do you mean?" I ask.

"It's just," she exhales slowly. "I just want to make sure you're not going to get hurt. You're my best friend, I know how much she means to you but I also saw what she put you through when things got tough. I just don't want you to make the same mistake twice."

"I get what you're saying but a lot of what happened wasn't Aspen's fault. She was just trying to make it through, just like me. I love her, Riley. I never stopped. And I want to be with her. That's all I've wanted since we first kissed."

"Okay, I hear you. Just be careful."

"I will."

"Charlie, one more thing."

"Yeah?"

"I'm happy for you."

"Thanks."

I hang up and crawl into bed. I should be exhausted after everything that's happened today but my mind is racing, replaying today's events. Aspen is the last thing on my mind when sleep finally overtakes me.

Sunday morning, I decide that I have to tell my grandparents and Matty about Aspen and I getting back together. I'm not sure how they're going to take it, but I'm not going to lie to them, not anymore.

I haven't gone to church ever since Reverend Charles came over to 'pray the gay away'. I expected a full-blown argument from my grandparents but when I told them my reasoning, they said okay but hoped I would change my mind.

I made plans to hang out with Aspen today, so I have to tell them at breakfast, before everyone leaves.

No big deal. Like ripping off a band-aid. You got this, Charlie.

Once everyone is seated, I clear my throat. "There's something I need to tell you."

They all glance up, there's eyes swimming with curiosity. I take a deep breath and then spit it out. "Aspen and I are back together."

"Since when?" Matty asks.

"Last night."

He raises a brow, nodding his head slightly. I tell them a much shorter version of the story I told Riley, once again leaving out the intimate details.

I can see Matty mulling it over, but then he grins. "I'm happy for ya, sis."

"Thanks." I glance between Gramps and Nana, the knot in my stomach growing with anticipation. Are they going to be angry? Yell? Jump for joy? Ha, yeah right.

Gramps leans forward, patting my hand. "Just as long as you're happy, sweetheart. That's all we want."

I peer at Nana when he says the word 'we'. Her expression is placid, but I can see the hint of irritation behind her facade. She looks up, her eyes meeting mine and I force myself to keep her gaze.

"Are you sure about this? That this is really what you want?" she asks.

Here we go again.

"Yes," I say, straining my voice to remain calm. "I want to be with Aspen."

She presses her lips in a taut smile. She finishes buttering her toast before she says, "I may not agree with your decision, but I love you and your grandfather's right, we just want you to be happy."

I pause, expecting her to say more but she doesn't. She sets the knife down and takes a bite of bread.

Well, that went better than expected.

I step outside just in time to see Aspen pull into the driveway. When I slide in the passenger seat beside her, the familiar sensation of butterflies flutters through me.

I lean over, pulling her in for a long, sensual kiss. "Hey," I whisper when we separate.

She gives me another kiss before saying, "What do you want to do today?"

"I don't care. Just as long as I'm with you." I interlace my fingers with her, lightly stroking the back of her hand.

"Well it's Sunday so everything is closed. But Aunt Beth is going into the office today. She apparently has a really important meeting this week and wants to be prepared. We could go over there and watch a movie or something?"

"Sounds good to me. I'm eager to see what Aunt Beth's house looks like."

She flashes me a smile. "Great."

"What does Aunt Beth do again?"

"She's a freelance accountant. She handles the accounts for most of the business in this town. She's taken on a couple more clients so she's been busy. But she's her own boss so it's flexible hours. That's what she likes most about it, at least that's what she told me."

"Sounds pretty cool."

"You should talk to her about it. You're really good with math so maybe that's something you might be interested in doing."

"Yeah, maybe."

A few minutes later we pull into the driveway of a cottage style house. The inside is warm and inviting, with numerous artworks hanging in the foyer and hall that leads to the living room. I inch closer, examining the ones closest to us.

"These yours?" I turn, looking at Aspen.

She nods.

"Damn, baby. They just keep getting better and better. I can't wait to see what you come up with at the Walton Institute."

She grins, her face turning a light shade of pink. "Thanks."

I trail behind her as she gives me a brief tour of the rest of the house. We pass through the living room with a large, comfy-looking couch taking up a significant portion of the space, until we come to one of the two bedrooms in the back. Her bedroom at Aunt Beth's house is much smaller but there's a sense of homeliness that wasn't present in her old room.

"There's no TV in here so we'll have to watch it on my laptop. Is that okay?"

"Sure."

I let her pick the movie, some romantic comedy I've never seen before. It doesn't take long for our limbs to become tangled, our mouths pressed up against each other.

Our kisses deepen, both of us frantic to remove the barriers keeping our skin apart. I rip off her shirt, wasting no time to unfasten her bra. She does the same to me, her lips leaving a warm trail on my skin as she kisses down my torso. I run my hands up and down her back, the softness of her skin igniting the nerves in my fingertips. I welcome the familiar tremble tingling in my belly and without a second thought, I allow it to take over.

Later, we lie in bed, snuggled up next to each other; the soft drone of the movie playing in the background. I shift to my side, trying to take in every perception that I can, from the softness of her skin, the warmth of her body, the hint of coconut when I breathe her in, the color of her hair. I could keep going, the list continuing to grow. I want nothing more than to savor this moment forever, locking it away deep inside me where I'll always be able to find it.

"I love you," she whispers into my hair.

"I love you too."

The rest of the day consists of us cuddling on her bed, watching movies (okay, maybe we're making out instead of paying attention to what's playing on the screen.) When she drives me home, we make a detour to the abandoned park I showed her the night we played Crossroads. We pull into the empty parking lot and she shuts the car off.

"Do you remember when you showed me this place?" she asks.

I nod. "Yeah, I do." I reach over, interlacing her fingers with mine.

"I came here a lot after everything happened."

"Really?"

"Yeah. When I needed a break from all the craziness, this is where I would come. It reminded me of you; made me feel safe, even if it was only for a little while."

I use my thumb to stroke the back of her hand, then I bring it to my lips and place a gentle kiss on each of her knuckles. "Did it help?" I ask.

"For a while. It was the one place I could get away from everything and be alone."

"I know what you mean."

We're silent for a few minutes, both of us staring out at the empty lake in front of us. The moonlight dissipates its white-silver glow onto the surface, illuminating everything around us. The trees towering around the lake, become silhouetted against the deep velvety sky. I haven't been here since I showed it to Aspen, months ago. Looking out, I sense the slight change in the air, as if this place too has evolved.

I shift my gaze back to Aspen. "You don't have to be alone ever again," I whisper.

"You promise?"

"Always."

Chapter Sixteen

The first week of summer vacation seems almost unreal as it settles upon me that there is no high school anymore. As the first few days pass, I grow more excited about being on the verge of a grand adventure. Soon enough, I'll be heading to Arizona, leaving BluHaven behind me, at least for now.

I've spent every day with Aspen. It doesn't matter what we're doing, just as long as we're together. It's almost as if we're trying to make up for lost time.

On Friday, we decide to hit up the mall. We've spent nearly the entire week cuddled up together either in the bedroom, on the couch, or in the car, and we figure it's time to do something outside for a change.

We wind our way in and out of different stores, stopping to try on clothes or anything else we see that looks appealing. When we come out of the first store, Aspen slips her hand into mine. I stop, pull back and glance around to see if anyone noticed.

She looks at me, her lips quirked into a cunning grin. "We don't have to hide anymore, babe. We can walk through the mall holding hands." She takes a step forward sliding her hand back into mine. The smile on her face is all it takes for my hand to relax in hers.

We continue wandering around the mall, not really having a specific destination in mind, just simply enjoying the comfort of being together. When we come across the lingerie store, Aspen heads inside, dragging me behind her.

I've never been in a lingerie store, never really felt the need to go in one. I glance around the store, taking in the copious displays of undergarments dispersed around the store. I shuffle awkwardly behind Aspen, not really having a desire to try anything on.

She turns around and flashes me a smile. "See anything you like?"

I shrug, taking another look around. "Not exactly."

"Not for you," she says with a devilish grin. "For me."

That got my attention.

I turn back to the lingerie hanging on the racks. The thought of Aspen wearing some if this makes my head spin. I adore seeing her in her bra and panties, but something like this, oh man.

I shift my head back to her. "I'm sure we can find something that'll suit you."

Twenty minutes later, Aspen decides on a red, lacy bra and a pair of matching panties. We spend the rest of the afternoon roaming aimlessly around the mall, our hands intertwined the entire time.

As the first two weeks in June peel away, we fall into a pleasant rhythm; one that begins with her picking me up and ends with a long make-out session before she drops me off. We take advantage of every opportunity we can to rip our clothes off each other, whether it's in her bedroom, the back of the car, on the couch, even in the kitchen once or twice. We've grown closer than ever, and I find myself falling more in love with her every day.

I've had Aspen over to the house a few times. Matty is always very friendly and welcoming and so is Gramps. Nana on the other hand, not so much. She may have had a revelation about me being gay and that she just wants me to be happy, but it's very obvious that Aspen and I being together, especially in her house, makes her uncomfortable. It could be worse though. For now, we spend most of our time somewhere away from people, where we can just be alone, and just be together.

Riley was apprehensive at first, wanting to make sure that I wasn't putting myself out there just to be stepped on, again. But she's come around. We even went on a double date with her and Tyler. I have to admit, it was much more enjoyable than when I got roped into that blind date with Noah.

"Aunt Beth wants to have you over for dinner tonight. She said she wants to celebrate our graduation and she enjoys your company. And things at work are finally settling down so she would love to see you before we leave for Arizona," Aspen says when I slide in the car that morning.

"Will your dad be there?" I ask, trying to hide the uneasiness in my voice.

"I don't think so."

"How are things with him? Have you two talked more?"

She shrugs. "He's started texting me more. He's asked me about college a few times, what I'm excited about, stuff like that. He talked about getting together sometime before I leave but I'm not sure. He almost sounds like my old dad, before everything happened. I miss him. I know how crazy that sounds but the last couple times we've texted, he's sounded different." She dips her head. "I don't know, maybe I'm just being naive."

I reach over, gathering her hand in mine, and gently stroke her knuckles. "What you're feeling is completely understandable and it makes sense. Maybe he really does want to try to fix things?"

"I don't know, Charlie. I mean what if it's too good to be true?"

"I can't tell you what to do, babe. This is completely your call and I will support you either way. But if my mom called me up out of the blue saying she wanted to talk, I don't think I could not go. Yeah, maybe it'd be a mistake and she'd end up hurting me again. But at the end of the day she's still my mom. And I think I would want to see her. Your dad's done a lot of messed up shit and I know he hasn't treated you with the respect you deserve, but at the end of the day he's still your dad."

"So you think I should see him? After everything he's done? After how he treated you?"

"I'm not condoning his behavior but maybe you need to give him another chance. I don't know if my Nana will ever fully accept that I'm gay, but that doesn't mean I don't want her to be a part of my life. And that's okay. Same goes for your dad. What's not okay is him treating you like a piece of property. But if it seems like he's at least trying, maybe you should hear him out."

"I don't know, baby. I'm not sure I'm ready. After everything he's done, saying sorry and asking me about college a few times doesn't magically make everything better."

"I hear you. Why not think about it for a few days and then decide?"

"Okay."

We spend the rest of the day driving around town, stopping at various places along the way. My gaze is focused on the landscape outside of the window when Aspen shifts the car in park. I look over to see the familiar structure of *The Book Worm*.

"You remember that day you showed me this place?" she asks, her eyes fixed on the door.

"Yeah. That was a good day."

She nods. "It was. C'mon, let's go inside."

We climb out of the car and make our way to the doors. The interior looks the exact same as the day we first stepped foot inside. We stroll casually around the towering shelves, grabbing a book here and there until we come upon a cozy spot in the back corner. Aspen takes a seat in one of the chairs, and pulls the other one next to her, motioning for me to sit.

We're skimming through the books we picked out when Aspen lifts her head, giving me a look that makes me put down the book in my hand.

"What's up?" I ask.

"Do you remember what we talked about that day you showed me this place?"

"Yeah. You told me about how your mom used to read you stories; how she made you fall in love with reading and getting lost in the story."

"I had never told anybody that story."

I reach my hand across and place it on top of hers. "So why me?" I ask.

"I don't really know. I just felt safe around you, like I could tell you anything and you wouldn't judge me or look at me differently because of it." She stops, raising her eyes to meet mine. "You were the first person that saw me for *me*. When my mom died, I never thought I'd even feel whole again, like there would always be a part of me that was missing. And then I met you. When I'm with you, I feel like I can conquer the world, that no matter what happens I'll be okay, because I have you."

I lean forward, not caring that we're in public, in the middle of a bookstore, and bring my lips to hers, for a long, delicious kiss.

"I love you so much," I say.

"I love you too, baby." She settles back into her chair. "Can you imagine all the amazing things we're going to get to do when we get out of this small town?"

"I know, I can't wait. Four years, and then it's just you and me."

"It's not that long," she says, the uneasiness in her voice seeping through.

"Hey," I say softly, taking her hand. "It'll be fine. We're only a train ride away. We can see each other every weekend. You can come to some of my games and I'll come to your art shows and then we'll graduate and be together."

"You're right, it'll be fine." She gives me a sheepish smile.

"Hey, if we can survive having to pretend we're not dating and being outed like that, we can survive anything."

She nods, her expression more relaxed. "Good point. I just want to be with you."

"I'm not going anywhere." I lean down for another kiss.

When we arrive at Aunt Beth's house later that night, Aspen and I walk hand in hand up to her door.

Aunt Beth pulls me into a hug as soon as we step foot inside. "Charlie, my dear, I have missed you. I'm so happy you could make it to dinner."

"Me too."

We follow her into the kitchen as a mouthwatering scent fills the air.

"That smells delicious," I say.

She smiles, pulling a dish out of the oven. "It's Aspen's favorite, chicken pasta bake."

"Aunt Beth makes the best food," Aspen says. "I told her for my going away present I want a cookbook of all her recipes so I can take them with me."

"I'm working on it," she says with a grin. "Take a seat at the table and I'll dish it up."

Aspen wasn't lying, Aunt Beth's chicken pasta bake is heavenly. It might be even better than Nana's famous lasagna.

"I'm so glad you and Aspen are back together," Aunt Beth says.

I swallow my bite, the heat rising to my cheeks as I chew. "Me too."

"Aspen told me about everything that happened. I'm sorry. Nobody should have to go through something like that."

I shrug. "It's okay."

"No it's not, but I'm glad to see you two made it through. I know it's not easy being gay, especially in a town like this." She sets her fork down and leans forward. "She also told me what my brother did, about showing up to your house and telling your grandparents everything."

I stop eating, my face turning a dark shade of crimson now.

"I'm sorry he did that, it wasn't his place. And I will not let him do something like that again," she says, her tone rigid.

I look up, meeting her eye. "It's okay, I think he was just trying to look out for Aspen, even if his methods were a little…harsh."

"How are your grandparents with things now?" she asks.

"My grandfather seems to be okay with everything and Matty is super supportive. My grandmother on the other hand, wants me to be happy but it still makes her uncomfortable."

"Well I'm glad you have some support over there."

"Me too."

We spend the rest of the evening talking about our plans for college, move-in day, classes, adventures we want to go on in Arizona, and how happy we are about finally being out. Aunt Beth brings out a small cake that says, "Congrats" and a tub of vanilla ice cream for dessert. After our bellies are stuffed, Aunt Beth gives me a hug goodbye with the promise of doing this again before we leave for school.

Aspen received her official welcome package to the Walton Institute in the mall the other day. Along with a packet of 'Welcome Info', financial aid details, and a map of campus, was a list of recommended necessities for freshmen moving into the dorms. Aspen takes this as a sign that we need to start packing.

"But you still have like a month before you leave." I say. I'm lying on the bed, while Aspen shuffles around me, throwing clothes in different piles.

"But you leave in a couple of weeks and you haven't even started."

"It won't take that long, and besides all the stuff I'm going to pack I still use so I'll just have to repack it again."

She shakes her head, feigning irritation. "You can at least start sorting some of your things."

"Like you're doing with your abundance of clothes." I motion to the various mounds scattered all over her room.

"There's a method to my categorization. You gotta sort your clothes by season, so you know which ones you can pack away for a while and which ones you'll need to have available."

I roll my eyes, "Babe, you've seen my closet right? I don't think I need to sort my clothes based on seasons unless you can tell me which t-shirts I should wear when."

She wads up the shirt in her hand and throws it at me, smiling. I toss it to the side of the bed, sit up, and scoot to the edge. I grab her arm and pull her closer to me, stretching up to taste her lips.

"Baby," she says, stepping away, "You said we could be productive today."

"And we have been," I wrap my hands around her waist. "I think we deserve a little break, don't you?"

Her eyes meet mine and for a second I think she's going to argue and pull away. Then she places her hands around my neck and leans in. "Just a quick break," she whispers.

I close the inch between us, brushing our lips in a slow, soft kiss. I press her body closer to mine, my hands sliding underneath her shirt as the kiss deepens. I shift back to the head of the bed. She slowly crawls on top of me, her gaze locked with mine as a shudder flutters down my spine. Our hips connect, our bodies molding together. Aspen leans down, kissing me so hard and so quickly that I lose all sense of existence; unable to focus on anything but her tongue and how her body fits so perfectly into mine. We tumble around on the bed, a tangle of arms and legs as I once again surrender to her.

We spend what's left of the afternoon sorting the rest of her clothes. I had no idea there are specific colors that go with each season, or exactly how many different types of shirts and pants combinations Aspen actually owned.

"Oh shoot," she says as she rifles through the cluttered mess atop her desk.

"What's wrong?"

"I think I left my pastel set at the house." She glances at the clock hanging on the wall. "My dad should still be at work. Can we swing by the house before I drop you off?"

I lift myself up off the bed. "Sure."

It doesn't take long to drive across town and pull into the familiar driveway.

"Garage door is closed which means he's probably not home." Aspen gets out of the car and heads for the front door. "We'll be quick."

She unlocks the door and I shuffle behind her as we enter the dismal residence of her father. Aspen switches on the lights as I follow her through the house. The living room is a mess; various containers of take-out are scattered across the table. The kitchen is filthy, with an assortment of beer cans littering the counters. A musty smell fills my nostrils as we climb the stairs.

Her bedroom looks about the same as the last time I was here, except for the lack of personal items and clothes. Aspen begins by rifling through her desk, hastily moving from one draw to the next.

"Can I help?" I ask.

"I'd say yes but you don't know what I'm looking for." She moves on from the desk and heads for the closet.

"Any luck?"

"No," she huffs. She moves on from the closet and positions herself on her hands and knees beside the bed. A few minutes later, she snaps her head up with a smile on her face. "Found it." She pulls a thin, black container out from under the bed.

"Aspen?" someone hollers from downstairs. "Is that you?"

Aspen's head snaps up, her eyes wide. "Shit," she hisses. "I didn't think he'd be home this early."

The distant thump of footsteps rumbles up the stairs and three seconds later Mr. Sullivan is standing in the doorway. There's an uncomfortable silence that envelopes the room as he glances at Aspen. A look of disgust flickers behind his eyes when he shifts his gaze to me.

He's wearing a plain black suit but it's wrinkled, the right side of his button-down untucked, and there's what appears to be a stain on the front. His hair's longer, unkempt, like he barely tried to fix it this morning. There are dark circles around his eyes and he looks tired but it's more than that. He looks like a disheveled mess compared to the man I met the first time I was here.

A few more seconds pass before he finally speaks. "Well this is a surprise."

Aspen's eyes flicker from me to her father. "Uh...I needed to get some art supplies."

"I see." He glances at me, and does a poor job of trying to mask his revulsion before turning his attention back to Aspen.

After a moment Aspen takes a small step towards the door. "Well we should probably be going now."

"Wait. You just got here and it's been so long since I've seen you. Wouldn't you at least like to stay for dinner?"

Aspen looks from her father to me. I stare back at her with the same bewildered expression. She turns back to her father. "Aren't you going to at least make some sort of acknowledgment to Charlie?" She gestures in my direction and my face immediately begins to blush.

Mr. Sullivan glances at me, his lips turning downwards as his mouth drops into a small *O*. After a beat he says, "Uh..." He pivots on his feet, turning his body so he no longer has to face me.

"Unbelievable," she snaps, charging past him through the door.

He grabs her arm. "Honey, wait," he pleads.

"Why? So you can continue to ignore Charlie and act like she's invisible? I can't believe you."

"Aspen, please. I'm trying."

She wrangles free from his grasp and throws her hands up in the air. "You call that trying? You couldn't even say a simple 'hello' to her? Does being around my girlfriend make you that uncomfortable?"

He takes a gradual step towards her. "Aspen…I…"

"What Dad? You said you wanted another chance. Well, here it is." She spreads her arms out wide, motioning to the area around her. "Show me you're trying." She walks back into the room, gripping my hand in hers. "Try acknowledging my girlfriend like she's an actual person and not a stray dog you're trying to get rid of. Why is this so hard for you to do? I'm not asking you to convert to Buddhism, I'm simply asking you to support me."

"I do support you," he seethes. "I've given you everything you could possibly want."

Her voice rises as she takes another step towards him. "Everything except acceptance. Don't you get that? I don't care about the fancy house, or the nice clothes, or the shiny car." She exhales a long, slow breath as her shoulders sulk. "I just want you to love me for me. Is that so hard? Mom did. So why can't you?"

"Because I don't want you to end up like your mother!" he spits. The second the words are out of his mouth, his demeanor falters. He takes a step towards Aspen, his hand outstretched as if to touch her. "Aspen…I…"

She recoils at the sight of his hand, stumbling backward as he inches closer.

"Aspen," he whispers. "I didn't mean that. I—"

She snatches the pastels off the bed and charges through the door before he can finish his sentence. I awkwardly trail behind her, doing my best to maneuver around her father before I pick up my pace as we retreat to the car. We make it several blocks down the road before she pulls over, buries her face in my shoulder, and cries.

The last week of June is supposed to be windy and stormy with a prediction of over six inches of rain—which pretty much mimics Aspen's mood. Ever since the run-in with her dad, Aspen hasn't had the energy to do much of anything. I thought she would snap out of it after a few days but every time I suggest doing something other than lie around she makes up some excuse about not feeling up to it. I know she's hurting and I want nothing more than to take the pain away.

So today I've come up with the idea to surprise her. I stopped at the store and bought all her favorite snacks—Twizzlers, popcorn, strawberry ice cream, Cheetos, and pickles. I went to three different shops—the last one being forty-five minutes outside of town—to pick up her favorite movie, *LoveStruck*. I personally don't care for the movie but she loves it so much she can practically recite it in her sleep.

I gather the various assortment of goodies and knock on the front door. Aunt Beth answers and ushers me inside.

"What's all that?" Aunt Beth asks

"I thought binging on junk food and watching her favorite movie might cheer her up."

"That's very sweet of you."

"How is she?"

"About the same. But I'm sure she'll be happy to see you. She's in the bedroom. I've got to run to the office but I won't be too long."

"Alright, I'll see you later." I turn and head towards the bedroom.

"Hey, baby." I lean over and give Aspen a kiss on the top of her head. She's sitting up in bed, reading a book and I take that as a good sign.

She smiles. "Hey."

"How're you?"

"I'm okay."

"I brought you something."

"Oh yeah?"

I grab the snacks from the grocery sack and begin tossing them on top of her covers. "I've got all your favorite snacks and…" I pull the movie out last and hand it to her. "Your favorite movie."

She looks up and smiles. "Baby, you didn't have to do this."

"I know how upset you've been the past few days and I thought this might help."

"But you don't even like this movie."

"But I like you." I lean in and give her a kiss. "And it brings me so much joy to hear you quote the movie word for word."

A soft laugh bubbles out. "Thank you," she whispers.

We spend the rest of the afternoon snuggled on the couch, snacking on junk food, and watching the cheesy romantic comedy. I don't know what it is about those movies or why Aspen likes them so much but apparently it was just what she needed.

Aunt Beth comes home not too long after the movie is over and joins us in the living room. "I take it a movie and snacks did the trick?"

Aspen nods and reaches over to grab my head. "It was perfect. Thank you, baby."

"Anytime."

"You stayin' for dinner, Charlie?"

"I actually need to get home. I promised Matty I'd help him with his summer robotics project tomorrow."

"What kind of project?" Aunt Beth asks.

"Something for the advanced Engineering and Design class he wants to take next year. I'm not sure how much help I'll actually be though."

"I bet he just wants to spend time with you before you leave," says Aspen.

"Are you kidding? He's already talked about turning my room into his workshop the second I'm gone."

"I'm just saying, to me it looks——"

Aspen's phone rings, cutting her off. She looks at her phone and glances at Aunt Beth and me before getting up and walking towards her room. She leaves the door slightly ajar as she brings the phone up to her ear.

A few minutes later she returns to the living room, twirling strands of hair between her fingers.

"Who was it?" I ask, unable to hide my curiosity.

"My dad."

"What'd he want?"

She doesn't answer right away. Instead, she slowly walks over to the couch and sits back down.

"Aspen, honey. What'd he say?" Aunt Beth says.

Another moment passes before Aspen speaks. "He wants me to come over. He said he wants to apologize and try to work things out. It sounded like me meant it."

I glance at Aunt Beth, trying to mask the apprehension on my face. "Really?"

"Yeah. He said these past few months he's been all alone has given him a lot of time to think about things—think about our relationship. And seeing me the other day really put things into perspective. He wants me to come over so we can reconcile. It sounded like he'd been crying, like he really wants to fix things."

"So are you gonna go?"

"I don't know. I'm still not sure if I actually believe him. What'd you think?"

"I don't really know if I can answer that for you, but I have to admit I am a little hesitant."

Aspen looks to Aunt Beth, her eyes questioning.

She smiles at her. "I think this is for you to decide. But if it sounded like he meant it then maybe you should at least hear him out."

"Whatever you want to do baby, I'll support you…" I pause, glancing up to meet her eye.

"I feel like there's a but coming," she says.

"But I just think you should be careful. I know how much your father means to you but I don't want to see you get hurt again."

"So you don't think I should go?"

"That's not what I said. I just want you to think about it. But in the end it's your call."

"Okay." We sit in silence for several minutes before Aspen looks up and says, "I think I'm gonna go. If he's willing to try then so should I."

"Alright. Do you want me to come with you?" I ask.

She shakes her head. "No. I think this is something I need to do by myself."

"Okay. You mind dropping me off at home first?"

"Of course."

"Please be careful, you two," Aunt Beth says as we rise from the couch. "The weather is just supposed to get worse and the roads can get pretty slick in the rain."

Aspen gives me a subtle eye roll before plastering a smile on her face saying, "Whatever you say, Aunt B."

The drive home is silent, the only sound coming from the windshield wipers streaking across the glass as the rain pours down.

"You sure you don't want me to go with you?"

"I'm sure." She reaches over, taking my hand. "But thank you."

I kiss the back of her hand. "Will you call as soon as you leave and tell me how it went?"

"Sure."

Aspen pulls in the driveway and I lean over to give her a kiss goodbye. "I love you, so much."

"I love you too."

When I step inside the house, I'm met with the decadent aroma of Gramps' famous BBQ chicken.

"Hey, Monkey," Gramps hollers when I close the door. I walk into the kitchen and greet him with a peck on the cheek. "You're just in time for dinner."

"Great."

"Where's Aspen?" Matty asks when he sits down at the table.

"Uh, she had a thing with her dad."

"Oh, well are we still on for tomorrow?"

"Yep."

"Isn't it so nice to have dinner just the four of us?" Nana says when we've all sat down at the table.

Gramps gives her a reassuring smile as he passes the plate of chicken around. I focus on my glass of water, ignoring Nana's comment. Our dinner conversation mainly consists of Matty talking about the project he's been working on all summer. I do my best to feign interest as he goes into detail about the switchboard. I don't even know what that is.

After dinner, I head upstairs to my room, double-checking my phone to see if Aspen texted or called. She didn't.

I'm not sure why but I have the sudden urge to pack. Welcoming a distraction, I begin rifling through my closest, dresser, and desk, sorting items into different piles. I'm about an hour into it when my phone buzzes.

"Hello?"

"Hey babe, it's me," Aspen says, the sound of thunder booming in the background.

I lift myself up on the floor and settle on my bed. "Hey, is it still pouring out?"

"Yeah, it's only gotten worse."

"Should you really be on the phone if it's that bad?"

"But I couldn't wait to tell you everything."

"Oh yeah? How'd it go?"

"It went pretty good...I think."

"Really? What'd he say?"

"A lot actually. When I first got there it was really awkward. We both kind of sat in the living looking at anything besides each other. But the house was clean and didn't smell bad." I can hear her smile coming through the phone as she speaks. Maybe she and her father really can fix this.

"Anyways, he said he's been miserable these last few weeks without me. He's missed so much these past couple months and he can't stop thinking about how much more he's going to miss out on. He wants to work things out—wants to make it right."

"Do you believe him?"

After a moment she says, "Yeah... I think I do. Charlie, you didn't see the look in his eyes—the desperation as he waited for me to say something after he was done. He sounded like he meant it. He even asked about you."

"Seriously?"

"Yeah. He asked if you made me happy."

I can't help the smile that tugs at my lips as I say, "What'd you tell him?"

"What'd you think I told him? Yes, of course."

"I'm really happy for you, baby," I say sincerely.

"Really?"

"Of course. I want you to have a relationship with your father. And I'm really excited to get to know him."

"You have no idea how much it means to hear you say that. I'm really——"

The piercing screech of the tires squealing and the deafening sound of metallic scraping against concrete howls through the phone before the line goes dead.

Chapter Seventeen

What began as a simple drizzle has now become a wall of water. The raindrops strike the concrete, beating the Surface like they're bullets from above. I rush to my car and climb in, my shirt already sticking to my back. I put the car in reverse and slam on the gas, nearly running over the mailbox on my way out.

The wipers go into overdrive trying to keep up with the torrential downpour. Visibility is reduced to less than ten feet. Any depression in the road is filled and becomes a hydroplaning hazard.

What should've been a quick ten-minute drive to Aspen's house has now turned into an agonizing race to get from one stoplight to the next without veering off the road. I try calling Aspen back, knowing damn well I should put my phone away and focus on the road but the knot in my stomach expands with each fleeting second. I need to hear her voice; need to know if she's okay.

No answer.

After what feels like hours instead of minutes, I slowly crawl to the end of her driveway. I slam on the brakes and lean forward to peer out the windshield—looking for any sign of her shiny black Lexus. The lights positioned on the side of the house illuminate the driveway as the torrential downpour continues to fall.

The lump in my throat plummets to my stomach when my hunch is confirmed. Her car is nowhere in sight.

I pound my fist on the steering wheel as the panic slowly sets in. My hands tremble as I reach for my phone and press *call*. It doesn't even ring before I hear the high-pitched tone of her voicemail.

Where the fuck is she?

I rest my head against the steering wheel, trying to calm my nerves long enough to consider my next move. I shift the car in reverse, peeling out of the neighborhood and down the same route Aspen would've taken.

I make a left on main and head for the other side of town, the rain showing no signs of letting up. I force myself to focus on the road in front of me—refusing to let my mind consider all the devastating what-ifs.

The red and blue flashing lights twinkling in the distance snap me back to attention. I slow down to a crawl, inching the car closer. I come to a stop when I notice the flashing lights are attached to a police car idling on the other side of the road. There's an ambulance and firetruck parked haphazardly in the middle of the road.

What the hell happened?

A stroke of lightning surges across the sky in brilliant streaks, giving me just enough light to recognize the black Lexus with a Texas license plate laying upside down in the ditch.

The clouds above me ooze and billow, casting a shadowy darkness across the sky. I climb out, wincing as the icy raindrops pierce my skin. The winds increase, my pace slowing as if I'm trudging upstream against a tenacious current.

When I finally make it across the street, it's as if time has ceased to proceed. The seconds stretch out in front of me like a never-ending abyss. People in uniforms hustle past, their voices drowning in and out as the scene unfolds in front of me.

A swell of nausea rises up and I force it back down, trying to get a grip on myself. My eyes dart back and forth, attempting to decipher what's happening around me. Uniforms keep rushing by, only this time I'm able to catch bits and pieces of what they're saying.

"…Single driver…"

"…Female…Teenager…"

"…No pulse…Starting compressions…"

"…Let's get her loaded up…On my count…"

I try to articulate the words 'what happened' but all that comes out is a choked gasp. The tender grip on my arm causes me to turn to my left as a female police officer, who looks vaguely familiar, approaches me. Her lips are moving but several seconds pass before I actually hear what she's saying.

"Charlie? What are you doing here?" she shouts over the pouring rain.

"What happened?" I mumble, my eyes welling with tears.

"Do your grandparents know where you are?"

That's when it dawns on me—church. She goes to the same church as my grandparents.

"What happened?" I say again, my voice pleading. "Please."

She nods towards the overturned car, her expression dismal. "Not entirely sure. We think the driver hit a slick spot and lost control. This is one of the worst storms we've had in a while. If you're not careful on these roads it can be really dangerous when the weather gets bad."

"The driver?" I shout through the rain. "Where's the driver?"

"Loading her up now. Rushing her to the hospital for—"

The second she confirms my suspicion about who was driving the car, I march towards the ditch, my feet becoming heavier with each step. The only thing coursing through my mind right now is Aspen. I need to get to her; need to make sure she's okay.

The ground is slippery and muddy. I trip, nearly tumbling down the rest of the ditch when someone grabs my arm, pulling me back.

"You can't be down here, miss. It's too dangerous," a man says. He's wearing a fireman's uniform and his face is streaked with black residue. He gently nudges me back to the road before I have time to respond.

The female officer, whose name I still can't remember, is back by my side, motioning to the fireman. "I'll take care of her." He turns back and heads down to the car.

I take another step forward. "No, I need to see if she's okay!" I holler, though no one seems to be listening.

She holds me back, her grip firm but gentle. "See if who's okay, Charlie?" Her tone is soothing and even.

"Aspen," I stammer. "I think she was driving the car...I...I think..."
I turn back to where the Lexus is slumped against the ditch, my
hands perched on the top of my head. "I was just talking to her...I...
What happened..."

She places her hand lightly on my shoulder. "Charlie dear, you
shouldn't be out here."

"But how did this happen?" I spread my arms out wide, gesturing
to the area around me. "I was just talking to her."

I run my fingers through my hair, shaking my head over and
over. The tears continue to stream down my face as the rain descends
from the sky in a white velvet blanket.

This can't be happening.

"Is she going to be okay?" I ask.

Her gaze dances around the area, surveying the scene around us
before she turns her attention back to me. "I don't know. They've
rushed her to the hospital. Do you want me to call your grandparents?
I'm sure they're worried sick about you."

I shake my head. "No. What hospital are they taking her to?"

"Blossom Valley Medical Center, over on Tenth Avenue."

I turn and walk back to the car, my body going through the
motions while my mind catches up. The officer hollers at me but I
ignore her. I climb into the car, not caring that I'm soaking wet at
this point. I make a U-turn and head straight for the hospital, sending
up a silent prayer for Aspen.

I have no idea how but I manage to make it to the hospital in
one piece. I call Matty on the way over, doing my best to reiterate
what just happened.

I hang up and pull into the parking lot of the unfamiliar hospital. I've only been here a handful of times and never for anything
this serious.

I reach the large automatic sliding doors with their dull chrome
outline. The hospital corridor is stuffy and a draft of air hits my face,
warm and with an undertone of bleach. Ahead of me lie magnolia
white walls with cheap benign prints of uplifting scenes. Above the
double doors are large grey plastic signs indicating the different areas
of the hospital. The light is blinding compared to the darkening gloom

outside. I bring a hand up to shield my eyes and squint, trying to decide where I need to go.

I walk up to a tall, circular desk. An older lady in scrubs with bushy hair and too much eyeshadow glances up, her expression impassive. "Can I help you, dear?"

"I'm looking for Aspen. Aspen Sullivan. She was brought in from a car accident."

"Are you family?"

I shake my head. "No, I'm her girlfriend," I whisper.

The lady gives me a once-over and begins typing away on her keyboard. I tap my fingers on the desk, anxiously waiting for a response. What is taking her so long?

"They took her back into surgery. You can wait down there." She points down the hall. I follow with my eyes and see a sign that says SURGICAL WAITING AREA, and an arrow underneath it.

"Thank you," I mumble.

The waiting area is small, with red faux-leather chairs cramped together. A couple that looks to be about my grandparents' age sit in the two chairs across from the TV, their hands clasped around one another.

The rest of the hospital is buzzing with nurses, doctors, patients, families, but I've never felt so alone. They all pass by in a blur, rushing to their destination. I walk to a chair in the corner, my shoes squeaking on the tile floor, and sit. I'm trying so hard to think of Aspen—of the possibility that I may never get to see her again or the possibility that if I do, she might not be the same person. I've spent nearly every waking second with her these last few weeks and the thought of something happening to her is just…

I can't think about that.

I drop my gaze to the floor below me, remaining motionless and still as I count the scratches on the tile floor, over and over.

There's a kind of waiting that feels like a gentle onshore breeze. It isn't warm but there is a sense of peacefulness, of nature, of things expected. It's like the waiting you do in a drive-thru line, at the dentist, when you're getting your car serviced, in the pickup line at school.

Then there's the kind of waiting that feels like the end of a medieval mace is loose within your belly, disfiguring your insides while your head is being slammed into a thick brick wall. As I sit in these stiff, uncomfortable chairs, staring at the dreary wall in front of me, I know it's the latter.

They say waiting is the hardest part. But I don't think they've ever experienced the kind of waiting like this.

I drop my head into my hands, pushing the nausea back down, while every worst-case-scenario runs through my mind like snakes twisting around my brain.

This isn't fair.

I lift my head up at the faint sound of footsteps approaching. Matty and Riley quicken their pace when our eyes meet. I stand only making it two steps before I collapse into Riley's arms, my tears flooding out like a broken dam.

She holds onto me, gently stroking my back as I sob into her shoulder. After a few minutes, when my sobs have turned into soft hiccups, she pulls back, cupping my cheek in her hand.

"Matty, called me," she says, her voice comforting. "Thought you could use some support."

Matty moves closer, holding a bag in his outstretched hand. "Thought you might want a change of clothes given the weather," he says.

I take the bag from him, hoping my eyes will communicate what my words can't. "Thanks," I whisper.

Riley places her hand on my upper arm. "Go get changed, we'll wait right here for you."

I nod and head for the restroom down the hall. When I come back, Matty and Riley are sitting in two of the chairs. I take a seat in between them, no longer soaking wet but still shivering.

"Have you called Aspen's aunt or her father?" Riley asks.

I shake my head, it didn't even cross my mind. "No, I...I didn't think about it."

"Well I'm sure somebody will."

It's as if Riley's words were like a spell; seconds later Aunt Beth comes marching into the waiting area. The ghost of a smile touches the corner of her mouth when she sees me. I stand, meeting her in the middle. She doesn't wait for permission before she buries me into a hug.

"Oh Charlie. I'm so sorry," she whispers.

I pull back. "Did they tell you what happened?" I ask, feeling the tears start to boil over.

She nods, wrapping her arm around me and gesturing to the corner where Matty and Riley are sitting. "Come, sit."

I take my place between Matty and Riley, while Aunt Beth pulls a chair around, creating a circle. She leans forward, her chest rising and falling several times before she begins. "They think she lost control when she was driving. The storm made it damn near impossible to see and the road back to my house can be dangerous if you don't know where you're going. They think she hit a slick spot on the road that caused her to end up in the ditch."

"But is she going to be okay?" I mutter through quivering lips.

Aunt Beth leans forward, gently patting my knee. "She was alive when they brought her here. Her injuries are extensive but they're hopeful." She glances up, meeting my gaze. "She's a fighter, Charlie. She'll pull through."

I nod, no longer having the ability to form any comprehensible words.

The sudden burst of commotion is loud enough to make the four of us snap our heads up the same time Aspen's father comes barreling into the waiting area. Aunt Beth immediately stands up and walks over, meeting him in the middle of the room.

"What happened?" he fires at her. He glances around the room; our eyes meet briefly as anger crackles across his face like a bolt of lightning. She guides him to the empty chairs on the other side of the room. They sit with their heads bent as Aunt Beth reiterates the information in a hushed voice.

I keep my gaze fixated on the floor, willing my breathing to settle.

"You," he hisses. It's not until I lift my head that I realize he's standing in front of me, his face beat red and anger radiating off of him like smoke.

In the next instant, Aunt Beth is between us trying to guide him back to the other side of the room. He's at least twice her size so it doesn't take much for him to shuffle around her.

"You," he spits again. "This is all your fault. I should've known that her getting involved with another girl would lead to something like this. This is exactly what happened last time and now I stand to lose both my wife and my daughter."

I stare at him, unable to articulate any intelligible words. Aunt Beth grabs his arms, trying to usher him back but he doesn't budge. His face is creased in rage as his words continue to seethe through. "What are you even doing here? You don't belong here." He points towards the door. "This is not your place."

Aunt Beth steps in front of him and uses the palm of her hands to push him backward. "Charlie has just as much right to be here as you do." She propels him towards the opposite wall. "Now sit your ass down before I call someone to escort you out."

He slumps down in the chair as if all the muscles holding his body up suddenly gave out. He leans forward, bracing his elbow on his knees as he dips his head and sobs.

Aunt Beth walks over and takes the seat next to us. We sit in those rigid chairs for what feels like an eternity. No one talks, there's just the dull drone coming from the TV above us.

Chapter Eighteen

When I was ten, Matty fell off the monkey bars at the park and broke his arm. It was one of those days where the temperature was just right and he'd been talking about finally getting across the monkey bars in one try all week. He went from confident to terrified in a matter of seconds. I remember him screaming bloody murder when he realized what happened, the look on my grandparent's faces when they hauled him into the car to rush him to the ER. And the entire time I was just standing in the background, wondering how a day that started out so wonderful could end so badly.

Waiting at the hospital back then feels like nothing compared to the waiting right now. Back then I knew Matty would be okay, knew that in the end he would get to come home.

But this time? This time I'm not so sure everyone's going to come out of this in one piece.

A man in green scrubs and a surgical cap hovers at the entrance to the waiting area. My first thought is that he doesn't look like any of the doctors I've seen on TV. He looks older, tired, worn-out from countless hours of cutting, and delivering the news that no one's ready to hear.

I trail behind Aunt Beth as she rises and walks over to him. Mr. Sullivan gives me a look of indignation and I brace myself for another outburst. Instead, he just shakes his head before turning his attention to the doctor. The man's expression is impassive, and I can't decide if that's a good thing.

His eyes dart back and forth between the three of us and I'm reminded of the way Aspen's ocean blue eyes twinkle when she laughs. I push the thought from my mind as he opens his mouth to speak.

"We did everything we could, but there was just too much internal damage. I'm so sorry to tell you that she didn't make it."

My knees buckle as the weight of his words come crashing down like waves on frigid sand. Aunt Beth cups a hand over her mouth, muffling her cry, the other clutches the sleeve of Mr. Sullivan's shirt as he buries his face in his hands.

In the next second, Riley is beside me, grabbing my arm and guiding me to a chair as my legs give out. I bury my face in Riley's shoulder, as the familiar agony of wondering how everything could turn so unbearable so fast, increases with each passing moment.

Aunt Beth shuffles over, mascara running down her face as the tears continue to fall. She sits beside me, resting her hand on my shoulder for several minutes. Aspen's father takes his place on the other side of the room looking just as terrible as I feel.

I lean forward, burying my face in my hands. "This isn't fair," I murmur.

Aunt Beth gently rubs my back. "I know, sweetheart."

I stand up, the rush of anger surging through me. "No." I shake my head back and forth, my hands tremble and I rake them through my disheveled hair.

"Charlie?" Riley says, hesitantly

"No," I say, even louder. "This can't be happening." I begin pacing back and forth, running my hands through my hair as the anger only increases. I turn back towards them, dropping my hands to my side as if to signal defeat. "This isn't fair."

Riley takes a small, cautious step forward, "I know," she whispers. "Why don't you come sit down for a minute."

I shake my head, unable to stop my feet from moving as the words from the doctor echo through my mind. I glance towards Aspen's father, our eyes meet and in that moment I focus all my hate and rage towards the man sitting six feet away from me. The man who took one look at me and immediately decided I was less-than. The man who couldn't get past his own insecurities and support his daughter. The man who tried too little too late.

Burning rage hisses through my body like a deathly poison, screeching in demand for release. "Are you happy now?" I spit at him. "This is what you wanted right?"

"Charlie," Riley snaps but I ignore her.

"Admit it. You hated the fact that she was gay. All she wanted was your support and you couldn't even give her that."

In less than two strides, he's inches away from my face, the words seeping out through clenched teeth. "You don't have any idea what you're talking about. I love my daughter, more than you know."

"Then why didn't you tell her that? Don't you get it? That's all she's ever wanted from you."

"I gave her everything she could possibly want."

"Everything except being loved for who she is, not who she dated. She just wanted your acceptance. She tried so hard to make you happy, but you couldn't see past her being gay long enough to realize just how incredible she really is."

"You have no idea what you're talking about. You—"

"*Enough!*"

In the next instant, Aunt Beth is standing in between us, her gaze shifting from the two of us. "Do you really think this is what Aspen would've wanted?"

At that, Mr. Sullivan turns and stalks out of the waiting area without another word. Aunt Beth takes a gradual step towards me. "Charlie," she says, cautiously.

I shuffle backward, unable to look her in the eyes as everything comes flooding back to me, only this time there's no way to stop it. I turn, leaning my head against the wall as I try to force the ache in my chest back down. I pound my fist into the wall, my knuckles turning white as the pain boils through me. After one more punch that leaves my knuckles bleeding, my legs give out and I slump to the ground, tears streaking down my face.

In that moment, my world collapses, like a limb had been torn from my body, without the chance of saving it. The door that was once open and welcoming is now locked and disinviting, the connection severed like a tether cut in the middle of a storm.

The mild sound of footsteps echoes throughout the room as Riley and Matty stand on either side of me, hauling me up from the floor. They half-carry me to the chairs in the corner and sit me down. I don't protest, no longer feeling the anger boiling inside me. Instead, I feel hollow, like the shell of the person I used to be.

Riley wraps her arms around me, rocking me gently as I let the tears continue to descend down my cheeks. We stay like this for what feels like half a lifetime. "She loved you so much," Aunt Beth whispers, her eyes spilling over with fresh tears.

"I know," I choke out. "I loved her too."

She cradles my cheek in her hand, wiping underneath my eyes with her thumb.

"This isn't fair," I mutter. "I didn't even get to say goodbye."

She shakes her head, her lips trembling, "I know, none of us did."

Reluctantly, Riley and Matty pull me to my feet to guide me to the car parked out front. I try to object, wanting nothing more than to stay right where I am.

"Charlie, there's nothing else you can do."

I stare at the floor, refusing to hear her words.

"You can't stay here all night, honey. You need to go home," Aunt Beth whispers.

Begrudgingly, I shuffle my feet along the tile floor, following behind Matty towards the exit. They usher me into the back seat, the rain finally letting up. Matty climbs behind the wheel and Riley slides in next to me.

The drive home takes less than twenty minutes. Gramps and Nana are anxiously waiting for us when we get home. Their mouths move, firing questions at us like a drill sergeant but I don't hear a word. I tread past them, my feet beginning to feel like lead weights as I make my way upstairs.

I flick the lights on in my bedroom and the first thing I see is the piles of clothes, toiletries, books, and shoes scattered across my room. I collapse on my bed, shutting my eyes as the pain shatters through me. The plans we had for each other—college, the adventures we were going to take, the freedom we were going to experience. The way she made me feel, like I was whole again. The time we spent together, the memories we made. It's all gone now.

The next couple of days pass in a foggy haze. I can't eat. I can't sleep. I barely get out of bed. Gramps and Nana try to get me to come downstairs and Matty has tried several times too but I just can't bring myself to do it. Matty eventually just started bringing me a plate of food to my room but it usually sits on my desk, untouched.

I can't get Aspen out of my head, can't get what happened out of my head, and I can't stop replaying the scene over and over in my head, but the outcome is always the same. I thought if I had Aspen, I wouldn't need anything else, wouldn't *want* anything else.

But maybe, you never really had someone. No matter how much you loved them, how much you wanted to protect them, they could slip through your fingers like water, and there was nothing you could do about it except watch. I now understand why people talk about their hearts literally 'breaking'. It feels like mine's made of cracked glass, the shards like tiny knives, puncturing me until I slowly bleed out.

There's a soft knock as the door slowly creaks open. I don't bother looking over or getting up, I know who it is. Riley's been over every day since it happened. Most of the time she just sits beside me, trying to coax me out of bed until she eventually gives up and promises she'll be back tomorrow. Today is no different. She comes in and the mattress shifts as she sits down next to me.

She gently rubs my back. "Hey, Charlie."

I respond with a barely audible grunt.

"I talked to Aunt Beth," she says.

My ears perk up at the sound of her name. I roll over and lift a brow.

"There's going to be a funeral service for Aspen tomorrow at ten. She would really like you to be there. She knows how much Aspen meant to you."

The thought of seeing Aspen, lying motionless in a coffin makes me shudder, but this is my only chance to say goodbye. I have to go, even if I'm terrified of what seeing her like that might do to me.

"Will you come with me?" I whisper.

Riley brushes my matted hair off of my face. "Of course."

Riley stays with me the rest of the day. When she leaves she promises she'll be here early tomorrow morning to help me get ready. I spend the rest of the evening staring at the ceiling. My eyes remain sore and swollen, no longer producing any more tears for me to cry out.

There's no longer a feeling of searing pain, but instead a feeling of emptiness, like a never-ending dark void. But I've noticed something these past several days. The happiness I felt before is like a pleasing weight—surrounding you in the same way air pressure surrounds us: unnoticeable. But when you're sad, the weight drops off, giving the illusion that you're empty. But the thing is, you're never really empty, just full of the wrong thing.

Chapter Nineteen

When I was eight years old, I watched Nana pack up the last of my mother's things and tuck them away in the attic. That was the day I realized staying with my grandparents was going to be permanent. I was still holding on to a sliver of hope that one day we might be reunited with our mother. I was young, naive, and didn't have a clue about how things really worked.

I spent the rest of the day in my room crying. Crying for the life we were never going to be able to experience with her, and crying because of the relief I felt when I realized she couldn't hurt us anymore. Some people just aren't meant to be parents but knowing that didn't make the pain any easier.

I always thought that was the saddest day of my life. But it wasn't until I saw Aspen lying inside a cold, bleak casket that I felt the pain of loss erupt inside me.

The morning of the funeral, the evanescent color of the summer day is offensively bright and cheery. It's as if they conspired against me to show me just how easily the world would go on without her. It shouldn't.

Everything should be as miserable and dreary as I feel—bitter and dank with silent air. But the birds still chirp and the flowers still bloom, continuing on as if nothing has changed. I walk through the doors of the church like a silhouette of myself, wishing I really was as insubstantial as the darkness.

The minute I step inside the auditorium all the emotions come flooding back to me. The mahogany brown casket housing Aspen sits upfront. The sunlight glistens through the stained-glass window casting a spotlight on the podium directly above her. The rest of the room is decorated with simple bouquets of calla lily flowers on each end of the rows. It's beautiful.

Riley gently places her hand on my back, guiding me to one of the empty rows as Gramps, Nana, and Matty follow, taking a seat next to us. I fix my gaze on the podium up front, drowning out the crowd that's slowly padding in. I catch a glimpse of Aunt Beth and Mr. Sullivan as they take their seat on the first row, beside two other people who I assume are Aspen's grandparents.

I completely zone out as a pastor, followed by Aspen's father, stands behind the podium, and begins. Instead, I let my mind wander, lingering on memories of Aspen—wondering what she might think if she were here.

I snap my attention back to the present when I realize Aunt Beth is standing behind the podium. She's in the middle of her speech when our eyes meet, the hint of a smile tugging at the corner of her mouth.

"…She had her whole life ahead of her, a life that should've been spent with people she loves…" She pauses, her eyes locked on mine. "Doing things that made her happy, like art, hiking, traveling, going to college and starting her life, experiencing the world in her own way." She stops, her gaze falling to Aspen's casket in front of her. "Unfortunately the universe had other plans. Aspen was more than just another face in the crowd, she was a daughter, a grandchild, a friend, a student, a niece, a partner, and a fighter, up until the very end. But most importantly, she was loved." The slow trickle of tears begin to spill down my face. Aunt Beth looks out at the crowd, her eyes scanning the room. "Aspen was too young, too young to die. She'd barely gotten a taste of what was out there. But I know she won't be forgotten, she'll live on through the people that are here today. The people that love her."

The pastor says a final prayer before everyone stands and begins filing out of the room.

"We'll meet you out front," Matty whispers to me as he follows everyone else out.

I stay towards the back, waiting for the bulk of the crowd to exit before I walk up to Aspen's casket. She's lying inside, her hands on top of one another on her chest; it almost looks as if she's sleeping. I stare down at the face I had grown so used to over the past several months. The features I knew like the back of my hand. But this time, there's no hope that lingers behind the heartache, no hope for the thought of us being together.

There's just a desolate feeling of despair, knowing this will be the last time I get to see her like this. But there's no such thing as a beautiful body when death has claimed the soul. There's nothing romantic about this scene. Death is death. The flesh rots, the bones follow, the hair mats into the soil. It is the life that is beautiful. The life we cherish; the part of our life that we spent with the ones we love.

I take one last look, whispering a final goodbye before I turn, leaving the room behind me. Aspen's family stands off to the right directly in front of the door so I have no choice but to walk past them as I head for the spot where Riley and Matty are standing.

Aunt Beth grabs my arm, stopping me from moving forward. Before she says anything, she steps forward and pulls me into a hug. After several moments she releases me, taking half a step back. "She loved you so much, Charlie," she says through soft sobs. "I'd never seen her happier than when she was with you." She cradles my cheek in her hand, wiping a tear away with her thumb. "It's not fair how things turned out. But she would want you to be happy."

A low sniffle bubbles out and I choke back a sob. "She made me really happy, too," I murmur.

Aunt Beth wraps her arms around me for one more hug. "I know, sweetheart." She steps back, holding onto me at arm's length. "You call me if you need anything, okay?"

I nod, giving her a weak smile as I turn to continue towards Riley and Matty. I'm stopped by the outstretched hand of Mr. Sullivan blocking my path. I glance up, meeting his gaze. His dark blue eyes look almost black now; the light that was once in them now extinguished.

"Charlie," he whispers just loud enough for me to hear. I stare at him bracing myself for what comes next. "I'm sorry." He exhales a long and staggering breath. "I messed up. I thought I was doing what was best for her. I thought I was protecting her. I grew up being told that people—people who were gay were sick. That they had an illness that was immoral. That they could be fixed. I knew the kinds of things that happened to them. I was scared. I didn't want that for my daughter. I thought if I did everything right—gave her everything she could possibly want, a stable home, a nice car, a good school. But…" He dips his head, shaking it back and forth. "But you were right. I failed her and now it's too late." He snaps his head up, his cheeks streaking with fresh tears. "I know how I treated you was wrong and I don't expect you to ever forgive me. But if I've learned anything these past couple weeks, it's that you loved my daughter and she loved you. You gave her something I never could and for that I'm grateful. I may never be able to fix what I've done, but I promise to spend the rest of my life trying to make up for it—for Aspen. She deserved so much better."

If I wasn't standing directly in front of him, watching as the words spilled out of his mouth I wouldn't have believed him. I continue to stare at him, my mouth slightly agape at his confession. Then, I do something neither one of us expected.

I hug him.

He immediately goes rigid but after a moment his body relaxes as he wraps his arms around me. Never in a million years would I have thought I would be willingly hugging Aspen's father, especially not in front of all these people. But if he can make an effort at turning over a new leaf, maybe I can too.

When he releases me I hold his gaze, and it's like I'm seeing him for the first time. "Aspen called me," I say. "That night after she left the house. She called me on the way to Aunt Beth's. She told me you wanted to try and work things out, that she believed you. Hearing her voice when she was telling me everything; I hadn't heard her that happy since she found out she'd gotten into art school. She told me she was willing to try if you were."

My eyes spill over with tears as I think back to that phone call, replaying the memory like a projection on a film screen. "I know neither one of us wanted things to turn out the way it did. We both made mistakes, Mr. Sullivan. But I'd like to think that Aspen had some sort of closure before she died, and that is all I can really ask for."

"Thank you, Charlie."

When I'm on the other side of the room, I look around and I notice for the first time just how many people showed up. I'm surprised; I didn't expect this many people. There are kids from all over school, older men and women that look to be parents or business associates, and several families from church, one of which Gramps and Nana are deep in conversation with.

I take one last sweep over the room, completely caught off guard when I turn around and Skylar is standing in front of me.

"Hi, Charlie," she says.

"Uhh hi," I mumble as I glance around to make sure she is in fact talking to me.

"I know I'm probably the last person you want to see. But I was wondering if I could talk to you for a second?"

I raise an eyebrow at her, still not sure about where this is going. "Uh okay?" She pivots and walks towards the back corner. I glance at Riley and Matty before cautiously following behind her.

She turns to face me. "I....I wanted to apologize. I had no right doing what I did. I grew up being taught that homosexuality was wrong, that gay people have no place in this world. It was ingrained in me the same way as being told that lying and stealing are wrong. But Riley was right. I was also taught to be kind, to be respectful even if I had a different opinion." She glances up as if waiting for me to speak.

I stare at her, not sure what to say. After a moment she continues, "We may have different opinions on how we want to live our life but that didn't give me the right to treat you the way I did. It was none of my business and I should've respected that. I really am sorry, Charlie... for everything."

"Uhh... thank you, Skylar."

"Well, I'll let you get back to it then. Goodbye, Charlie."

I nod before turning and heading back to where Matty and Riley.

"Well that was unexpected," Riley says as she wraps her arm around me. "Saw you talking to Aspen's father. You okay?"

"No, but maybe someday."

Matty shuffles to the other side of me and I lean into him as tears stream down my face.

We spend a few more minutes standing towards the back, watching the interactions, and waiting for my grandparents to finish their conversation before we exit the church. I head straight for my bedroom, my appetite nonexistent when Nana mentions something about lunch.

The second I'm inside my bedroom, I collapse onto the floor, my knees giving out at the realization that Aspen is gone. And she's never coming back. What comes next is more than just crying. It is the kind of inconsolable sobbing that comes from a person drained of all hope.

I don't even realize I'm not alone until I feel Riley sit down next to me and wrap her arms around me, holding me close until I've cried so much that there's nothing left inside but a raw emptiness.

I know I should be packing and getting ready for college. I should be looking forward to the day I get to leave this place behind me and the memories that it holds. But I can't bring myself to get out of bed. BluHaven is the last tangible thing I have of Aspen and I'm not sure I'm ready to give that up yet.

Riley still comes over nearly every day to check on me. I can tell she's trying to give me space and let me grieve in my own way, but I know she's starting to get worried. It's written all over her face, the flicker of concern that flashes behind her eyes when she looks at me, curled up in bed like I'm withering away.

Matty checks in on me too, always bringing me food and not leaving until he sees me take at least a couple bites. I know he just wants to make sure I'm healthy but it's starting to get on my nerves.

Gramps and Nana have no problem giving me some space. They did their best to try and cajole me out of my room but after the first few failed attempts, they've left me alone. Nana offered to have Reverend Charles over to talk to me about everything. And although her offer seemed genuine, I politely declined, letting her know I'm doing just fine on my own. She gave me a skeptic look before heading back downstairs.

I'm in the middle of watching some house hunter show when my bedroom door creaks open and Riley walks in. She stands just inside the room, her eyes scanning the surroundings. There are clothes scattered all over the place, wrappers tossed aimlessly on the floor, the blinds haven't been open in days, and for the first time I notice the musty smell coming from inside the room.

She takes a step forward, grabbing my laptop and closing it. "Charlie," she says with her hands on her hips. "I know you're hurting but you can't stay in bed forever."

I just stare at her, not sure how to respond.

She sits on the end of the bed, the mattress sinking from the weight of her. "Have you even started packing for college?"

"I'm not sure I still want to go," I whisper.

"Why? You've worked so hard for this. You can't just throw it away."

A gentle burn spreads over my cheeks as fresh tears spill down my face. "But I can't leave her."

She repositions herself so she's sitting beside me. "But Charlie, she's gone."

"I know. But it's not fair. We had all these plans, for college, and afterwards. And now she's gone. And it hurts, Riley."

She wraps her arm around my shoulders, lightly massaging my arm. "You can still have all that. You can go to LittleWood and be out and live your life the way you want to."

I wipe my face with the comforter, the tears flowing in tiny rivulets. "But we were supposed to do it *together*, supposed to experience those things together. It's just not fair."

"I know. None of it's fair. But do you really think Aspen would want you to stay here, in BluHaven? Give up your scholarship that you worked so hard for?"

"No, but the thought of leaving her…" I shake my head, letting the sentence hang in the air.

"You can't hide in your room forever. You know that's not what she would want."

"I can't do this right now," I mutter, sliding back under the covers.

"Charlie," she says, dragging out the last syllable. "I'm just trying to help. I know you're hurting but lying in bed all day isn't going to make it any easier."

"You don't know that," I snap back.

I know Riley is just trying to help but I just can't bring myself to do anything other than lie in bed. Everything reminds me of her and it's just too hard. Nothing feels right anymore.

The door creaks open and Matty shuffles inside with a sandwich and fruit on a plate. Riley exhales loudly, then gets up off the bed.

"How's it going?" Matty asks quietly.

Riley throws her hands up in the air, shaking her head. "I told her she can't hide in her room forever. But apparently she thinks she can."

I pick at a loose thread, my gaze fixed on the fibers in my fingers.

"I brought you some dinner," Matty says.

"I'm not hungry," I respond without looking at either of them.

"You need to eat something," Riley says with a hint of irritation.

"Maybe later," I mutter.

Riley lets out an exasperated breath. "I'm gonna go but I'm coming over tomorrow and we're going to start packing whether you want to or not."

I continue fidgeting with the loose thread as if it's the most interesting thing in my room. I look over to Matty when I hear the door shut behind her. He gives me one of his *you know better than that* looks, before plopping down next to me and shoving the plate of food in my hands.

"Riley's right, you need to eat something."

I take a bite of an apple slice and chew. "Happy now?"

He sits up, crossing his arms over his chest. "Look, I know you're going through a really hard time right now. But you can't just push everyone away. We're just trying to help you."

"Maybe I don't want your help," I snap.

Matty drops his head, gently shaking it from side to side. "This isn't who you are, Charlie. You're better than this. Aspen would want you to be better than this."

"You have no idea what she would want," I spit, the anger starting to boil over.

"I sure as hell know she wouldn't want you to waste the rest of your life stuck in a town like BluHaven. Not when you have the opportunity to get away from this place."

I set the plate down, leaning back against the headboard.

"Look, sis," he says, his tone softer. "I can't imagine what you're going through, especially with everything that's happened this year. But I know you better than you think, and you're not the kind of person to just give up. Ever since we were kids, you've always had my back, always made sure I was taken care of." He leans forward, resting his hand on my knee, "Well, this time let me help you. You've worked too hard to throw it all away. And you may not realize it now, but if you do, you're going to regret it."

I stare at the wall, refusing to look at him, not sure if it's because he's right or because I'm ashamed or both. After a moment, he pats my leg and gets up off the bed.

"Please, Charlie. Let us help you through this."

I continue to stare at the wall until the door clicks behind him. When he's gone, I glance down at the plate of food balanced in my lap and move it to the dresser. I slide back under the covers, letting the tears fall once again.

Crying has become an expectation now. The sullen feeling washing in like an unwanted wave, knocking my sandcastles flat. I let them fall, not raising a hand to stop them. They splash down onto the comforter in a rain-like pattern, leaving dark splotches on the coffee-colored fabric, until sleep finally catches up with me.

Chapter Twenty

When I hear my door squeak open the next morning, I expect to see Riley standing in the doorway, ready to scold me again for not getting out of bed. To my surprise Aunt Beth is standing in the doorway instead.

"Hey, Charlie. Can I come in?" she asks.

I nod, sitting up.

She does a quick glance around the room before settling in at the foot of my bed. "How are you?" she asks, her tone soothing.

I shrug. "I'm okay."

"Oh Charlie," she says with a sigh. "I'm so sorry you have to go through this. It's not fair."

"I don't know what to do. It feels so wrong just moving on without her."

She leans forward, patting my knee. "I know, but you can't spend the rest of your life hiding in your bedroom. That's not what Aspen would want for you."

I cock my head slightly to the side. "Did Riley call you?"

A soft smile spreads at the corner of her mouth. "No, Matty did actually. He's worried about you. Thought you might need someone to talk to who knows what you're going through."

"It just doesn't feel real."

"I brought something for you." She reaches into the bag that's leaning against the bed legs and pulls out a slim, black briefcase-folder with two handles on the side. It takes me a minute to recognize that it's the same case Aspen used for her art portfolio.

Aunt Beth unzips it, opening it up to display what's inside. "I found this when I was going through some of her things the other day." She pulls out the pages inside, laying them out on the bed. There are several photographs taken around BluHaven, a few sketches of landscapes. I flip through them, stopping when I get to the last couple.

The first one I notice is the sketch she did of the basketball court that looks like a stage. The other one is a bookstore with the bookshelves drawn all askew, reminding me of our trips to *The Book Worm*. Another one is a drawing of what I guess is the two of us sitting in front of the lake, like when I took her to my favorite spot all those nights ago.

There's another sketch of the different places we went to, the diner, the mall, all connected using a road that resembles a page in a book. The last one is a drawing of two people, standing on either side of a large, deep valley. There's a bridge that connects the two different sides and when you look at it just right you can see the word 'always' written across it.

"I had no idea she drew all these," I say, wiping a single tear with my thumb.

"She showed me a couple of these not too long ago. She said you inspired her, and she wanted to keep the memories that you two shared with her."

"They're beautiful."

"I want you to have them," she says, gathering them back up into the portfolio.

"Are you sure?"

Aunt Beth smiles. "Of course. She would want you to have them. And I know it's not the same as having her here, but at least you get to keep a part of her with you, no matter where you go."

I lift my gaze, meeting her eyes. "Thank you. You have no idea how much this means to me."

She leans forward, pulling me in for a hug. "She was so ready to get out of here. I'd like to think that taking her art with you, would be like a piece of her getting out of here too."

Aunt Beth cradles my face in her hand, wiping the tears from my cheek, "You deserve to be happy, Charlie. Promise me you'll go to LittleWood? That you'll live out your and Aspen's dream of moving away and seeing the world? I know it's not how you pictured things working out, but you can't spend the rest of your life trapped in this small town. If not for me, for Aspen."

I glance down at the portfolio sitting on the bed. All that is and ever was my love of Aspen Sullivan plays out in my mind: innocence, self-discovery, first love, intimacy, risk, and yes, heartbreak. What we had was something I'll cherish forever, something that will always be there, lingering in the back of my mind. But a sort of lingering that reminds me to savor each moment.

"Okay," I whisper, "I'll do it."

A smile spreads across her face, as she gives my cheek one last caress before standing up, "I'd still love to come see one of your games next year, if that's alright."

"I'd like that."

I leave for LittleWood in two days. It's been almost a week since I talked with Aunt Beth and since then, I've managed to pull myself together. I took a long hot shower—several of them actually—finished my meals, cleaned my room, went outside for the first time in I don't know how long, played a little basketball with Riley, and now Matty is helping me finish packing.

I spend my last two days with Riley and Matty. She catches me up on what I've missed that's going on in her life while we hang out at the old park down the road from her house. In the evenings I hang out with Matty and Gramps and Nana, all three of them excited to see me eating dinner downstairs at the table for a change.

The day before I leave, I spend the morning with Riley, picking up some last-minute things before we both set off for college.

"I'm proud of you, Charlie," Riley says as we turn onto Park Avenue.

I shrug my shoulders, waving her off.

"I'm serious, you've come a long way. After everything you went through at school from being outed, getting back together with Aspen, coming out to your family, dealing with her loss, and now going off to college to play ball. You've worked hard. You should be proud of yourself."

"Thanks, Riley. I couldn't have done it without you though. You stuck by me every step of the way."

"And I always will."

"Can you believe we're about to go off to college? It still doesn't feel real. What am I going to do without you?"

"Hey, I'll be going to Silver Oak University which isn't too far away, so we'll still see each other."

"I know, I'm just so used to you always being right there. But I'm happy for you, I know you're going to kick ass over there."

When Riley drops me off, I choke back a sob as she pulls me in for one last hug before letting me go. We say our goodbyes, with promises to keep in touch throughout the year.

I spend the rest of the evening with Matty, Nana and Gramps. Nana makes my favorite dish, spaghetti, and we all enjoy a nice family meal together. I hang out in Matty's room listening to music and talking before retreating to my bed for the night.

Early the next morning, the sun peeks through, dawning on a new day, and a new adventure. I load the last of my things into the car. Gramps, Nana and Matty follow me outside where they take turns hugging me during our goodbye. I can tell they're all trying to hold back their tears as I pull them in for an embrace one by one.

"Call us when you get there?" Gramps says.

"Of course."

Matty steps over, wrapping his arms around me. "I'm proud of you, sis." He steps back, holding me at arm's length, a goofy grin stretching across his face. "I'm gonna miss you so much but I'm so happy for you."

"I'm going to miss you too, Matty. But I'm only a phone call away, call me anytime, day or night."

He nods as a single tear trickles down his face. "Okay," he whispers "Same goes for you. I want to know everything that's going on; parties, game stats, classes, all the incredible people you're going to meet."

"Sure thing, but only if you do the same here. I may be moving away but I still want to be kept up to date on everything happening with you. But steer clear of any more ideas to help out around the house."

A soft laugh bubbles out. "Sure, sis."

He pulls me in for one last hug before I move on to Nana.

"Oh Charlie." She cradles my face in her hands. "I'm so proud of the woman you've become. I may not have understood your relationship with Aspen, but I could tell how much you loved her. I couldn't be more proud to call you my granddaughter."

"I love you so much, Nana."

"You'll come home for the holidays?"

"Of course. They'll be here before you know it." I say, more for myself than for Nana.

With one last wave through the window, I tuck Aspen's portfolio safely away in the backseat and reverse out of the driveway. It only takes about fifteen minutes before I come to the stoplight at the highway. There's a bittersweet feeling that ripples through me as the thought of this chapter of my life coming to a close. I take my foot off the brake and gently accelerate onto the ramp, toward new, distant horizons.

Epilogue

It's been nearly seven years since I waved goodbye to my family and headed off to Arizona. Seven years since they lowered Aspen into the ground. Seven years since I discovered who I am.

It's a hot and muggy afternoon as I pass the *'Welcome to BluHaven'* sign, the sun peeking out behind a thick layer of clouds. It doesn't take long to realize the cityscape looks exactly the same as when I left it.

I wend my way through town, passing the familiar shops that I've spent so much time in; the little diner where Aspen and I shared our first milkshake, the used bookstore where I learned so much about her in a matter of a few hours, and the old abandoned park where I realized I was falling for her, hard.

I drive through downtown towards my old neighborhood. As I turn the corner onto our street, my eyes instantly lock on the house where my grandparents raised us. I half expect my family to be outside waiting for me like they did the few times I came home for the holidays. But of course, they don't. Gramps died three years ago from a stroke and Nana shortly after that due to heart failure. They could never stand to be apart from each other for too long. They lived a long and happy life and I'll be forever grateful for the time I did get to spend with them.

Matty moved out as soon as he graduated from high school. He managed to obtain a scholarship to MIT which wasn't surprising at all. He graduated two years ago with a degree in Engineering and now works for a computer tech company in Boston. He also found a girlfriend while he was in college and is head over heels in love with her. I couldn't be happier for him. He's grown up a lot since I left for Arizona and although I don't see him nearly as often as I would like, I'm proud of the person he's become.

I pull over and park next to the curb, craning my neck to get a better look at the house. The exterior looks just like it did the day I left, except for a giant letter *C* hanging on the front of the house. My old basketball goal is still sitting in the driveway and I flash back to the countless hours I would spend out there, shooting hoops until dark.

I snap out of my daydream when the front door opens and an older couple with a small dog emerges from the house. I smile to myself as the dog runs in a circle around the front yard. Life goes on—my old house now has another family's story to tell. I take one last look at it before I drive away.

My next stop is the high school. I pull into the familiar parking lot and stare up at the building. The old sounds of the morning commotion as students hurried in for class whisper in my ears. I think back to the traumatic events that occurred during my senior year, and the people that played a role in them—Skylar, Brandon, Will. I no longer feel the resentment simmering in my belly. We were young, naive, and ignorant about the real world. I don't condone what they did or how they treated me, but I've grown up a lot since high school, and so have they. Everything I've endured and overcome has made me who I am today.

I take a look at the gym, the place that was my sanctuary all throughout school. I almost expect to see Riley standing out front with a ball in hand but I don't. The place is deserted.

Riley and I were able to stay in touch all throughout college, we even visited each other a couple times before we graduated. After college, she got drafted to the WNBA. I remember that day so vividly in my head. She was ecstatic when she called me and I was so happy for her. About a year and a half in, she blew out her knee, ending her professional basketball career. Now, she coaches the girls' basketball team at a high school in Santa Fe, New Mexico.

My gaze traces the outline of the rest of the school, the courtyard, the football field, the main entrances, and the *Go Falcons* sign hanging in the front window. So much of what I learned about myself and who I am is tied to this place—this single building, in a little, small town.

I pull out of the parking lot and head for my final destination. I take a few deep breaths, psyching myself up for this last part. I knew when I was planning this trip down here that it was going to be difficult, but I wasn't prepared for the emotions I would feel surging through me as I head for the only cemetery located in BluHaven.

I slowly climb out of the car, fidgeting with the gold band in my pocket as I maneuver my way around the different gravesites. I take a moment to place fresh flowers on Gramps' and Nana's graves, before continuing on to my last stop. I wander around the cemetery, my feet treading lightly on the soil until my eyes are resting on the headstone with the name 'Aspen Sullivan' engraved into the marble.

A gentle smile pulls at my lips as memories of Aspen replay in my mind like waves crashing onto shore. I reach out, touching the slab of marble that bears her name but not who she was. She was never gray or cold; she was radiant—from the day I first laid eyes on her to the day she was lowered into the ground.

"Oh how I miss you."

I glance up towards the hazy clouded sky, my eyes prickling with tears as I reminisce on the past several years.

"You told me I could make a difference in this crazy world. I think you were right. What started out as a support group for LGBTQ youth with unsupportive parents turned into a non-profit center downtown—all because of you.

"Every year on your birthday, your dad donates to the center as a way to honor your memory. He's kept his promise and will be celebrating six years of sobriety in December. You'd be so proud of him; I know I am."

I close my eyes as the tears begin to spill over and it's like I can hear the sound of her voice as if she were right here with me.

"I still keep in touch with Aunt Beth. She came to several of my games, my graduation, and the grand opening of my non-profit. She and your dad reconciled their differences and she seems really happy."

My gaze falls back to her grey speckled headstone and I'm reminded once again of all that is and ever was my love of Aspen Sullivan.

I reach into my pocket and take a deep breath before pulling out the gold band with a diamond stud.

"I met someone. I think you'd like her."

I dip my head, shaking it back and forth as I chuckle to myself.

"Her name is Lucy; we met at a fundraiser for the center. We've been together almost three years now."

I turn the ring over in my fingers as the tears continue to fall.

"She makes me happy. You know, she was the one who suggested I come down here to visit you. Funny, isn't it? She thought it would be good for me to return to the place where it all started."

I wipe my face, taking a moment to compose myself before I hold the ring out to the headstone.

"I plan on proposing soon. This ring belonged to her grandmother; it's been in the family a long time and I know it means the world to Lucy that she gave it to us. I'm excited to build a life with her."

I shift my gaze to the sky, and I can't help but wonder if Aspen's even listening or if I'm simply just standing here talking to a rock.

"Every decision, every moment, every opportunity, has led me to where I am now. And it all started the day you walked into the cafeteria at school. I thought a scholarship was my only ticket out—oh how I wanted nothing more than to escape this place. I was wrong. You showed me everything I was missing; opened my eyes to the beauty of this world, and for that I'll always be grateful."

A flicker of sunlight cuts through the sheet of clouds, as if the color that had once been stolen, now returned. I take one last look at her permanent resting place, as a tear slowly descends from my cheek. I kiss my fingers and lightly touch the top of the headstone before whispering my last, and final goodbye.

Did You Enjoy "My Ticket Out"?

If you enjoyed this book, please leave an honest review on Amazon and/or Goodreads. As a self-published author, reviews are greatly appreciated! I look forward to reading your thoughts and opinions. Thank you so much for taking the time to read this story!

For any questions or inquiries, please email
jnmartonauthor@gmail.com

About The Author

J.N. Marton graduated from the University of Central Arkansas with a Bachelor's degree in education. Along with educating the future of our nation, she enjoys taking her daily morning run, reading any book she can get her hands on, and binge watching the latest shows on Netflix. Marton happily lives with her wife, Hollis, and their Lab/Basset Hound mix, Sam.

Email her at jnmartonauthor@gmail.com and follow her on her favorite social media platform, Twitter @jn_marton.

Made in the USA
Coppell, TX
27 November 2020

42196987R00163